William Rivière

William Rivière was born in 1954 and brought up in Norfolk. After leaving King's College, Cambridge, he spent seven years in Venice. Later he worked in Japan and travelled around the Far East, paddling sampans in Sarawak and sailing lateen craft in the Indian Ocean. His prize-winning first novel, WATERCOLOUR SKY, was published in 1990, followed by A VENETIAN THEORY OF HEAVEN in 1992, and his latest novel, BORNEO FIRE, is published by Sceptre. He has one son and is married to a painter, and has returned to Italy where he teaches at the University of Urbino.

SCEPTRE

Eros and Psyche

WILLIAM RIVIÈRE

SCEPTRE

Line from 'Lady Lazarus' by Sylvia Plath reproduced
by kind permission of Faber & Faber Ltd.

First published in 1994 by Hodder and Stoughton
A division of Hodder Headline PLC
First published in paperback in 1995
A Sceptre Paperback

10 9 8 7 6 5 4 3 2 1   06378010

A CIP catalogue record for this title
is available from the British Library.

ISBN 0 340 60967 2

Printed and bound in Great Britain by
Cox and Wyman Ltd, Reading, Berkshire

Hodder and Stoughton
A Division of Hodder Headline PLC
338 Euston Road
London NW1 3BH

Eros and Psyche

ONE

"What I love shall come like visitant of air . . ."

THE VISIONARY, Emily Brontë

Night hour by night hour, the net hung in the sea. It was borne up by floats every four or five yards, and by a buoy at each end. The floats were chunks of white polystyrene; the buoys were white too – old plastic jerrycans.

The net had been laid from the fishing-smack after dinner, laid by starlight where old Achilles had thought fish might move that night. Between waking and sleeping, Imogen Scottow lay in her hut by the Ionian shore and remembered how they had paid the net out over the slimy gunwale. Then she imagined how the pale mesh must be swaying in the black sea, swaying slightly because even on a still night the sea rippled and the floats bobbed, and swaying because a current set through the strait, the depths had their lightless draggings, and swaying too when a fish was caught and then fought to get free. Sometimes while it was entangled and fighting a bigger fish came and began to devour it and often was entangled too.

Imogen lay on her back. If she turned her head she could duskily make out Angelica's cot. Then if she waited a few heartbeats the lighthouse on the islet opened its radiant eye, the sparse rush walls of the hut couldn't keep out all the shimmer, for a moment the cot's rails appeared to have grown a phosphorescent lichen. Imogen had always liked that lighthouse. When she was a girl, it had been her

1

philosopher. Nocturnal, like all the best contemplatives. A soul of such austerity that he had chosen to live on a limpet-embossed, weed-bedraggled outcrop that was one of the few juts of the reef that broke the surface whatever mistral or scirocco blew, because there in saintly discomfort and solitude and usefulness to shipping he might train his thoughts in clairvoyance. Oh, not quickly and not easily; not certainly, either. But surely, Imogen had often prayed for him, such self-discipline and service to others might be rewarded.

Outside the hut, the calm sea lapped on the boulders. There were Scops owls in the eucalyptus; she heard one call. The cicadas of the day were quiet, but all through the scrub the crickets of the night were chittering.

She tried to imagine what it was like to be a squid and to know you were knotted into the cords of death. Or to be a mullet snagged by your gills, to be hanged alive and then to see one of the big eels, that ghostly snaking approach. How did they feel, the mouth's first moseying, then the first bite into your flesh, the ripping, the second bite? Or did the eel just take one gulp, she'd seen them caught with fish wedged in their gullets, was that how it was? Imogen tried to sense the panic, the frenzied thrashing, the agony; she was afraid that once she fell to imagining these things she wouldn't be able to stop; but she was sleepy, she couldn't even start imagining very convincingly.

The owl's soft call couldn't be heard down where the mullet was being torn apart by the back-jagging teeth of the eel. Well, no, naturally it couldn't. Ah but it was fine to be back in Greece, and fine to have brought Angelica to this peaceful island. They would fish by day too, not only by night. The net was for night. But then after sunrise you took the long weighted line. It lay, hundreds of yards of it, carefully coiled in its crate. The uncountable hooks that depended from the line would each have been jabbed through a gobbet of octopus and then snicked into the crate's cork rim, all in the right order so they could be paid out freely, would go overboard without snagging, slide slanting away down into the blue.

I must sleep, Imogen commanded herself drowsily. I have to be up at first light; I must sleep.

And yes, it was pleasant to be back on her cousin's coast again. She could never recollect whether Laura Rodostamo was her second cousin once removed or her first cousin twice removed. And Laura's daugher Anna? At another remove? Anyhow Laura was also her godmother, and the lighthouse was watching over her once more, and watching over Angelica too, so all was conclusively well. It would be pleasant to brace a foot against the gunwale of the smack and to haul up the dripping net. Anna and she would take turns to haul, and old Achilles would laugh as he had laughed since they were girls because they still didn't enjoy picking out of the net those fish that were still alive, and they were also a little hesitant about getting to grips with the unidentifiable lumps of slithery carrion which the sea's predators had chewed and left.

Sleep. Sleep. But why now suddenly did she have to see again that eel, not a particularly large eel, not a conger, a moray it had been, a brown and yellow moray eel caught by day with the hook well sunk in its throat? It must have fought and whirled and fought and whirled down there, because by the time they heaved it up it had knotted the line again and again round its neck, almost finished cutting off its own head.

"Imogen?" a voice softly asked. "If you want to go fishing, you ought to get up."

"I love you whatever you have decided, I shall love you whatever you do," Laura Rodostamo had remarked two years before amid the sober twittering of the tea-room of a London hotel, had pronounced with that same softness and had smiled at her goddaughter's swollen waist which cradled an undecipherable essence, which cherished her Minoan Linear A, Imogen said. (Linear B, poor charmless cracked code, was the banal fact of her pregnancy, her doctor's kind dull chat.)

"I can't make out a word!" Imogen had rejoiced wonderingly, playing her fingertips on the front of her ample dress, on her cocooned future daughter. And even after Angelica was born, she now mused as in the foredawn freshness she got out of bed to go fishing, it had been magnificent how tenaciously she kept her meanings to herself. She would be inscrutable – she would! She would divulge a little, a few smiles and murmurs, apparent graces – but in order to retain far more, to let her resonances deepen where her own conscious self would only ever nebulously discern them, superficially betray them. Of course, now Angelica was nearly one and a half a few scratchings of the script could begin to be interpreted. A few, and they didn't say much. And even after decades of thinking and feeling, Angelica would not fully have mastered the language of herself, her mother supposed. She would have toyed with only a few of the ambiguities of which she were capable, however many in her case they turned out to be, legion or scarce. Imogen pulled her shorts on over her bikini. Where was her shirt? "I'm coming!" she promised in a whisper that would not wake her child but was so faint it was unheard by the old lady who had been born Laura Salthouse, born long ago in that far-off world of before the war, brought up in Malta because her father had commanded the destroyer flotilla, and who was now standing patiently outside in the gloaming.

"If you do not wish anyone to know the name of your baby's father, I shall not dream of questioning you," Laura had concluded quietly. And then, as a codicil, with a puff of laughter: "I may even try to stop one or two people berating you."

4

And had she? Imogen wondered. Had she reasoned with her father, who was one of those English landowners who buy a new car every three years, send their children to expensive schools, and opine that there is no money in farming these days? Or with her mother, who was dependably eloquent on the redecorating of a bedroom or the replanting of a flower-bed, who gave fêtes indefatigably in aid of the cathedral and the children's hospital? Had their bewilderment and anger and pain been mitigated by Laura Rodostamo, baffled a bit? And what about her brother, to whom naturally the house and the acres would go? Her brother who after failing to get into Oxford had gone to Edinburgh and shot grouse; had then sniffed the air and had decided that the ability to buy cheap and to sell expensive was the only skill his society valued at all highly. Mark who had not wished to trade in oil, shipping, stocks and shares, ores, building sites, forests, nothing so vile. Who had found, at first in a fashionable gallery, soon thereafter in a famous auction house, friends disposed to reward generously this adroit way of his with cheapness and expensiveness. And who after his first Fragonard and his first hundred Mayfair lunches had gone and decided he was – ah Imogen didn't know – a scholar! Was he still labouring to compose something coherent enough for the badgered editor of the *Burlington* to accept? A respected figure in the London art world, a connoisseur for pity's sake! His sister no longer cared to bring to mind his pomposity, he made her sick. ("Yes of course, Mark, if the *Burlington* is being narrow-minded, try *Apollo*, what a good idea!") Give her men who bought and sold grocery shops any day.

Probably Laura had not found she could be bothered to speak in her goddaughter's defence in that quarter. But because Imogen Scottow was one of those who, when their love has been given, lavish on that soul gaiety, devotion, tenderness – unless their single-hearted love is perverted, becomes perhaps a single-hearted hate . . . because she was happy to decant more libations, because blithely she would anoint yet again the chosen head, she opened her hut door with a flourish, she astonished and enchanted and worried her hostess with a kiss as warm as that of her arrival the evening before. Then she drew Laura inside. "Come and have a look at Angelica," she whispered. For Laura's loyalty and tact had been superb that day in the London hotel and ever since. And was not her old ally the philosopher on his islet not opening his blazing mind for an instant right now, so you could see a swathe of silver on the bay? Was Angelica, whom only darling Laura knew was occasionally referred to by her frivolous mother as Linear A, not sleeping the vernal sleep of a script just beginning to be read by others and written by herself? Could she not be imagined to be dreaming a truth just beginning to burgeon and be revealed? Yes – and now it was obscurely but suddenly an incomparable joy to step out of your hut into the violet transparency, into the briny softness. A solid joy it was, to hear the first cock crow from the farm. A solid joy to see the stars had started to fade. Imogen took her water-jug, splashed her hands and face, filled a glass, began to brush her teeth, listened to Laura.

Surely the old lady had not been this vague last year. This shrunken and this grey, yes. But quite so flittery? "Put some shoes on, my love; remember how rough the track is." That was straightforward, useful stuff. Imogen tried to scuffle her feet into her espadrilles at the same time as rinsing her mouth, spitting froth onto the thyme. But what was all this wool-gathering about how it was no trouble to call her early, she was always up at this hour, old age she supposed? And had she mentioned to Imogen that Natasha Schomberg was arriving today? Oh yes, the car would have to go to the airport. Natasha and all four daughters, each more ravishing than the last, that meant they would be twenty for dinner, no, twenty-one, Dario was meant to be turning up too, she didn't know how, on the ferry probably. Maria would need help in the kitchen. Daphne must make beds. Yes, truly it was remarkable how

Natasha was reproduced in all four children – long golden hair, long legs, they were their mother lock stock and barrel, the two different fathers didn't seem to have . . .

"Dario who?" Imogen asked, but too faintly, tucking the sheet around her daughter's shoulders.

Now it was beds again. There weren't enough down in the huts here, Laura rambled. She had thought Natasha could sleep up at the house – she might find it preferable, what did Imogen think? And company for Ben Thurne and for Demitri, they'd been roosting together up there far too long. Natasha would surely liven them up a bit, those two sad old men. Imogen was not to fret, she was to be off to her net and her fish, the baby would be fine. Ben got so morose. No, that wasn't fair. He got tragic. Oh, didn't Imogen know? It was that boy of his, Stephen was his name. Ben had been wild about him for years, had him in the flat in Paris whenever he could. Boy in a manner of speaking. He must be forty, she guessed. Anyway, he was dying. The usual disease. Truly the moment Angelica woke she would be doted on. Would Imogen be a darling please and wake Anna when she went past her hut?

Death, Imogen thought. The sun has not yet risen, and already we have death. She leaned over the cot to touch her child's face with her lips, the child who might cry but it wouldn't matter because Laura would be sitting by the hut door to watch the dawn and wait for her charge to wake – but then she checked, drew back her head. For it would be a kiss with a vague, vague taste of death in it, wouldn't it? Early in the day; but yes. There was a man in Paris, a man immune against no evil, a man open, of extraordinary vulnerability, who would be spirited away by the next corruption that stole by.

Waiting for Anna to dress – had a woman ever taken so long to choose clothes in which to heave a net, clothes then to chuck in the scuppers while you swam? – Imogen reflected that Laura must get lonely often on winter nights with only her brother-in-law in the house. Dear old Demitri, he wasn't a great talker. No doubt that was why she burbled to her visitors. But was it simply that? Indistinct, somehow, she seemed. Laura in her widowhood might own the whole place, the high crags and the cypress woods and the terraced slopes, the spring with its roofless chapel and its fig tree, the stream where the frogs croaked – but with a shadowiness, her goddaughter felt. Was it shadowiness? But as if she existed every year less emphatically. Perhaps it had just been seeing her stand thin and colourless in the twilight like that, stand on the shore of her estate and say she would be grateful if they brought home a good catch, even if they only caught half-a-dozen squid she would be grateful, she would have a fire lit, for lunch they'd grill the squid and whatever else the sea yielded up, these things were best eaten fresh. Of course it was splendid the way she managed her land and her household. Nothing shadowy about that. And splendid the way she kept having people to stay, from May till October friends came and went, and the finest thing was to get yourself invited for Christmas. But still – indistinct . . . As if each day she managed without a few more of what had been her ideas and feelings. No, no, that wasn't the whole story. Ah, nothing! Nothing, probably. No ill that daybreak wouldn't show to be chimerical.

Day was breaking. Already the mist was white, the gulf mother-of-pearl. The crickets had stopped; all you could hear were the ripples, except when a gull cawed. What was Anna up to? Low in the east, the sky was flame. The moon, which when they had laid their net had not yet risen, was a crescent in the western sky, and that sky was not violet now, it was dark, dark blue.

Dear Anna. Not a woman to let herself proceed far into her thirties without a fiancé. A doctor from Padua called Fabrizio Something. He was turning up next month apparently, they were to be married at the end of summer. She was already pestering her mother about whom to invite. And the catering for such numbers – were Maria and Daphne up to it? Who else should be enrolled? The old lady was already wearying of this engagement. The men from the farm would roast a few sheep on spits like they did for the village weddings, she had been heard to mutter, what was wrong with Ionian feasts of the old kind?

While I, Imogen thought with a moment's grimness – but it was mere impatience with Anna's dressing, they would miss the sunrise – I am amusing. I divert. At dinner parties, people discuss me. Still, at least Anna's Italian doctor couldn't be duller than the English poet she was towing about a few years back. And there was more than one man in the world called Dario, it was silly to be even faintly agitated, she bustled him out of her mind.

As a child Imogen had been convinced that the sun was a vast buoy of fire that every night somehow got anchored down on the sea-bed. Then it was freed. Slowly it floated upward. And as its radiance rose, it spread a prayer-mat of gold and scarlet on the surface above, on the grey water it laid a miraculous weave that became more dazzling and more intricate as the blazing leviathan came up under it, up, up, up. Seafarers, she was certain, must have spied this marvel – seen it far off, naturally, for it was always spread to the east of where you sailed, always a little farther east. Still, there must be yarns; there would be fabulous reports. And then the unimaginable touch of the ascendent sun on the silken stuff, the eruption of the light of the world through the tattering warp and weft. She saw the light of the world lie for a moment awash like a great orange sea-mark, then the fiery sea streaming off its flanks as it rose again.

"Achilles will be waiting for us," she urged with what good humour she could command. She took off her straw hat; she tapped it against her leg. Beyond the headland, at the eastern horizon the prayer-mat must have been reverently laid, its arabesques must be brightening momently. And what quiet traveller had laid it down and now knelt to make his morning orison? "Do you have to stick a comb in your hair to go fishing?"

Temperately Anna said, "It keeps it out of my eyes."

Cool brackish air in her nose, throat, lungs. Shoes kicked off, the dewy feel of the deck. In the lightening anchorage, a refracted warp coming into its slantedness, a sea anemone on the quay-side coming into its purplish redness. And here a flanged spectral squid came slowly valving its way along, and there one of the night's last bats was jinking – it was magnificent to be afloat again, Imogen rejoiced. For the bat, the sky was all quiverings, rhythms, echoes, the sky was sheer information . . . Look how the black thing went ricocheting between ideas!

It was not magnificent. It was irritating. Ben's lover in Paris who would die – an evil start to the day. And now to go late to meet the sunrise – it was all damned Anna's fault, how had she got so dull? – to go peeved, ill-prepared . . .

"Ready?" Achilles asked, casting off from the bollards, cigarette in mouth. Winter nights fishing in drenched clothes had given him rheumatism at forty, now at seventy he was crooked with it. Imogen shoved the engine into reverse, reached for the tiller, heard Anna say "You steer" quickly. Not a star remained, they were going to miss the sunrise, probably it was being engaged to be married that made Anna so placid, so unalive to things. No, it was more likely because Anna was profoundly and happily in love that she wasn't fussed by the nothings that made Imogen plough her nails into her palms. The helmswoman opened the throttle, the translucencies around the rudder were churned to choppy cloudiness. Of course no vessel ever reached the prayer-mat and sheered it; but they were too late even to have made a creditable effort to salute those heavenly intricacies and hues floating far off, the sun would burst them asunder any moment now. She swung the smack seaward. They left the sloop *Nineveh* lying at her anchor in

10

the bay, lying at her anchor because the mooring needed a new chain, the old one was pitted with rust. That was something she could usefully do one day soon, dive down and wrestle to shackle a new chain onto the mooring, Laura would be grateful. What was happening beyond the eastern headland? Perhaps they were not too late; the cypresses stood very black against the conflagration, which was beginning to die down. Or was the kneeling pilgrim already being consumed in the uplifted fire?

She was not too late. Steering with the big curved tiller in the small of her back, Imogen revelled in the surging bow-wave, in the dwindling fires in the east, in the throb of the diesel engine beneath her soles. She took off her hat, she chucked back her head – glorious the wind of their passage in her hair, she could feel its ends fluttering across her shoulder-blades. This was freedom. (But she must remember to put her hat back on in an hour. In the high summer sun her English white face would scorch. Anna was dark, Anna was lucky, Anna had been dark gold all her life.) The bluffs fell astern, the gulf widened. Opalescent mist wreathed on the water that every minute was becoming deeper and deeper blue. Yes, she was free all right. At last . . .

There had been times which she had been afraid might be distressing. Going home, for instance. For after the London art school, after the Geneva textile design company, after the Milan fashion company, three months pregnant with whom she hoped would be the keystone of the arch of her freedom, Imogen had gone in the most prodigal fashion to her father and had asked for her share now. She had sat in the Wiltshire drawing-room that always smelled of her father's pipe smoke and her mother's flowers.

"I know this is all entailed for Mark," she had said. "That's fine. But you must have reckoned to leave me something when you died."

"Shaw Cottage," her father had replied. "Shaw Cottage is left to you in my will. And a little money. Not as much

11

as I'd like. But Mark will need all the help we can give him to keep the estate going."

Imogen had glanced out of the window; had tried to imagine her infant self, her befrocked and pudgy-footed and endearing-enough self learning totteringly to walk on that lawn; had tried to be moved by that image; had failed. Doubtless this scene now with her father would not be as distressing as morality might have required.

"Still, if you'd like the cottage now," he was saying, "I'll see what I can do. The lease doesn't have to be renewed next year. I can have the place done up a bit for you. Are you thinking of coming home, my darling?" Awkwardly not regarding his daughter's waist, his face had brightened nonetheless. "Your mother and I would be delighted if you came home. And perhaps we could . . ." Greyly, furrowedly, he had blushed. "Could help with – with our first grandchild . . ."

"Shaw Cottage? Thank you. Could we sell it, please? This business I'm setting up needs cash. I want to have to borrow as little as possible." (And she had founded her firm. Imogen Scottow was no longer a mere woman; she was a company. You could buy an Imogen Scottow dress. Soon you would be able to buy an Imogen Scottow handbag. Nothing prodigal about that.) "And another thing." Her father had listened – her father who had not yet made himself realise that the beloved heir would never live in Wiltshire, it was too far from the Garrick; Mark would put in a farm manager, he'd come down at weekends. "I know that Mother and you always wanted to give me a splendid wedding," she had pursued without discomfort, pursued lucidly. "Well, I shan't ever want that. So I'd like the money you would have spent on it, please. For the same reason," she had added. "Interest rates are so high."

For a moment her father had flushed with anger. He had begun to bluster. Then he had given up. "Yes. All right." He had turned to sadness like dust that turns to mud when it rains. "But you cannot," he had uttered steadily, "expect me not to hope I shall live to see you happily married one day."

Imogen had not felt as much remorse as would have been flattering. She had telephoned the railway station, ascertained the time of the next London train. Nor when on the platform her mother had summoned the courage to enquire, "When the child is old enough to ask about its father, what will you say?" had she shown the anguish or even thoughtfulness that might have been tasteful when replying simply, "Oh, I don't know. The truth, I expect. Or perhaps not." Nor now, steering across the gulf with her hat in her hand and her heart exultant because the sunrise was still to come, the horizon ahead was waiting for her, did she regret much. A flash or two of ruthlessness were necessary if anyone was ever to cut herself even a little bit free – whoever imagined otherwise? And the tendency not always to feel the expected sentiment, and the ability not always to show what you felt – these were graces, weren't they? and made society slightly less horrible to inhabit, unlike predictable reactions, which made it more. And Laura had agreed with her on the subject of freedom, or at least had not disagreed.

It had been on one of the old lady's infrequent visits to London. She had invited her cousin and goddaughter to her hotel; they had drunk tea; they had talked. And then, one pregnant, the other missing her dogs – who always pined for her when she was away from home, lay in the dust and grieved, would not eat, there was nothing Achilles and Maria could do with them, nothing! – the two women had walked into Kensington Gardens to admire the autumn trees.

And there, with Laura's love for her earthed deep in her mind like the tap-root of an oak, with that love a strength to be counted on, blessed, lived up to, Imogen had tried to explain a little. For Laura would not interrogate her – she had just said she would not, over tea in the hotel. She might, therefore, be spoken to. Unlike her daughter Anna whose first demand, whose first cajoling, wheedling, teasing, cooing demand had been to have the baby's father's identity confided to her. Who now was standing in the bow peering for buoys – the white dots glimpsed so far had all proved to be gulls. Who believed that Imogen's behaviour in regard to both Angelica and the wretched dupe her father was selfish, exploitative, cruel; she had said so. Imogen had not wanted a husband, she had made clear while Laura admired a maple in blustery gold. She had not wanted, and she would never want, a family in the customary sense. She had wanted to be independent, forever. She would rather not explain what events and what feelings had led her to this. Oh, well, perhaps, one evening in the haziest of futures, if Laura would swear never to breathe a word to a soul. Anyhow, such was the case. And she had seen no reason why any of this need mean she should never bear a child. On the contrary, she was longing to bear a child who should be the very symbol of her freedom.

Laura had frowned at a resplendent beech. It was all wrong – wasn't it? – for people to be treated as symbols of this and that. Vainglorious. Empty. Wrong. And it was awful to think of her spaniels in the dust believing that she would never come back, she was dead.

There had been, Imogen had allowed, the problem of financial independence; but she had reckoned she could solve that. No, the chief thing, the crux of the – what? Ah yes, Laura was right, the dusk falling was lovely, she'd always liked the London parks at that time of year, at that hour. As she'd been saying, the heart of things was – "My love, I *suppose* you're listening to me" – was more or less this. Men were not invariably as scrupulous as they might be about making sure a woman did not conceive a baby. Putting it politely, that was. So . . . might a woman not be – just once! one time in a million – comparably unscrupulous? Might she not be so not carelessly but deliberately, as a trick? To satisfy her own ends, yes. An egotism for an egotism, did Laura think? Mmmm, she guessed she had to accept that. No, Angelica's father

14

had been sweetness itself. The most considerate of men. Easy to fool. And that – Imogen had laughed, had taken her godmother's mackintosh elbow – had been the point. She had wished to conceive; her lover had not. She would keep the consequence of her selfishness to herself; she would defend her dominion over that adored consequence fiercely; to do just that was her cardinal desire. The child would be hers utterly, hers alone; the responsibility hers alone. Her lover would never know he had a son or daughter on the face of the earth; would never know his loss, to be tormented by it. Oh yes, Laura must believe her, she'd covered her traces pretty well. And – here she had laughed again, had squeezed Laura's arm as they wended their way over the damp grass – her lover had enjoyed unwittingly conceiving his child. She had tried to make sure he enjoyed it very much.

"I don't know much about freedom," Laura had said. And had thought: So – so – you have been a succubus.

And why indeed did I ever imagine she did? Imogen wondered, watching the sunrise which had never borne much resemblance to her childish fancy and didn't now. A dark red cusp broke the sea's rim. The globe was still dark red when it was clear of the horizon. She gazed into the sea-level light. She had never listened to anything, never watched anything as silent as that sunrise. Soon now it would be orange; then yellow; then nearly white, just heat and light, she wouldn't be able to look at it any more, she'd have to bow her head.

But why had she imagined that dear, quiet, respectable old Laura would have a feeling for how detached you could be? Watching the day breaking at sea, for instance, you could be extremely detached, and then freedom would flicker in your head and you would feel your heart thud. Freedom would flicker in your head with such a pulse of joy, shed such a delicacy of radiance on spars and sea and coast and now on a butterfly jigging merrily and waywardly offshore that you would do damned nearly anything, you would invoke suspect powers, you would sacrifice trumpeted values, anything to fool that feeling into coming again, fool it or yourself. Sometimes freedom would flash almost virulently – you liked that too. Odd, though, the way she had assumed Laura suffered from comparable illuminations and desires. Ah, here was their net. Closer to the cliff on the other side of the gulf than they had remembered. Yes, curious how that evening in Kensington Gardens she had burdened the unprotesting old lady with all that self-indulgent confession. Doubtless she had been driven to come at least fractionally clean with one living soul, and Laura was her only thinkable confidante. And no doubt too, like every pregnant idiot, she had thought and thought about her poor share of the commonplace till she made it vacuously grand.

Or maybe it was that old rumour about the war – old cloudy myth of forgotten drawing-rooms, old vagueness in old air. Was that why Laura Rodostamo had the aura of a woman wise in stories of passion and intrigue? (Had she merely imagined that other people were aware of it too? Imogen brought herself up sharp, beat a fretful tattoo on the cypress tiller with her fingernails. Had she decided it was true and then found confirming evidence?) But a woman whose blood thrummed to the music of magnificent loves tragically lost ... A woman who by right – not like the safe twitterers, the shallow domesticated ones – took her place at tables where tales of forlorn passion, late at night, were rehearsed ... Any reality in this, any truth at all? And what was the war vagueness? Something about Laura Salthouse when she was working at the War Office in Whitehall, bicycling about in the Blitz. And a young German officer – called what? – to whom before the war she had been engaged – or she had married him – or they had been lovers – or at least had danced. Anyway he had been killed before peace came. Killed somewhere, by someone, by some method. Or he had perished of a disease; or of his wounds; or had been drowned. But on active service.

Imogen's mother perhaps in a soft moment had alluded

to him – but had told nothing of substance. Or at a London dinner party a lady, a friend of Laura Rodostamo's, knowing she was talking to her favourite goddaughter, had been unable not to let fall some hint – so that bedevilments, otherwise opaque, might one distant day be clear, so that honour in the end should be accorded where it was due. At any rate, then Laura in the fifties and in her own thirties had married Alexis Rodostamo. She had gone to live in Greece. A couple of miscarriages; then Anna had been born. And Alexis, who doubtless knew quite a bit, was dead. He had in his will left Imogen an Egyptian ring, which she wore.

Still that nagging idea . . . And would Laura ever, would she perhaps one tolerant evening, give some explanation of her admission to noble story-tellings? Overestimating the importance of her impending death – for she was ailing – rather like she herself had doubtless been overimpressed by her own pregnancy, would Laura recall – what?

Imogen hauled at the net.

She dropped it in rough coils in its crate. Water ran down her arms and legs. No . . . that her baby was a sure defence against all her enemies – crazy to have dreamed Laura would understand that. And yet she had seemed to intuit that vulnerability as that strength. Like, in the Kipling story, the naked Saxon child who held a ford against a mounted Norman knight. Oh, nonsense. Imogen hauled, arm's reach by arm's reach. The important thing when you hauled was not to reach below the gunwale and grab where you couldn't see, because there might be one of those evil little scorpion fish – evil except that they made delicious soup – which had poisonous spines. Even if you quickly borrowed Achilles' knife and dug them out of your hand the cut generally went septic.

Anna stood beside her. When there was weed in the net, she yanked it away. When there was a fish, she detached it gingerly. There were not many fish, and all so far had been small.

Away astern, the lighthouse had shut his eye, stood pale.

17

Here the cliff reared over the motionless smack. At sea-level, aeons of waves had cut an overhang. Ripples sucked at the limpets' holds. Overhead, a few scrubby trees had latched their roots into the scarps. Cormorants were roosting on a pinnacle. Imogen craned her neck, saw how higher up the tufts of bushes gave out and the rock-face went on up and then there were jags against the light where wild goats scrambled but she couldn't see one now, perhaps at daybreak they were still asleep in a hollow of thin brown grass. And then a shadow soared out from the crest, a buzzard or a kite, it wheeled – what? – a hundred, two hundred metres over their masthead and her eyes, but to gaze that perpendicularly heavenward made her dizzy so she looked down.

Alexis and Laura Rodostamo had fished this sea, dusk dark and dawn, all their marriage. Balancing a netted and twitching scorpion fish on the gunwale so Anna could club it with the boathook, Imogen hoped they had been happy. But how could she tell? She had been a schoolgirl.

Alexis had died on a winter morning of harrying squalls which battered one hamlet with water for half an hour but missed another, ripped thunder clouds to rags on this summit but rucked them into a mound on that, gave the Rodostamo valley's orange grove a fit of St Vitus' dance so frenzied it would surely prove mortal, Imogen had thought, staying in the house for her first Cambridge vac, watching the trees' ripe gaudy baubles judder. Achilles, disheartened by his old captain's long painful decay, had leaned on his pitchfork beside her. They had fought the fascists together, Alexis Rodostamo and he, he had told her – not for the first time. Italian fascists, German fascists, any fascists that had shown their faces. They were stories he liked to tell. How the Italians had come over in the autumn of '40, regiments of them yapping and swaggering, with a whole lot of equipment the Germans had given them, but the Greeks had bundled them home. Italians weren't men. They puffed themselves up like owls, Italians did, he'd seen them. And they bolted like rats, he'd seen them do that too. Yes, the Italians had come with their ships and their aeroplanes, they had come with their field guns and their armoured cars and their machine guns, columns of them marching in the dust, and a handful of free Greeks had knocked hell out of them. Alexis Rodostamo and he had fought. Old rifles, hand grenades, shotguns. They'd ambushed them. Scythes and pitchforks (he had clenched the one in his gnarled fist) and knives when need called. At night they'd come down from their mountains and killed the fascists while they snored. It hadn't been till the panzer divisions turned up the next year that Greece had been lost. The only country that had stood by Greece had been Britain. The British army had fought, and a few Australians and New Zealanders, but the British hadn't been much use on land. Good at sea, yes, but no good on land. Had Imogen seen the village memorial to the fifteen local men the Germans had taken to the ravine and shot? Then, "What do you think?" he had demanded abruptly, nodding at the garden pyre of lop and top, rotten seed-boxes, raked leaves, "is it dry enough to burn?" Imogen had said, "I hope a tortoise hasn't chosen it to hibernate in." And then Maria had come out of the kitchen door and stumped along the gravel path and stood beside them and the kitchen door had slammed and she had said, "He's dead."

Anna took over the heaving of the net. Tired, Imogen made her way aft, sat beside Achilles. He was too seized-up to lift nets, usually he fished with his son Tasso or with Yanni the fat odd-job-man. And in the village, Imogen smiled as she remembered, they said the only thing that kept any semblance of life in his ugly cadaver was the summer month when he had his two half-undressed young women to watch working. And Alexis, she smiled as she remembered this too, had been the soul of kindness when on his London visits he had come down to that depressing school and taken Anna and her out for lunch – the soul of kindness, wearing his English suits and shoes, talking

19

his accented English, making his wry little jokes about the difference between her country and his.

Achilles rummaged in a locker, took out a bottle of wine, hoiked out the cork, passed it to her. She raised it to her lips. The farm's wine was passable, and at sea at daybreak it tasted pretty fine.

What did she think about Anna marrying an Italian? the old guerrilla asked in a low grumble. The estate going to an Italian one day. A bad business, he reckoned. Well, he wouldn't live to see it.

One evening the summer after Alexis Rodostamo died, fire came over the hill.

The north-west wind was blowing, the mistral; in the offing, white horses champed. For a few minutes the flames massed along the crest of the hill; then they leaped down ridge by ridge at cypress and eucalyptus and maritime pine, at juniper and broom. The eagles and the swifts flew up. The rabbits ran, beside them ran the stoats who before had gone for rabbits' throats and sucked their blood till they stopped jerking and screaming. The wild dogs and the pine martens ran. At least, down in the valley Laura Rodostamo, as she marshalled her household in the courtyard, found herself distractedly hoping the pine marten she had surprised by the stable the other night was running fast and would get away. The lizards and the mice could not run fast enough, they caught fire and burned. A swarm of bees on an olive bough began in panic to disintegrate, and some flew fast enough and high enough and others were lulled by the smoke. The butterflies shimmered into flames. The bats hanging by their heels in a shed roof looked charred already. They were made cinders in an instant; were flecks in the ash of the bracken thatch; as ash and smoke were blown aloft, played their part in putting out the sun over several parishes.

What about my snakes? Laura wondered. What about my beautiful emerald grass-snakes and my zigzagged vipers and my golden and reddish brown Aesculapian snakes? For since she had been widowed she had loved every growing thing and every creature on the estate more fiercely than before, loved with a protectiveness half consolation and half despair. And now with the roaring and the smoke and the skyward gouts of flame that were trees' deaths, were trees tied to the stakes of themselves and martyred, now with her milling frightened nephews and nieces about her she prayed for every pounding heart, every being that crawled or scuttled or galloped, that fluttered or bounded or slithered, every mind stampeded by horror, every stampeding foot and paw, every mind emptied of everything except the agony of being burnt alive, every choke, every fall, every shriek. Mercy on them, she prayed. Let mercy be shown to every soul – because of course if any living thing had a soul then all had, she had never doubted that; either all or none. Either every atom was sublime or it was all a delusion. The latter probably, but one steadied one's nerves with what notions the air carried drifting about.

They shall not hurt nor destroy in all my holy mountain. That had been in the English church in Valletta when she had been nine and at the carol service she had read one of the lessons, had read it standing at the east end of the nave because even if she stood on a stool she couldn't see anything on the lectern. *The wolf also shall dwell with the lamb, and the leopard shall lie down with the kid; and the calf and the young lion and the fatling together; and a little child shall lead them.* That was the kind of holy mountain Alexis and she had dreamed they might ordain here on his family's estate. That was the kind of harmony they had tried to nurture. *And the cow and the bear shall feed; their young ones shall lie down together; and the lion shall eat straw like the ox.* Now the peaceful mountain was being ravaged. It would be laid waste. Marina, Sophia, Alexis who had been named after his uncle, there had always been an Alexis Rodostamo, little Adonis, yes they were all four there. "Don't make a fuss, everything will be all right," she told them, and wondered how long one went on saying that sort of thing, and heard her soul cry: They shall not hurt nor destroy. Not in Olympian calm but in impotent fury her soul, her flustered shrill old woman's soul, raged: They shall not hurt. They shall not destroy. They shall not fire my groves. In contempt of evil divinity, in hatred of this evil world, her soul cried its defiance. They shall not burn alive my bellowing cattle. They shall not by evil fiat turn my bright moths to sparks. Who is it that harries my people? "Adonis darling, don't cry." What mindless power would make my green fields ash? *And the sucking child shall play on the hole of the asp, and the weaned child shall put his hand on the cockatrice's den.* What had happened to that old dream of peace? Why did it have to be made a mockery of with such brutishness? And why ah why did the countryside have to go up in flames when Demitri's children were staying but not Anna who was older and would have been sensible? Anna would have helped – Anna who was on the other side of the continent, and probably right this minute in her room at Newnham dressing for yet another May ball. Or Imogen. Imogen would have been decisive, lucid, brisk. She would have stood firm. (But there was nothing to her! the figure of a ballerina.) She would have planted her slightness in the middle of the courtyard and would have been immoveable and would have given orders: You do this, you do that. Doubtless now in her rooms at Clare – for of course Imogen had been one of the first women to go to a men's college, of course she had! – she was putting on a dress more dashing than Anna's, she would enchant, be envied, hankered after, might outrage, had always been a—

This was ridiculous, Laura grappled with her wisping thoughts. Marina, Sophia, Alexis. Where had Adonis got to? Ah, old Maria had picked him up, bless her. Any child putting his hand anywhere near a cockatrice's den would be cuffed. Along the lines of a basilisk, weren't they? Born of a serpent and a cock? With a barbed tail? And their look was fatal, she remembered that.

They could not fight the fire, Laura made herself reason stolidly. Look at them, those that were not sixty were not yet ten – oh, except for Yanni, but he was useless, always had been. Her duty was to get her household away to safety. The buildings would have to take their chance, it would depend on the wind. Ah why had Alexis left her to face this alone? She was old. She was sad. She was unsurmountably tired. No, she was glad he had never seen his woods charcoal, his meadows ash, never seen his house burned, his family portraits in the hall, the Edward Lear watercolour in the dining-room, the library with the books for winter nights and the painting of Anna by John Ward, the gun-room, dear God where were the dogs? It was difficult to remember everything and to make the right decisions with the roar of the fire coming nearer. That darkness billowing down the hillside and shot with horrifying scarlet assumptions into the heavens looked as if it had got to the top olive grove. And the reek of burning! Hard not to be frightened. It had her by the throat.

The boats. To the boats. Right. Had they lost anybody? Here came Achilles. He had unbolted the stable door, he reported. He had unbolted the byre door. He didn't look alarmed. He put leashes on the whimpering dogs. Maria and he stood to lose everything if the fire came this way just as she did, Laura thought, her mind at once a lonely black bedroom where not quite silently the door opened and then a floorboard creaked. Well, Tasso had taken the truck into town today, he was all right. Now, there must be no scurrying back into the house to fetch things they believed were precious. Nothing was precious. "Right." She squared her shoulders. "Follow me."

Laura Rodostamo marched her people out of the court-yard gateway, down the valley path beside the stream toward the shore. A scared cow gallumphed away through the olive trees. Sheepbells tinkled peacefully. "So long as they don't get cut off," Achilles muttered.

It had not rained for weeks, the stream was a trickle, all the land was tinder. It will not rain, Laura as she led her procession of fugitives made herself know, and gave a little encouraging jiggle to the hand Alexis put in hers.

"I hope the frogs and the terrapins will be all right," he said, who sometimes transferred terrapins from the stream to a bowl in his bedroom and had to be urged not to keep them in captivity very long.

"I'm sure they'll be fine," his father Demitri Rodostamo replied, hobbling along with his stick. He had married late, a wife young enough to be his daughter. Soon after their fourth child was born, she had gone back to Athens – in which ugly, meretricious, philistine city it was the general view in the family and among their friends that the silly bitch belonged, though it was miserable that she only dispatched the children to their father once a year. And since her departure he had suffered from gout.

The walk to the sea took twenty minutes, which is what it always took. The old, grey captain of the retreat would have no unseemly scampering. Was the fire at their very heels, pray? The children would be so kind as to behave with dignity. Had they forgotten Achilles' rheumatism? Their father was lame too, it could hardly have escaped their attention. Did they intend to leave them behind?

And Demitri had not told the others to push on ahead. He had let his sister-in-law be gallant; had not insisted on being gallant himself. Fearful for his brood and ashamed of himself, he had pegged along as briskly as he could – or as briskly as he thought Laura would let him, people suggested afterward when the fire was discussed. They could just imagine that ancient child of empire with hell-fire only a few terraces away, they declared; could imagine her regarding the poor fellow with pity; could hear her voice. "Do not get agitated, Demitri. Walk slowly." Of course he had deferred to his brother all his life, they judged if they felt like elaborating on his wretchedness, and now he deferred to his sister-in-law, anyhow that old lady domineered in a hundred soft and not so soft ways. Demitri's trouble had always been that Alexis was the elder brother. No, it was being captured right at the outset of the war that had unmanned him. It was spending years in an Italian prison camp from which he had not, so far as one knew, made any very resolute attempts to escape – whereas Alexis had proved a dogged guerrilla leader, at the end came down from his fastnesses in something very like glory. No, it was never having any money, that was what had crushed Demitri. Having to go and be manager of that factory on the edge of town for twenty years, what did it produce, ginger-beer somebody thought, no, either plastic mugs or some special kind of biscuit, ah taps that was it, well naturally it had broken a spirit not the most robust in the first place. And now being practically a pensioner of Laura's didn't help, sleeping by her grace in the bedroom he'd had all his life, and in a turmoil of anxiety before his children came in the summer, then unable to cope with them when they were here, fretting over whether he could afford to pay a girl to look after the little one, imploring his jibbing banker for tolerance, nothing funnier than a gentleman with no credit. The sort of good manners you die of didn't help either, the opinion ran. No wonder he played that mournful thing all the time, what was it? pipe, recorder, penny-whistle? No wonder during the fire he let Laura take command. Just look at the way even with his gout he insisted that young healthy girls take his seat in the bus.

From the shore, the hill looked twice its usual size; the fire's reds and greys battened on brush, vineyard, copse, orchard, they grew. And what was worse, Alexis thought, clutching his aunt's hand, what was more dreadful still was that now the hill was a thing of air, of deadly air, it kept changing its shape. It is a tiger, no, it is a castle, no, a witch, he thought. In its rage it will fall on us. Or it will fall on us

25

because it cannot help but fall, the towering darkness has lost control of itself, no longer knows what it is doing, could easily topple this way. Now it is a dragon. Its breath will shrivel us.

Up the valley, the abandoned house waited. Its fate waited to be declared. It would depend on the lie of the land, on the veering of gusts, on whether this scarp provided tinder, whether that spinney caught when the sparks blew by. The guns in the gun-room, abandoned, waited. Among the sabres and the riding whips they waited, English shot-gun by French shot-gun, Venetian flintlock fowling-piece by Russian musket. (There had been in the eighteenth century a Venetian and in the nineteenth a Russian marriage.) Would polished stocks be burned, engraved breeches and smooth barrels be melted? If the Angel of Death, deliberating whether to annihilate things and creatures and their souls in this valley or the next, opened the gun-room door and glanced in, would he be moved by the weapons' gleaming indifference, their tranquillity akin to his own? Standing on the quay struggling to collect her wits and make sensible decisions, Laura knew that souls too were annihilated; there was no eternal life; even the numinous visitor was only an idea she had blurredly imagined. But would the angel – who was real enough as he picked up the dead master of the house's revolver, handled it a moment, put it down again – be moved smilingly to spare or smilingly to destroy? As real as godhead or dust or as unreal, did he share our human delight in earning prayers of gratitude and our delight in snuffing life out? Laura suspected he might not. No, the Angel would have nature's divine disregard for joys and tortures, rights and wrongs, births and deaths; and finding this a strangely heartening suspicion she gave Alexis' four-year-old hand another jiggle and said cheerfully, "You see? Here we all a͏ safe and sound, just like I said." For then if the Angel the gun-room door, if he paced slowly musing across - taking, possibly, from the table that old Byzantine

26

dagger and sticking it into his presumably sumptuously begemmed belt where the damascened blade would look very handsome – then there would be a communion between the deserted house and him. The haunted and the haunter would understand one another, no? Peace would find itself in harmony with peace.

That is what above all I love, Laura suddenly heard her mind announcing. But then she frowned, because it would do the peaceless souls gathered about her no conceivable good to be even mildly and silently despised. And who was she, bedevilled by apprehensions and distractions, to do homage to indifference, to coldness and stillness and quietness above all things?

It was very likely the approach of her own death, Laura's mind added in an off-hand, sardonic tone of voice. That was a plausible explanation. Her abstract self shrugged its shoulders, allowed itself a flutter of exasperated laughter.

"Demitri, take the children in *Nineveh* and sail well out," she ordered with uncalled-for brusqueness.

That the Angel should be immovable was pleasing to her own increasing ghostliness – that was what Imogen had called it once, who could herself be immovable, cold. Yes, it was her own diminishing ability to exist very convincingly – for that was often what it felt like. On occasion she would most dismally fail to convince herself. This was the reason why she was far from displeased to envisage the uncaringness with which the Angel of Death would finger her jewellery. She hadn't got much. But there were a few pretty things on her dressing-table, things that had been her mother's or her mother-in-law's. Ivory combs and brushes. A tortoise-shell box with a few rings and brooches. Yes, if the elegantly caparisoned Angel went upstairs . . . If wearing a dagger fit for one of his majesty (the lovely chasing on the blade had always beguiled her, and the garnets set in the sheath, and the jade hilt) he explored the quietness from which the people had been easily routed; if he stepped into her bedroom, approached her dressing-table, bent his eyes on its neatness and ordinariness . . . If with white indifferent fingers he picked up one or two of her trinkets, put them down again, she would be far from displeased. Take my pearl necklace out of the drawer, she told him, dangle it a moment from your hand, drop it back. (She heard it drop.) Finger this. Finger that. Have your way with my things. Have your way with me. (Far, far off, she heard Wagner's music for Iseult's death. Extraordinary, she thought, the wild echoes that throb in a respectable old widow's thin blood.) Touch my ruby earrings. Touch me.

That what little Rodostamo jewellery there was had during the war been buried at the foot of the third cypress on your left as you came up the drive – this might make the Angel smile faintly; but would not make him less likely to consign the unbeseeching stones and metals to the furnace now. Nor that the guns had endured the Nazi occupation under the library floorboards – from which sanctuary they had been easy to take out when required. (Her father-in-law had not let infirmity prevent him, when the coast seemed temporarily clear, from doing his country's invaders some old man's cunning and pitiless damage. With respect for his justice and his courage the village had noted the deaths; and with terror of reprisals.) Nor that the japanned box where she kept Otto's letters was in a drawer of that dressing-table – the few letters he had written, or the few that had reached her. None of these facts amusing or touching would deflect the Angel from his arbitrariness. The celestial would be as amoral as ever, Laura was pleased to reflect, loving that cold eyeing and cold fingering with her dying woman's cold heart but warmly kissing Adonis as he was lifted whimpering aboard the sloop. The rest of them would take the fishing-smack, she explained with a forcefulness that startled old Achilles into recognising that her husband's spirit was alive in her. Her husband's or her father's. Achilles had never known Captain Salthouse, but he had seen his medals in the cabinet in the drawing-room.

Hooves came drubbing through the olive grove. Laura's

mare had been well trained, she was a pleasant ride; but now her mane rippled and her eyes rolled. She swerved around the thicket of prickly pear. She saw the figures on the quay, she snorted, she shied. Shingle shelving under her hooves, she plunged back into the trees.

They would stay close inshore, Laura decreed as the smack put forth. Someone running from the fire might appear on the rocks. One of the village people might have been on this part of the estate, might try to escape this way. The goat-boy, had anybody seen him today?

She stood on the foredeck as they patrolled the coast, she peered. Inshore the mistral hadn't thrown up much of a sea, but farther out where *Nineveh* had vanished in the ashen murk it would be rough. Such combers of smoke were breaking over the land, she couldn't tell if the flames were blowing toward her house or not. With the sloop bashing through the waves, how would Demetri ever stop Adonis crying? And then Alexis might start, poor love. And the girls weren't much older. Away on the mainland, fires sometimes raged for days – when would this one be exhausted? Well, at least the summer evening would be light for another couple of hours – not that light this evening looked much like light. The tide of smoke had lapped down the olive grove to the driftwood, it was lapping out to sea, she could make out less and less, everyone on board was coughing and rubbing their eyes. So you could pray for every creature to be saved, but at the same time be glad the world's meaninglessness was not going to be tampered with just because of human hopes and fears – she was learning, maybe old age had a lesson or two for her yet. You could be inconsequential in this interesting new way.

What about firefighters? Any chance of aeroplanes droning in over the hills, mercifully debouching water? No, not much chance. Certainly not today. You're in Greece, she reminded herself. Ah, to hell with it. Let it be as in the prophecy of the ruin of Babylon, she thought – what did they call it? *the glory of kingdoms*, that was right. This must be whispering to her from another childhood Sunday in Valletta, she supposed. Let her house be blackened. Let her harvest be consumed by flames. Let it come to an end. *And their houses shall be full of doleful creatures; and owls shall dwell there, and satyrs shall dance there.* Why not? Alexis was dead. She didn't like the world so much that she couldn't take a macabre pleasure in seeing it suffer. Was that a man on that headland, a man waving? "Closer in!" she called to Achilles at the helm. And what malign chance had set the country alight? Or what malign man? That happened sometimes. Not so often as in Sardinia, say. But it happened. *And the wild beasts of the islands shall cry in their desolate houses* . . . Yes, there would be satisfactions. Let the wild beasts of this island cry in her house. No, it wasn't a man on the headland. A spectre, a smoke wraith. With the fire roaring as it devoured the hillside, how would she hear if someone called? Ah, let her Babylon fall too, she didn't care. *And her time is near to come, and her days shall not be prolonged.*

What was Yanni saying? The fire reached the huts where she often lodged her summer guests; she heard the whoosh as the wattle walls and thatched roofs blazed, she saw the flames spout up. When the fire reached the kitchen hut she heard the drums of gas explode. Yanni was coughing as poignantly as he knew how. "Mrs Rodostamo, I cannot breathe." He choked. He gasped. Then with sudden inspiration, "Mrs Rodostamo, your dogs cannot breathe."

Truly the man was contemptible. "I have explained to you," she pronounced without turning her head to where no doubt through a rip in his loathsome shirt he was scratching his bulbous gut – that was what he was usually doing when her gaze happened to fall on him. "We are staying close to the shore in case somebody needs to be rescued. Keep an eye out for swimmers please." (Laura did not know it, but during the siege of Singapore something very like that had been her father's last words, spoken in a picket-boat crossing Keppel Harbour in the dark.) "If really we cannot breathe we will get into the sea. With our faces near to the surface, we will breathe what air there is."

"Ah Mrs Rodostamo I cannot swim! Alas, I am a poor wretch. My mother never taught me. The Holy Virgin never taught me. Mrs Rodostamo I beg you, I—"

She confronted him. The white hairy flesh seen through his shirt had never appeared more despicable. "Honestly, Yanni, sometimes you sound like a Catholic. Do not be afraid. We will put ropes over the side of the boat. Maria and Daphne cannot swim either – but are they whining? Indeed, put out some ropes now, and make sure you tie them securely. It will be good for you to have something to do." And then, because she felt a loyal head at her knee, she said more softly, "It's all right, Pan, I'm here." She stooped, she patted his head. Alexis had loved Pan above the other dogs. Her eyes brimmed. Luckily there was the excuse of the smoke. She was just a foolish old woman with no capacity to look after her own.

No one was killed by the fire, though after it was spent they found the carbonised body of a donkey which a smallholder from the village had left tethered to a tree. Also two sheep had blundered into a ravine from which they had been unable to scramble out when the smoke and flames came.

The fire spared the Rodostamo house and the cottage where Achilles and Maria lived. But it destroyed two outlying cottages and a number of sheds; it came far enough into the garden to turn the hard tennis court into a lava field palisaded with posts melted crooked, festooned with cobwebs of molten wire; and if the wind had been due north rather than north-west it would have taken the house, everybody agreed, the house and then the lower olive groves and orchards – the local saint, Saint Sosipatros, and the spirits of the air were to be praised. As it was, of the one thousand four hundred and thirty something Rodostamo olive trees the conflagration charred to death over a third, and olive trees were slow to grow, their mistress sorrowed. Olive trees were the richness of that land and of that people, but they took a generation to begin to bear. When Venice had held sway over its Ionian colonies they had paid the Greeks to plant olive trees for their children and grandchildren. That had been enlightened government. You only had to compare these verdant islands with the goat-ridden and dust-stormed regions the Turks had misruled for centuries. But would she be able to afford to replant at once? Let alone help the villagers to buy the hundreds of saplings they would need. Her savaged farm would next make a profit when?

The fire gutted the chapel by the spring, which was an evil chance. But it spared the butterfly chapel, which everyone could agree was miraculous. It was called the butterfly chapel because for some reason in the clearing there the swallow-tails and the Camberwell beauties flocked more gloriously than elsewhere. And all in all, Imogen Scottow considered eleven years later as Anna and she dumped the last coil of net in its crate and dumped the buoy, which had DIESEL written on it, on top of that, Laura and her household had recovered from their purgatory very well.

Each year when Imogen came, the young olive trees on the terraces had grown a little. In the upper orchards, the new lemons and oranges, the new plums and pears, the new mulberries and walnuts, could be seen to have put on new growth. One year a burned shed had been reroofed; it was a sty now; Imogen had leaned on the gate, watched the sow suckling her litter. And Tasso had carpentered away for months, he had rebuilt the huts by the shore. Happiest achievement of all, in time the last of the charred trees were felled. They no longer stood about the landscape like black ghosts waiting to be buried so that their souls could step aboard Charon's skiff and be sculled across the Styx. Fresh arbutus and myrtle and cystus had sprouted up through the charcoal that acres had been thicketed with, Imogen remembered, it had been impossible to walk in that desolation without getting pitch-black. Another year

Laura had been dowsing, a new well had been sunk. And this year she had doubled her apiary, another orchard was furnished with hives. Of course fire might come over the crest of the hill again. And then despair would put to flight the last remnants of her godmother, Imogen was sure; oh yes, then the last ethereal notions and feelings, faced with a reborn tempest of fire, would be whirled away to oblivion; she wouldn't exist at all. But for eleven years they had been fortunate.

Imogen stripped off her clothes. After hauling up the net, a swim. Anna was already overboard. Achilles was gutting their catch. No, he'd stopped. He was gazing out over the morning sea. (We triumphed, he was thinking. Those few of us who are still alive will be dead soon, but in the end we triumphed over the fascists, Greece is free). Over there the only village fishing-smack still in action was chugging toward land, towing her string of half-a-dozen dinghies each with a lamp, a man, a trident. They had been at sea all night. They would drop their net one last time in the cove, Imogen knew. Often with the other women she had helped pull the catch ashore, had taken her place on the rope and pulled and felt her feet slither on the shingle and seen the net inch shoreward, then tired among tired women had splashed into the shallows and laid her weight on the rope again and pulled again, and had then had to make an effort not to show how surprised she was by the meagreness of the catch. The sea was poor. Over-fished; beginning to be polluted; poor. When she was a child there had been three village fishing-smacks. Evening after evening she had watched them put to sea. Morning after morning she had watched them return. But now most of the men had left to work in those parts of the Ionian which had been turned into tourist resorts. Who could blame them? They sent money back to their families. Sometimes at the season's end they came home. No doubt it was more amusing to pick up foreign girls in nightclubs than to sit all night rocking in a dinghy with a lamp and a trident.

Imogen stepped onto the gunwale. She wavered; she balanced. Here came the ferry from the mainland too, heading along the coast to the town. The sunlight on the pale cliff was roseate. On boulders, cormorants were stretching their wings. A flying fish broke the blue calm and went winging away. She looked for what might be chasing it. Was there a school of dolphins? On occasion you were lucky, you saw them passing. No, there didn't seem to be anything.

It was good to be at sea, good to be free, good to watch the sun burning up the mist, feel it drying the dew off the deck. The dazzling water would be cool, would wash her clean. The gunwale stirred. Imogen swayed, she dived.

And the light? wondered Laura Rodostamo, sitting down stiffly and thankfully in the green deck-chair outside the hut where Angelica slept – for she was weary, could not remember a day or a night for years when she had not been. And the light? For dawn by dawn she was brought to light, and still she marvelled at the luminous peace that could seem to extend over the world for an hour.

Not that she could not be inspired by stormy days that broke with rain drubbing on her bedroom windows, with waves thundering at her cliff, with light not a radiant garment but tatterdemalion soused grey rags. But on a clear still dawn light came and brought her to light – or so it could seem. Anyhow the phrase had stayed with her. Mildly she claimed it as true. And at her age, so rickety, so sleepless, so wasted, with such a long list of boring things wrong with her, with pains here and pains there, with pills for this and pills for that – pills her swollen clumsy fingers frequently dropped on the ground, where her spaniels wolfed them – she reckoned she might while away her goodbye with what insubstantial illuminations and unsubstantiable truths she fancied.

Time was simplifying her, perhaps that was it. By day she honoured the sun; by night the moon and the stars. Often too she made her obeisance to fog, to cloud, to rain, paid homage to obscurities and velleities and regrets. So now with her head against the back of her chair, with her misshapen hands folded in her lap, Laura listened to the ripples, watched the rafts of mist shimmer on the sea. With her only virtue, which was this simple openness of hers to immediate things, she would let the daybreak lighten her mind. Humbly she would hope to partake of its peace. What was that poem, she had read it donkeys' years ago, during the war, before the war? About looking out over the Mediterranean early in the day. *Wait, don't bring the coffee yet, nor the pain grillé.* Something like that. *Odysseus' ships* . . . Who was it by? Ships . . . Ships . . . *Have not yet passed the islands, I must watch them still.* Fine poet, whoever he was. She had read poetry all her life – which was why her daughter's love affair with that conference-trotting versifier had dejected her so leadenly. Naturally she couldn't recall a single one of his formless lines. But it was irritating – her memory was ravelling dreadfully, it was a disgrace – when she couldn't bring to mind the true poets she had loved since she was a girl. And it was even more irritating when instead she recollected that man's bland views, his determination to be liked, his twitter about all the arts festivals he attended, readings he gave, editorial boards he sat on, prizes he judged, anthologies he edited. Imogen had so enjoyed making fun of the man that she had been almost disappointed when she succeeded in prodding Anna into alertness and the butt was dismissed.

Still, still, *Odysseus' ships* . . . Well, there was no point in sitting there being annoyed by her stupidity. To let the sea-light wash her mind clear . . . To let in as much clarity as she could; to hold Imogen and Angelica in that lucency; to turn their destinies in it, turn, turn . . .

35

Astonishing, the sight of pregnant Imogen in that hotel had been. "Shall we have some tea?" Laura had asked. But she had wanted to cry: You're sheer spirit, you can't have a child! For she had always thought of the girl as really spirit and only by some polite convention flesh, only for the sake of appearances flesh; and so it was all, she had helplessly confessed as her goddaughter took off her coat and sat down at the tedious frilly little table, about as easy to comprehend briskly as if a boy had been cumbersome with child.

"I'm not cumbersome," Imogen had said lightly. "A scone, please."

And it had not only been the trouble Laura had experienced in imagining those narrow hips giving birth (Angelica had, indeed, been delivered by caesarian section) or those small breasts giving milk (Imogen had breastfed her with manifest contentment). It had been that Laura's old sense that her stuffy Scottow cousins' wayward daughter was pure spirit, jolted into prominence by her pregnancy, had not then faded once more into the haze at the back of her mind. It had continued to stand out. Light had played on it. Imogen had always looked like a dancer, had always moved as lightly as a dancer, always seemed light as air. She was a mere breath – was that it? No doubt that was partly it. Then there was that fine china face of hers. She had a face with a beautiful glimmering glaze, white with the faintest flushes of rose in her cheeks. (Naturally these days she lavished care on her make-up. But Laura could remember her as a child, the light coming out through the clear thin whiteness had been the same.) It was the face of her ruthlessness – that had to be acknowledged of course. It could be, or could appear to be, utterly cold, that china face. Eighteenth century, a Chelsea figurine or a Derby figurine. Very pretty; but just glaze, a clever glaze. Oh certainly Jim and Margaret Scottow were not particularly exciting – but equally certainly their daughter had treated them with shameful unkindness. She had spoken to them by all accounts – and her own account had been the sharpest –

with a harshness there had been absolutely no call for. She had dumped their fatherless grandchild's existence in their consciousness like a derrick thudding a container down on a ship's deck – and then scarcely ever let them meet her; wouldn't let them help; didn't seem to care if they never came to know her well or love her more than dutifully.

Had she been disloyal to the Scottows? Laura worried. When she had seemed to take their errant daughter's side – had really done so – disloyal? (The rest of the day would be one distraction after another. She would forget things; she would dither; she would feel horribly old. But now for a few minutes she would hold the mother and child in her morning clarity.) Had she been beguiled – and not for the first time – by that face that might be the doll-like front of ruthlessness, even of cruelty, but was also the mask of a magnificent spirituality that naturally went disguised among men, went incarnate, but was superbly abstract nonetheless? Not for the first time. Laura shifted guiltily in her deck-chair. It went back a long way, this feeling guilty because Jim and Margaret Scottow sensed that their daughter's deepest affinity was with her. And Imogen had not helped; had never cared to help at all. Ah the flamboyance with which she invited herself to stay here sometimes several times a year, the insouciance with which she refused her mother's invitations to Wiltshire. It had been going on for years. It went back to when Anna and she were at the same boarding school and Imogen had made no secret of preferring her godmother's to her mother's Sunday lunches at restaurants in the neighbouring county town. It goes back, the reluctant penitent made her mind pronounce in its own flinching hearing – the chair creaking, for her awkward old limbs had tried to writhe – it goes back to my sometimes feeling disappointed in my own daughter.

Had it been a good idea, that boarding school? The Scottows were stinking with money, but Alexis had had to borrow to pay Anna's fees. Of course it had been he, being Greek, who had insisted on an English education.

Laura would cheerfully have sent the girl to school on the island. The Scottows had been an enormous help, driving Anna to and from the airport, having her in Wiltshire for half-terms. As for the school, which was meant to be terrifically fashionable and was certainly terrifically expensive, it had always seemed to Laura a barrack made intolerable by uniforms and bells and shuffling queues and lists, by social pretensions, by cretinous ball-games, by religion, by invented traditions, by miserable children . . . the more likeable children were generally miserable, the viler parents relentlessly blithe.

Anna had been quite happy there. The green deck-chair wobbled, it groaned. What sort of a woman was she who had to try to stop herself thinking ill of her own daughter for displaying equanimity?

Angelica cried.

Laura picked her up. She kissed her. She changed her. She was useful, she was happy, suddenly love made her throat prickle. It was a blessing, she reflected without being embarrassed by her cynicism, how the tricky mind sloughed off its guilts.

With the child in her arms she stepped out of the shady hut into the halcyon air. "Look," she murmured, "Isn't it a glorious morning? Can you see anyone else up and about yet? Perhaps it's all for you and me. We'll go and find some breakfast, shall we?" The chatelaine made her way along the footpath through the boulders and scrub. In the first warmth of the day's sun, the cystus was beginning to scent the stillness. Light rippled around the baby's head and her head as she walked. Her dogs padded at her heels. "Who will we find?" They were coming into the heart of the encampment where the kitchen hut stood and the arbour where they ate. "Oh look, there's Tasso watering his tomatoes. Good morning, Tasso!" she cried. "Good morning, Mrs Rodostamo." He waved his hosepipe so the arc of water glittered in the sun.

Laura cut bread, she poured milk. Would Angelica like an egg for her breakfast? She would boil an egg, they would dip soft bits of bread in the soft yolk. Angelica toddled among the dogs; she toddled this way, that. Laura made herself some coffee. She carried everything out with a light heart and a light tread, set it on the big round table beneath the arbour. She lifted Angelica into her high-chair. At lunch the wistaria cast its dapples on the pale scrubbed wood; but now the sun had only just cleared the headland, the brilliance danced across the bay and in under the fronds and into her eyes. "Is the egg good?" she asked, cutting off the crust of the rough brown bread because it might be too hard. Angelica was cheerful too, she chucked her spoon to the dogs. "Your mother will be back from fishing in an hour or two. What shall we do till then, you and I?" A fresh spoon; a dip into the egg; the wavering approach of her hand toward the childish mouth; the deft advance of the spoonful when she judged the moment propitious; its insertion between the sticky lips; its unloading; its withdrawal; its reloading. "Shall we go to the butterfly chapel?" And then, as Laura picked Angelica up from her high-chair and held her a moment before lowering her to the dust, she murmured, "You're my last adventure, you know that?"

You're my last adventure. She had heard herself thinking those words the first time she had laid eyes on Imogen's baby. She had stood beside the London hospital bed, in her hand a little *papier mâché* box which contained a coral necklace that her father had brought back from the China Sea. She had explained to a very flat goddaughter in whose wan countenance the blue eyes flashed with a triumph that was positively indecent, that although it might seem an odd present for somebody two days old she hoped the girl might

39

be amused to wear it when she grew up. It was just an old Chinese necklace, a thing of her father's, she had said. Pretty enough in its way, but nothing grand. It was just that she had been unable to come without a present for the baby, she had said; and had averted her gaze from the arrogance on the pillow – truly it had been a Head of Victory that lay there – and had looked into the cot and had thought: You're my last adventure. It had brought her up sharp a moment, thinking that. But only for a moment. It was so obviously true. And now she had said it aloud.

She might perhaps live till Angelica were three, could not hope to live till she were six. The girl would remember her vaguely or not at all.

That was neither here nor there, she thought, setting off with the child once more in her arms, her dogs once more at her heels, and thinking also how agreeable it was that most people got up late. To have the shore to oneself . . . To have the encampment in the sun and a breath of cystus and a breath of thyme, and the sheep-bells chiming from a high pasture, and the stand of eucalyptus which the fire had touched but by unaccountable grace not mortally . . . To have these things for an early hour, with only the admirable company of Tasso sprinkling his vegetable patch and Angelica mumbling her egg, was princely. The nearness of her own disintegration and the distantness of the child's made not an iota of difference to anything. It was an adventure. The track to the butterfly chapel was steep, Laura stopped to draw her wind. It was an adventure because . . . oh, because she had not been entirely straight with Imogen.

Or rather, she had only been superficially straight. If Imogen did not wish to be questioned about her baby's father, she would not dream of prying, she had declared. But it was not just love, if she had it in her to be austere for a minute, was it? Not simply loyalty. It was more than the ready ability to love your goddaughter whatever she decided, whatever she did. Laura stiffly swung Angelica into the air again, went on up the stony path through the olive grove. "Come on!" she exhorted her dogs. "Sappho, Juno, come here!" (Pan was dead.) "You can hunt lizards when we get there." No, it was not only that blind urge. The cause was that despised Margaret Scottow's anguished question, What would Imogen tell Angelica when she were old enough to ask who her father was? – an enquiry for which the luckless woman had by her daughter been condemned with renewed frigid hauteur – had been a good question. It was that in Imogen's bravura there lay concealed, didn't there, a ducking and dodging? (She would return merry from her fishing, bear her child off to the beach to paddle.) It was that she herself, puffing in her faded cotton shirt and skirt across the dry watercourse, on up through the broom, had often hoped that possessing Imogen's pretty unconditional love she might – what? Find a possible answer to Angelica's future question? (She would be dead. The girl would never know that long ago her phantasmal hand had fumbled anywhere near Imogen's scruples – if she had any.) Find some unknown man's unwanted daughter for him? A meddling, an impertinence. But how could she renounce her hope that one day Angelica should know her father? But, then – find someone who might resent her? And she, perhaps, might be appalled by him. But, then – exploit Imogen's trust, tamper with her resolve, conspire to warp that true spirit of hers, trick her into kow-towing to tribal conventions when until now she had stood with her back straight and her head high? No, no! Not that.

What, then? Perhaps she was no less respectably sentimental than Margaret Scottow, only less honest about it. Or perhaps she would condone any immorality to shelter the flame in that china face. If only she knew whether Imogen intended one day to tell Angelica the truth . . . But very probably she had not decided, Laura recognised with a spurt of panic, seeing the resolution of the enigma recede into the decades ahead when she would be mouldering beside Alexis beneath the butterflies' glade. Yes, Imogen would wait, would see who Angelica became. She would wait and see what the truth looked like after a span of years, see how different it appeared. Or no – she would tell her a lie. Send her imagination off on a wild goose chase. Something to stop her fretting – her father had been killed in some war or other – something anodyne, a touch romantic maybe . . . And that might be the happiest issue. Angelica's conception might have been squalid, might have been violent even. Things might have gone sickeningly awry after some party where – ah, Laura didn't know! but her wincing mind wouldn't stop guessing luridly – where alcohol and drugs, she old-maidishly assumed, had played their destabilising parts . . . The version of events related in Kensington Gardens might be fantasy. No, she mustn't think that!

What, then? once more. To lead Imogen to confront more penetratingly, possibly more bleakly, what she was doing – because she hadn't yet met her ghostly lover's eyes squarely, her godmother could tell, hers wasn't a haunted look. To lead her deeper into the person Angelica would become – because though Imogen was brave, no question of it, she had conceivably not yet been brave enough. But how? Laura panted, she stumped forward. How? That Angelica should one day be at peace . . . What that peace should be was Imogen alone's concern; but Imogen must establish it, mustn't she? Perhaps Imogen was doing that very thing. Perhaps a necessary or merely stylish concomitant of this coming serenity was Laura's ignorance, hers and all the world's, she was sure that if she did not know no one knew. But no – no – Imogen hadn't yet met those ghostly eyes – had not looked back into that look openly and steadily – she had not . . . And how take her hand, lead her to do it? Especially when you were dying, time was short. How? Where was her opportunity, her way? That damned girl has us all most cunningly boxed in, she thought. Including you, you little sweetheart, including you.

Perhaps it was just vulgar curiosity. Her dogs were

disgracefully ill-trained, they were hounding something, refused to come back. Paltry, futile, if she merely wanted to know who Angelica was, know what had occurred. And what did one's father or mother matter? She knew several examples of people – two in her own cousinage – who believed unquestioningly that they knew their own fathers, but were wrong. And what, at Angelica's conception, of any interest other than erotic could have occurred? Doubtless Imogen had chosen a lover with looks, with intelligence . . .

Laura tipped the child back, studied her face. No, you can't read people, she reminded herself.

The chapel by the spring had not been rebuilt after the fire. The scorched walls encompassed mounds of charred timbers, cinders that were by turn winter mud and summer dust. Leaf-mould was beginning to overlay all that remained of roof beams, screen, altar, icons. Grass and wild flowers grew in the holy ground. The spring still came splashing out of the fissure in the rock, was still held in the old stone trough, still then flowed away in a stone channel of Alexis Rodostamo's devising to irrigate part of the garden. But the fig tree which had always leaned over the spring had been burned, its blackened vestiges had had to be hacked down. True, of recent years Laura had noticed that its roots were alive; but the new stems sprouting up from the stump were still only a bush, it would be a long time before the old shady canopy were restored.

It was a melancholy place. In the early years after her husband's death and the fire, Laura had come there to be peacefully desolate on days when to be cheered up added insult to injury. But it worried her household that she should haunt the ruin. (Doubtless it had been ruined more than once, she reflected. Doubtless too before the conversion of the Roman Empire a pagan shrine had stood here, the place had been sacred immemorially.) And Anna did not approve. "Mother, I think you should make an effort not to become morbid," once she had said. So the old lady hardly ever went there now. Scarcely anyone ever went. Occasionally somebody from the village or from the house, working on that part of the estate, took his donkey to drink from the trough, but not so often as before the fire.

"You see how obliging I am?" Laura had remarked to her daughter, and had taken to haunting the butterfly chapel instead.

It had always been idyllic, not desolate at all, but she found she could be just as peacefully desolate there. It was a small white-washed building, with a stone bench on its south side where she sat and looked down to the sea. She sat there now, Angelica sitting at her feet. Naturally her peace and her desolation were one, she mused. The unmoving brilliance of the early morning brought her to light; like the land and the sea, she was revealed; she was revealed to herself; dazzled, she might see only mistily, but she saw. Sometimes she could almost watch the elements which had been her heart and mind loosen their grips on one another, watch them begin to undo her, go their everlasting ways. It was unfathomably tranquil; there might be a ripple, a cat's paw of sadness here and there on the surface, but certainly nothing you could call a wave. And sometimes she could almost see – what was it? Not see, that was wrong. But she could sense in some blind way ... She could seem fleetingly to know that the butterfly chapel was one of the places that could be the end of the world. Not dramatically – not like that time in Ethiopia when Alexis and she had been stranded in their jeep in a sand-storm, nor that other time up Etna wandering on the lava in fog. But the end of the world because in the bright stillness time could slow down; slow down; very nearly stop. Of course there were no timeless moments. Laura was rational enough to know that, and to know that was the reason why redemption, like Isaiah's holy mountain where the lion should eat straw, was a sop fed to the fainthearted. But time could slow down . . . Slow down still more . . . It could pulse so slowly you were certain that if it beat still more sluggishly the world and you would come to a standstill together, you would stop together, you would die. Time could so nearly cease that as you leaned against the wall of the butterfly chapel and looked away down over the grey olive groves to the sea you could imagine a timeless moment. It could come to you to dream that. A meeting of time and eternity, of the things of time and the nothings of eternity. When the beginning of the day shone with its stillest radiance . . . When she could sense the feelings which were the warp of her soul and the thoughts which were its weft being unpicked . . . When time slowed its rhythm; when again it slowed . . . Sad? Only in a grave, triumphant way. Her tattered, fading soul was a warship's ensign hung on a cathedral wall.

Unfortunately Anna did not understand this at all. Of course the crooked little bell-tower and the mighty cypress had charm, she would allow. And the clearing where the tortoise-shells and the fritillaries flitted had charm. And the view of the sea was magnificent, she would be the last to deny that. But did her mother have to go every day? Sometimes more than once a day? On Sundays to light a candle for Alexis was the most fitting thing in the world. But to plod up there in all weathers – to hang about on that bench for hours – when it rained, to huddle inside in the gloom half the day – Anna didn't think it could be right. And what about that evening when after dinner Laura still hadn't appeared, and they had searched and had found her pottering in the glade among the night moths and exceedingly grumpy to be looked for?

"What kind of Godawful world is it where a widow can't weep in a graveyard?" Laura had demanded; and had at once been ashamed of such sentimentality – such lying, that was the clear word for it.

"I'm afraid of finding you dead up there one day."

"You're afraid of too much. I shan't mind, why should you?"

Her visits to the chapel had given Laura Rodostamo a reputation for religion which she did not deserve. "I've read the Bible," her niece Marina had remarked to her recently, and had tossed her black tresses.

Marina had just finished her first year at Athens University. She was in love with a young Virginian called Nick Morston, who happily appeared to be equally in love with her, and who was delightful, Laura thought. An absolutely splendid young man. Or at least he knew how to make himself agreeable to his hostess, which was one of the extremely few incontrovertible virtues open to mankind. They were asleep in one of the huts down by the tide-line right now. Asleep in each other's arms. Or making love – you couldn't doubt they did that quite a lot. Anyway they certainly wouldn't be up yet, it was only eight o'clock.

"The Old Testament is all dynasties and killings and hatreds and injustices and hypocrisies and rant," Marina had said. "The New Testament is all piety and dogma and hypocrisy and rant. Why should I give either of them a second thought?" And she had gone – with a smile, because she was fond of her aunt Laura, with a smile and another flounce of those curls. She had gone, the commendable, pretty, pagan girl, to make love with Nick probably, for it had been after lunch and they had strolled toward their hut arm in arm. She had gone before Laura had had time to concentrate her straggling faculties. (It hadn't been easy, what with Maria asking whether for dinner she should cook the cutlets or the octopus, and Daphne still clattering the washing-up from lunch.)

Marina had dawdled away into the blaze of day before she could hear that her aunt pretty much agreed. Laura might make a plea for *Ecclesiastes*, it had always seemed to her level-headed, but by and large, yes, she agreed. I don't go to the butterfly chapel to pray, she might have added.

I never pray. I rarely weep. When on Saint Sosipatros' day the village priest comes to give a service, Achilles and Maria, Demitri and I, Tasso and Daphne and Yanni are his congregation. That is the extent of my Christianity: courtesy to the priest. I never light a candle, except when somebody who would expect me to is present. If I were to light a candle, I should light two. One for Alexis of course, buried under our butterflies. And one for Otto, whom you dear Marina do not know about, who was in the North African desert when he was blown to smithereens. But no, I do not light candles. Partly because there is no transcendence; souls do not shine in the darkness; lovers do not meet again. And partly because . . . oh, I don't know. Perhaps I am ridiculously fastidious. And certainly at my age it is almost impossible not to doubt everything, my thoughts are worms in the carcass of likelihood, I should take that into account. But . . . I doubt . . . I doubt I was ever truly in love.

Would Marina understand at all? Laura stooped, she picked up Angelica whom the dogs were sleepily licking really rather too much, she sat her on her knee, smiled to think of Nick and Marina lying naked on a white sheet in their shadowy room – they were both goodlooking enough for it to be a thought to make one smile. "Look!" she whispered to the child, and pointed out over the tree-tops to the dazzling sea. "Odysseus' ships!" she whispered, and laughed. For indeed there was a vessel creeping across the blue – the smack coming home? a yacht? her eyes were not what they had been. "Don't bring the coffee yet, don't bring the *pain grillé*!" Gaily she bounced the child on her knee. She hugged her. "Odysseus' ships are still there, they haven't passed our island yet!" she cried. "My darling and I want to watch them!"

For if Marina had checked for a minute before she went back to her love-making, if she had asked, "What do you do up at the butterfly chapel for hours on your own?" what could she have replied? "I feel myself being undone. I die. I don't dislike it." No, no!

47

"We can't laze away the whole day up here. I wish we could, but we can't."

To stay. To stay sitting against the chapel wall in the sun that was getting warm now. To stay watching the cobwebs on the lilac shimmer, listening to Angelica's burbling in which quite a number of real English phrases could be made out. Ah how Laura would have liked it! To stay looking out through air that would get more and more translucent as the sun reared higher and higher, looking at colours that would get harder and brighter and coarser, for instance the blue in the anchorage down there where *Nineveh* lay and the smack was right now slowing down as she approached the quay. To cuddle Angelica; to make sure her games with the spaniels were gentle games; never to fret about half-forgetting Otto by whom when she was young she had been wildly carried away, merely wildly carried away, and Alexis whom she had married and had loved dearly, merely loved dearly. (Probably some people were more profound in their passions, more true. Or else they told themselves a lot of grandiose nonsense, flaccidly let themselves believe it.) To remain. To gaze with half-closed eyes, and if she were fortunate be visited again by the Angel of Death. If she were fortunate. He did not often come, did not often really appear to stand among her imaginings, come as one of the nothings of eternity among the things of time; but of recent years in vacant hours up at the butterfly chapel she had sometimes seemed to see his slow pacing and stopping and musing, his folded pavonian wings. Senility, that was what it was. But no peacock butterfly in the clearing was more lustrous than he. He was nothing – she must remember that. He was nothing, an adumbration who occasionally loomed, or whom she could tease out of her thoughts, out of her consciousness's refractory ever-dissolving elements. Maybe, maybe. But the sun and the moon did not meditate on the world at once as intensely and as heedlessly – and since her husband's death and the fire, since her razing, he had been her preferred interlocutor, except of course when Imogen

48

was staying, when the Angel had to content his august self with second place in the local landowner's affections.

Well, other old women took to piety or the gin bottle, Laura reminded herself. She gave herself a shake. She stood up. And then, "Listen!" she murmured to Angelica. For she had heard her sea eagles. There were nothing like so many of them as she remembered from thirty years ago, but sometimes still from the crags over the sea she heard their wild cries, and more rarely again when she was watching a speck she had taken for a buzzard it wheeled closer and the grandeur and plumage were nothing like a buzzard's and she knew it was one of the kings of the sky. However, this morning although she scoured the air she couldn't see one.

But she had heard the cry. That was something. A good augury for the day, she couldn't help hoping, wondering if she had told Daphne to make beds for the new guests. Achilles and Imogen and Anna would be coming ashore with their catch. Some mullet almost without doubt. A bass if they had been lucky. Later they would light a fire.

The peace and the radiance were over for the day. Laura carried Angelica down the hill. She might have heard her eagles, but now she had recollected Stephen dying in Paris, that cast a wretchedness over things. Her solitude was over for the day too. Till midnight it would be people, people, people. Perhaps at midnight she would come up to the chapel again. Now, what was it she had determined not to forget? She must find a free afternoon to prune her roses, that was right. Well, not today. What time was the Schombergs' flight?

Laura walked into the encampment just as Tasso came jolting back from town in the truck. He had been to market, of course he had, she recalled now that she herself had written his shopping list. And he had met the ferry, sensible man. Because here, getting out of the passenger's seat of the truck with his suitcase, was Dario De Corvaro who otherwise would have had to catch a bus to

49

the village and then walk. And here were Nick and Marina, fresh from bed. Where was Sophia? Sleeping off her night's dancing, probably.

"You're just in time for breakfast," she told Dario as she kissed him. They must all sit down under the arbour, she declared. There was coffee. There was toast. There was honey from her own hives. There were peaches from her own trees. Now, who had Dario met before? "Have you met my goddaughter, Imogen Scottow?" – for here she was, appearing round the corner of the kitchen hut carrying a blue plastic bucket of fish.

So it was that Laura saw him – what? – not blush – scarcely hesitate – it was over so quickly she hardly knew what she had seen. But it was as if his eyes had been jarred.

Two

"Where do you think would be the best place for the marquee?" asked Anna Rodostamo, coming into the drawing-room.

Her mother stared at the swag of blue and scarlet silk knotted over her bikini – it was pretty, she wondered where the girl had bought it – and at her calm happy face as she sat down at the other end of the sofa. Truly it defied belief that Anna should have noticed nothing. Had it not stood out like – mockingly Laura ransacked her imagination for images of the unmistakable – like a piano in a ploughed field? Even right at the start when they had all stood in the morning sun, when Dario De Corvaro with his Roman suit of great chic and great age and great crumpledness, with his co-respondent shoes that needed cleaning, with his imperial Roman nose of great handsomeness, had stood in the dusty clearing among the huts and the olive trees where the dogs were joining in the boys' football game . . . had it not begun alarmingly to emerge? Right at the start, when for a moment Dario had wavered . . . had Anna had her head in the fish-bucket? As for the next few hours, they were composed of one agonising obviousness after another. But at the beginning . . . Only her daughter, Laura considered, could have failed to hear the tremor of strain in Imogen's low clear voice when she said, "Of course Dario and I know

51

each other," and stepped forward, and they kissed lightly on both cheeks.

Then the moment had been lost, what with Alexis and Adonis letting their ball roll to a halt and coming to the arbour for breakfast, what with the mullet and the squid and the one splendid bass being admired, and someone saying that Sophia hadn't got back from her nightclub till an hour or two ago, and someone else asking if they might take the smack down the coast to the beach for a swim. It had been lost, the moment of jolted spirits, of jarred eyes. But it had not been overwhelmed by distractions before Imogen had found another moment to deepen it. She had laid two fingers on her toddling daughter's blonde hair and said, "This is Angelica. Darling, say hello to Dario." And Laura had watched his eyebrows lift for an instant before he brought them under control again, had watched him stoop to greet the child, noticed there were grey markings in the hair at his temple. Angelica had not said hello. She had stared up into his face, then turned, gone stumbling away. And now it was afternoon and Anna wanted to talk about marquees. Do you think this is Wiltshire? suddenly her mother wanted to demand. And do you think I can afford the kind of grand wedding the Scottows always longed to give Imogen – still long to, for that matter, though she's so abrasive they don't dare mention it to her. And where on this island do you imagine I could lay hands on a marquee?

Anna met her mother's revealing stare. She was weary of being found disappointing. It made her miss her father, who had loved his wife with all his heart, but had not been loved with equal richness and had known it, his daughter was sure. She could on occasion weary of her mother's adoration of Imogen too. She had still been a schoolgirl when she had first been hurt by noticing Laura's efforts to appear to love her more – how she would turn to Imogen with brightening eyes and a lightening voice, then turn dutifully back to her. Still, she managed to sound friendly when she said, "Oh, I see. You've guessed, have you?"

52

"I've done more than guess," Laura responded. (She *must* stop underestimating Anna. She *must* love her more suitably, no, not more suitably, what a nastily indicative thought, more warmly for pity's sake. But she would die still trying, she knew.) "I've found out. Or at least," (it was of the highest importance to be more amiable), "I've begun to."

The idea that her last adventure might be upon her had been drumming a tattoo – at first soft enough to try to ignore – since Dario's bowing before Angelica under the nine o'clock sun. A shape had been looming. The hitch was, it had been looming in a mind overcast, in a *camera* truly and hopelessly *obscura*. Where were her translucency and lucidity of daybreak? They had gone! Gone when she needed them most vividly. So that she still, to start with essentials, had only the vaguest presentiments as to whether what was impending were good or bad – and this after an hour's private talk with Dario! No, more like an hour and a half it must have been; and still she was floundering among notions that kept changing their shape. Were it to prove possible to act at all, she had only the cloudiest conception of what – beyond a general benevolence, a readiness to pitch herself in – she might do. There had been the need to ascertain whether the smack were wanted for more serious purposes, such as the transport of canisters of gas or drums of kerosene, or before lunch might she be used to take a swimming expedition to the beach? (There was no sandy beach on the Rodostamo property. It had been a problem ever since Laura could remember, this desire for sand that people had. Herself, she liked swimming off her rocks. And what was wrong with the shingle in the bay?) Alas not a breath of wind had fluttered, so it was impossible that anyone should sail *Nineveh* down the coast. There had been the anxiety that Sophia, whose father was incapable of even attempting to keep an accurate eye or a steadying hand on her, was at seventeen plentifully young and hot-headed to be out all night more nights than not, with God knew

53

whom dancing God knew where – and were the few dingy discotheques in town really open till dawn? There had been Alexis who after breakfast had tired of kicking a ball around with his younger brother and had wanted to ride Tasso's decrepit motorbike on the farm tracks. Tasso had said that was fine. Laura had said it would be fine if he wore a helmet, which he had stalwartly refused to do. There had been Adonis to accompany to the quay so he might show her how well he could now dive; and the gloom implicit in Ben Thurne's non-appearance to be distressed by – up at the house, she couldn't doubt it, Demitri and he respected one another's silence resolutely; and Tasso to tell that she was afraid he'd have to go back into town after lunch to meet the Schombergs' aeroplane, unless he could bully Yanni into going instead; and this and that. So the upshot was, she was confused.

And now at the house, sitting with Anna in the drawing-room which with its thick walls and its shutters was cool even at mid-afternoon, Laura peered into her *camera obscura*, she tried to see. To bend sight back in upon itself . . . !

Through breakfast at the round table, with the sun by then high enough for half the company to be in the shade, Dario De Corvaro had not exchanged ten words with her goddaughter. He had, as fervently requested, given her something of his news. Of recent years Laura had almost lost touch with the De Corvaro family, it had been good to catch up. That castle of his. There really was a De Corvaro castle, sort of. It perched over a sorry little town in Umbria. And it wasn't much of a place, a tumbledown bit of fifteenth-century fortress with a tumbledown bit of seventeenth-century house, called a palace but it barely merited the name, stuck onto it. With outhouses against the ramparts. With a grubby chapel. With in the courtyard a well with no water.

The family had two branches. There were the rich cousins, who only ever worried about being kidnapped. In fact they got most agitated by the prospect of one another being kidnapped (ransoms extorted, it would no longer be so easy to dispatch their dim offspring to schools in Switzerland and England); and their ability to imagine for themselves the discomforts and dangers of being held hostage was, despite regular outraged reading of the newspapers in which these infamies were reported, a distant ability. They dabbled in politics, naturally. Half were so-called Christian Democrats, half so-called Socialists; sagely they hedged their venal bets. And they all wanted to be fashionable photographers, naturally. And they all depended upon regular sessions with Rome's most celebrated psychoanalysts, naturally. And they all ended up having people tempted into marrying them, and having babies and nannies, all very naturally indeed. And who yachted, of course, in the summers; and, in the winters, skied. Happily there existed the Texan extension of this cousinage, who all appeared to have a great ability to profit from the world, and who were generous, who were sentimental about the family seat in Umbria and its occupants.

Then there were the impoverished members of the De Corvaro clan, like Dario from whose grandfather the Texans did not descend and whom nobody had decided to take up and marry. Dario lived in three rooms in the stable block, lived there in the perennial expectation that one day his apartment might be required for a more important cousin, or for more Philippine maids. And the university? at breakfast Laura had asked. Ah, no news much. For ten years he had been in Rome three days a week; had held his course – in Aesthetics, of all things, in which once he had taken rather a good degree. The History of Aesthetics. But the professors who had prized his undergraduate efforts had never put his tall figure in the way of more than a provisional, temporary post. Why should they? He had no political friends. The book he had written was short, hardly wadded at all with footnotes and appendices, and was conspicuously scant with laudatory references to established luminaries. He kept on turning up, teaching, year by year, shabbily – but, word had it, effectively. And his crotchety mother – Laura had hardly felt she had to pretend to be pleased – was still alive. Hung over him like a cancerous but seemingly deathless vulture, her heart oozing with maternal and Christian and deleterious love.

After breakfast, Dario had been shown to the hut he was to occupy. Just an airy hexagon with a lantern for the nights, the same as all the others. But his hostess had tried to choose him one in a pleasing angle of thicket and boulder near the sea. What did a lot of the others – Marina and Nick, for instance, in their entwinings (it was to be imagined) such a charming nymph and satyr composition – notice or care? She had given Dario lodging near enough to the eucalyptus clump, she hoped, for him to hear the Scops owls.

It had been five minutes later, when he had emerged again, that among the clouds in Laura's mind a coming storm had begun to lour, to be unmistakable however persistently she tried to mistake it, some monstrous thing at once dread and excitement, something that made her eyes smart with pity and her heart shudder with the need to be brave. He had joined the stroll to the quay. There had been Adonis who would dive, she herself who would watch and praise. Dario in khaki shorts and a blue shirt now had sauntered, had chatted to Marina, chatted to Nick – he had a dozen phrases of Greek only, but his English was excellent. He had chatted with them, but he had not known they existed, Laura had been sure. Because his soul had been hurled out of the blue warm heavenly air like summer hail, and had been whipping down on Imogen's straw hat, which was probably of her own design, and had been melting helplessly on Angelica too, on the fetching little white and doubtless Imogen Scottow bonnet on her fifteen-month-old head . . . Yes, with her customary irrelevance Laura had marked what everybody had been wearing.

And now she must try to be meticulously accurate about this beginning of things – because if the very beginning were misthought and misfelt, what wrongs might not be generated? Anna had guessed too; that was a mercy; they would help each other understand. It would be good to confide in her daughter — a way of loving her better, Laura hoped.

"How have you found out?" Anna was asking, her question balanced between gravity and amusement. (I must remember to respect her reasonableness, her mother thought. And Goddamnit, if a marquee for her wedding is what she's set her heart on, she shall have one whatever the difficulties.) "And what have you found out?"

Laura heard herself laughing, and for a moment was shocked. But truly it had been ludicrous. Horrible things often were. "I caught Dario getting himself telephoned."

Naturally she had not intended to catch the poor fellow in his little subterfuge, the old lady protested. It was not her habit to spy on her guests. But Dario was such an amateurish deceiver. First of all, before lunch he had asked her if he might walk up to the house and use the telephone. He did not approve of visitors who used the telephone, he had expatiated pointlessly, and blushed. But alas it was rather urgent. His voice had stumbled.

Of course, Laura had replied, please go right ahead. And then after lunch she had been in this very room and the telephone had rung — it had been somebody wishing to speak to Dario — and he, could Anna believe it? had been back up at the house — she had only had to call his name on the off-chance and in a trice he had appeared at the door — ah it had been so transparent! He had stood there . . . She gestured with her eyes to where on a bamboo table the old-fashioned black telephone crouched in decent silence now, its receiver curled over its back so it resembled a monstrous but fortunately fossilised scorpion. He had stood

there and had tried to look worried. His mother was dying
– such a cliché, didn't Anna think? and far too good news
to be true, and darling Dario had made the feeblest efforts
to sound upset. "I'm afraid I have to leave immediately."
Laura imitated his mumble.

But what with everything else, what with the perturbing
profusion of signs, she had not hesitated a moment for her
reply, she told her daughter. "No you don't," she had
answered outright. And he had wriggled hardly at all
before he confessed it was a lie, like a pierced maggot
he had writhed on the hook for a bit but then ... Laura
spread her palms, she smiled. Dario had sat in that chair
by the window. He had remained for an hour or more,
jumping up and pacing about and leaning against the
chimney-piece and flopping down in this chair or that
and then starting up again and fretting about. He had
talked. He had disappeared scarcely a quarter of an hour
ago. Anna had only just missed him. Laura had had
nothing like enough time to marshal her wits, which as
usual were straggling like the deserters and the wounded
and the would-be prisoners scattered about the countryside
after the main bulk of a defeated army has retreated, events
have moved on, those capable of fighting another day are
elsewhere. But Dario had talked all right. He had told her
– well, no, not everything, naturally. He himself knew so
little – knew so much that was circumstantial, only one or
two things that might pertain to the essential thing. But
when you added it to what you had already guessed, when
you saw matters in the light of the signs ...

"Oh, the signs!" Anna gushed, unable not to be a little
proud of her perception of them. "Did you see how when
Angelica was playing in that rock pool Dario bent down
beside her but Imogen picked her up and carried her
away?"

"More than once!" Laura interjected, also somewhat
gushingly, because with this anguish wringing her heart
and mind like a brawny laundress grasping a sock in each

fist and throttling the suds out of them it was difficult not to lapse into conversational posturings. "And it happened again when we were all watching Adonis dive. Poor Dario knelt down before the child, tried to amuse her, tried to get her to say something to him. Looking into her little face with that terrible intensity all the time. Were you watching? Really a ghastly look, a haggard look. No wonder she didn't like it."

"And Imogen getting colder by the minute!" Anna cried, who righteously though she disapproved of the whole business could not help but be a little excited to be on stage even as a maid toting a tray while the heroine and her cavalier were stepping around one another with such elaborate cruelty and such poignant suffering. And did not her condemnation of Imogen take moral lustre from her compassion for Dario? And was not moral lustre a fine thing? "You know that cold look she gets in her eyes when she's decided not to use them for seeing with? When we were going down the coast to the beach she wouldn't speak to him. She was sitting on the gunwale beside me. Dario joined us. He tried to be cheerful. He said, I've scarcely seen Laura since I was a boy – otherwise we'd be bound to have met here. She didn't glance at him. She said to me, I think I'll go for a ride this afternoon. Xenophon isn't lame or anything is he?" (The horse had his noble name because Alexis had always said that Xenophon's book on horses and horsemanship was the finest ever written.) "My God, Mother, I'm glad you didn't see Dario's face," Anna went on – went on with relish, Laura could not but observe, dejectedly trying not to dislike her for it. "He tried to pretend he hadn't heard her, or that he thought she couldn't have heard him. Just imagine, he said, I never knew Laura was your godmother. Imogen scooped up Angelica, went down to the stern. Then Dario stood up. He went. To the bow, of course. But five minutes later he'd made himself recover, he was going nonchalantly down to the stern."

"I'm glad I wasn't on board," Laura remarked, who at

the time, thinking swiftly of an excuse not to join the boating party, had accused herself of cowardice. She had stood on the quay in the sunshine, she had talked plausibly about a swarm of bees that had been spotted in the big mulberry by the bridge – was the swarm on an accessible branch? if they could capture it, was there a spare hive ready to house it? – and she had thought: rat. However, a respite she had absolutely had to snatch before the spectacle presented itself to her flinching attention again at lunch. "But tell me, darling. Am I imagining it, or . . . Angelica truly *does* look like Dario, doesn't she?"

"Very!" Anna pronounced halfway between a wail of commiseration for him and a gust of exasperated laughter at the meticulosity of fate, its unkind care to get right a plethora of details that might perfectly well have fallen out differently.

"She hasn't got his nose," the older woman observed cautiously.

Her daughter admired one bronzed thigh as she crossed it over the other; she rearranged her blue and scarlet silk. She laughed. "Did you ever see a child of one with Dario's nose? When she grows up she'll have something like it I dare say."

"And she's fair."

"Well, so is her mother." Anna could see no reason to try not to focus on what they were confronted with. "But her eyes are brown, like her father's." It was Anna's nature to see things plainly, make plain judgements of them. "And a lot of people with brown hair were fair when they were children." Nor was it natural to her to feel hesitantly, to feel other than forthrightly, the immediate sentiment that presented itself to be felt. She brushed her hand across her eyes, in the shuttered twilight the diamonds on her engagement ring coruscated. "Does Imogen realise now how she treated him, do you think?" The demand was fierce. "And what do you imagine she proposes to do about it by way of making amends?"

Laura grappled her courage to her. "I still doubt," she murmured. But she had to be honest. "Not as much as I'd like to."

Anna had no patience with that. "Look at Angelica's chin, her mouth." She was dismissive. "Her forehead. Everything. And if Imogen hasn't suddenly realised today that her loathsome trick has been discovered, if she isn't scared that her scheme may not work, if she isn't beginning at long last to feel guilty, why has she been behaving in this crazy way? When Dario first turned up she kissed him, she was friendly. Then the rest of the morning she wouldn't speak to him. If he tried to play with Angelica, she whisked her away as if he were known as a molester of infants. Then around lunch-time she clearly decided she was betraying herself, so she went back to being friendly in a superficial, social kind of way."

"Perhaps Imogen knows that Angelica is not Dario's child. But perhaps she knows she very nearly might be, and she's been watching Dario imagining everything wrongly, and she's horrified by what he's feeling."

"It's true she's always been pretty promiscuous." With the confidence of a woman engaged to marry a successful practitioner of one of the liberal and liberally remunerated professions, Anna unveiled the mystery of things. "No, what she's horrified by is the beginning of self-knowledge. How she fended it off for so long is astonishing. But it looks like it's stealing into her now." Then with scorn, "If Angelica isn't Dario's, why doesn't she prove it to him, why doesn't she stop him suffering?"

"Perhaps she will." Anna was genuinely indignant, Laura knew. But why did she have to enjoy her revenge, her ascendency? "Perhaps it isn't easy to prove, but perhaps she's trying to convince him right now. They may be together somewhere about the place. She may be telling him that he's childless, that he's free." Imogen had never been a straightforward person to defend, and the task was getting more crooked not less. Imogen whose daughter was

61

her freedom, or so she swore, so maybe had been till today. Imogen who, it was unpleasant to have to acknowledge, had, it seemed, deceived her on a pretty big scale. And why? She was still a long way from finding out. Imogen who in Dario's arms had clearly found other things to murmur about than godparents – their shock at seeing each other had been genuine. Her Imogen, her coz. Sometimes in moments of tenderness, in moments of smiling, they called one another coz. "Even if it isn't true, she may be telling him that."

"Of course, she may not know who Angelica's father is," Anna mused. But with that suspicion she had shocked herself; she changed tack. "No, no. It's Dario. And what's jazzed her up today . . ." Imogen's habitual arrogant calm had been shattered, reduced to a few shards in a pit; her rival for Laura's love was an archaeologist picking over the fragments, checking whether any of them were worthy of note. "What's flurried her is Dario's natural feeling for his child." Anna dabbed her eyes with a corner of her silk robe. "It'll be the saddest love ever born." Again she had recourse to her silk. "Imogen is so perverted, it isn't sad to her, it's abhorrent. And do you really think it would do any good, her telling him Angelica isn't his daughter? How could he believe her? If she took the child to Peru he'd still ache for her. And when I think of Angelica . . . If Imogen never tells her anything she'll live haunted by darkness. If she tells her the truth she'll live haunted by the truth. If she tells her lies she'll live haunted by lies."

"I feel sorry for Imogen too."

"You would." Anna sniffed; she swallowed. "I can't. I don't even really feel one ought to, until she shows some repentance. Is that too exorbitant a gesture to ask? What she did to Dario is like . . ." The archaeologist chucked the last fragments of ware back into the mud; they were worthless; there was nothing to learn from them. "It's as if a raped woman were denied an abortion. You'd agree that was immoral, Mother, wouldn't you? Well, Imogen got Dario with child, she forced a child on him. Oh, I'm sure he

62

enjoyed being seduced. But to use deceit is to use violence, she raped his heart, why have you never understood?"

Even with the shutters closed, the afternoon heat was beginning to lap into the drawing-room, heat and the churring of cicadas and the resinous scents of cypress and maritime pine. A fly droned away from the portrait that might have been by Zoffany till you looked more attentively and it was only school of, headed toward the opposite wall where hung the skin of a tiger that Laura's father-in-law had shot in Kenya. In the dimness you could not see how tatty the paintwork on skirting-boards and cornices had become. The fireplace was a shadowy cavern; beside it, a basket of billets and fir cones waited dustily for winter. On the hearthrug the spaniels dozed. From upstairs came whisperingly the notes of Demitri Rodostamo's flute. In another bedroom Ben Thurne, who had spent an hour writing a short letter to his dying lover, and another hour failing to write the next paragraph of his new novel, was lying on his back with his hands behind his grizzled head.

Outside the house, the sunlight fell to earth in a blazing débâcle the more stunning for being silent and still. A donkey in the stable swished its tail; a lizard scuttled across the flagstones; nothing else moved. In a hut down by the sea, Nick Morston and Marina Rodostamo had made love, had drowsed. Now he was caressing her again. She sighed and smiled and stirred as she felt desire come back. A couple of hundred yards down the shore, Dario De Corvaro was sitting on a rock, his elbows on his knees, his eyes bent on the sparkling shallows at his feet, a crab's inching, a tiddler's twist and dart, light that swam down and showed off by turning somersaults underwater and then floated to the surface and lay awash. Inland, Imogen Scottow, who had left her daughter in Maria's care, was trotting the bay thoroughbred Xenophon through one of the olive groves. She pulled her straw hat more firmly onto her head, she clapped in her heels, the horse broke into a canter. On the high track that wound over the ridge toward the village, obese sweat-sheened Yanni, dispatched to meet the Schombergs, stopped the rattly Fiat, got out, looked crossly at the multitude of insects which had already been splatted to death on the grimy windscreen. Grit, gore, how could a man see where he was going? No water, no sponge. Just crags and scrub and emptiness for miles, no wonder all the goatherds he knew were mad, those that had not hanged themselves. He removed his sodden shirt, scrumpled it up, used it to wipe a patch of windscreen, put it on again, drove on bedizened with smears of dust and blood and torn wings.

At her end of the drawing-room sofa Anna Rodostamo, her eyes dried, her tranquillity restored, asked, "What did Dario tell you? What have you learned?"

Laura leaned toward her, put a hand on her knee. Almost as if to stop herself toppling onto the floor, the younger woman thought with a qualm of anxiety. If her mother died this summer, would she have to delay her wedding? "It isn't as we had supposed, my darling," Laura said. "They were in love." Anna raised her eyebrows. "And now, please, would you be kind and make us a pot of tea?"

"They were in love," Laura Rodostamo had heard her voice say, her voice that sometimes annoyed her by quavering in a doddery way she detested but on this occasion had rung with exemplary soft confidence. And she had heard a spirit add voicelessly: And they are still in love.

But now, because she had been clever and asked for tea, she had perhaps five blessed minutes of solitude. She leaned her head back against her end of the sofa, she shut her eyes. How had it come about, this learning?

At lunch she had made sure that Imogen with Angelica on her pale thighs sat between Achilles and Maria because they adored her. Dario had helped Tasso carry the platters of grilled fish, then she had called him to the chair she had kept empty next to her own. She had made sure the fishermen and the cooks were congratulated. She had made sure that the jugs of wine circulated, that the mullet and squid were dished out generously, that the bass was divided into tiny portions so that as many people as might be could taste a morsel. She had made sure that Alexis and Adonis were remembering to pass the salad and the potatoes to their neighbours politely, and she had gazed out from the wistaria shade and seen in the offing a yacht with her sails rippling slackly using her engine to cross the gulf, and she had heard Imogen call brightly across the table to Dario, "The trouble with that castle of yours is, it's not on the sea." He had looked taken aback a moment; but then he had grinned. "The trouble with my castle is, it's not mine." And then his smile had taken less precarious hold of his face; he had turned in his finest old Roman fashion toward his hostess – she recalled it with a stab of liking – and had inclined his head and shoulders a fraction, and had said, "And then – there's nowhere like Laura's house." It had, on the other hand, been disgraceful the way Achilles scowled at poor Dario throughout the meal. Truly after all these years his dislike of Italians was a bore. Valiant old comrade in arms of her dead husband's he might be, but she must remind him to treat her guests with courtesy. Or what shameful conduct might not be evident when – what was Anna's doctor called? – Maurizio? – no, when Fabrizio came?

Laura's first instinct, after the coffee had been drunk, after the fish heads and bones and tails had been flung to sizzle on the fire, had been flight. So had Dario's first instinct – that telephone farce – been flight. Cowards, were they, then, both of them? But they were returning to the fray.

Laura had fled slowly because the stream path had its steep stretches and the day was at its hottest, had fled pantingly and ignominiously up through the terraces and glades which at Easter were thigh-deep in asphodel. She had kept in the shade of the olive trees where she could. More than once she had stopped to rest.

Eleven years after Alexis' death and the fire, eleven years after she had been laid waste, she had not been hard to rout. It was one thing to conduct your widowhood decorously. It was likewise within the bounds of the achievable to initiate a long campaign to reclothe the burned slopes with olive trees and orange trees. Anyhow, that was a furbishing which Anna would have to see to fruition after her death. She only hoped the Italian doctor would wish to live in Greece. Probably he would not. But it would be bad for the estate just to be visited for holidays. Perhaps he would sell the place to speculators, perhaps he would build an hotel, if he did that she would rise from her grave, she would . . . Calm! She was an hysterical old ghoul. Still, it was a shame she could not have left the lot to Imogen. No, she mustn't think that. But now to join furious battle from one hour to the next . . . To fling your unprepared weakness into a skirmish that would not be less savage for being fought with airy nothings, with hopes and fears, with truths and falsehoods generally indistinguishable one from another, with loves and for all she knew hatreds . . . To be a fighter on both sides, a double agent . . . At the unexpected blast of a certainly ethereal and possibly delusory trumpet to charge into a short sharp mêlée – for so this last adventure promised to be . . . Because although she had bullied Dario into dropping that nonsense about his mother being mortally sick, she had only managed to extract the most stingy of promises from him. At least stay tonight! She had besought him. Give me a day! And he had undertaken to remain today. And the end she desired, whatever it was she had begged him to stay *for*, was a fishing-line that had got knotted, got into a hopeless tangle, between panic and patience she was fumbling with it, fumbling, fumbling . . .

Haltingly she had retreated up through the groves. Solitude she had longed for – which was the one luxury the day would unequivocally not permit her because, after Dario, here was Anna only temporarily held at bay by tea-making, and later, please heaven much later, she must find Imogen or Imogen would find her. She had thought of resorting to the butterfly chapel, but she had felt exhausted. The idea of her bedroom up at the house had appealed to her – the bedroom abandoned in the summer when she slept down by the sea. The walls were thick, it would be cool. She would lie on her brass bed. How random everything was! If she had turned aside to the butterfly chapel, Dario would most likely have left a charming dishonest letter on her desk, vanished before she came back.

She had entered the courtyard. Under the cedar tree she had stopped, because after tramping uphill in the sun her head ached. Her eyes had blurred too – they often did when she was tired – so that the outhouses were just splotches, were nearly abstract hazes of browns and greys. She had waited. Slowly her house before her eyes had come into focus, its faded pink plaster façade, its grey terrace balustrade where her father-in-law had been shot. Betrayed by villagers who didn't want any more reprisals, fetched from his library by a German posse, shoved against the balustrade, shot. His wife had been there, but they hadn't shot her. Alexis had not shared his father's taste for hunting African big game, but his attitude to the hunting of European fascists and collaborators with fascists had been the same, and during the civil war he had taken his revenge on known and presumed renegades.

The kettle would not yet have boiled. Providence was merciful, the nineteen-fifties stove in the seventeen-fifties kitchen was inefficient. And praise God she had made it into the nineties without anybody officiously giving her an electric kettle. A minute or two yet until Anna carrying a tray would come out from the vaults and up the worn steps to the sunlight and the weedy courtyard gravel and the dusty parterre where the cats, the far too numerous cats, scrabbled and wauled. A minute surely still until she turned, came up the steps to the terrace, came in and crossed the hall where the Angel of Death had taken the Byzantine dagger from the table and stuck it into his gorgeous belt; ah, a minute still . . .

After years of not inviting my daughter into my – my what? my sanctum? – this is very likely going to be neither easy nor pleasant, Laura reminded herself with weary sternness. Perhaps Anna will not come in. Perhaps I shall prove unable to open a door for her, open a convincing and attractive door. Or she will come to the door but come no further. Or she will see no sanctum in me, see nothing in my thinking and feeling that could be so described – and maybe she will be right, though she is rarely ambivalent she is often sturdily penetrative. This last I must not lose sight of – I who at moments of such fatigue long to lose sight of everything. Nor of the fact that though her weeping was unnecessary and off-putting, and her righteous vehemence will never be to my taste, a lot of what she said was unexceptionably sound. Dario is indeed being tormented by love and by doubt. Angelica will indeed grow up haunted. This is not a new truth, but it is true, though Anna's expression of it is simplistic. What will shadow the girl when she grows up is the knowledge that she will never be able wholly to trust any truth to be true, any falsehood to be false . . . our common quandary, but she'll suffer from it in an acute form.

Her head back, her eyes closed, Laura clenched her hands in her lap. Anna had again been right, hadn't she? Most intrinsic to the labyrinth of all questions was the question of Imogen's self-knowledge. Her goddaughter was brilliant, Laura realised defeatedly. When Imogen had made her own silent and invisible inner exploration the lantern that would light a way into the heart of the maze and out again, she had banished everyone else to insignificance. To make that the crucial formula, have all things depend only on that . . . brilliant, damn her. A fiendish stroke of design which, repeated a myriad times, had everybody twisting

68

and turning futilely, but which if its secret were understood would make every trap a game, every dog-leg a fairway, every right choice clear . . .

This I must unlock! Laura exhorted her unconfident intelligence. Today, tonight, quickly! Had Imogen been avoiding the inner reaches of this knowledge, but was she now beginning to venture farther into the galleries and stairways and crossing corridors and halls with many doors, beginning to turn her exploration of them to some account? Or was she idly pretending, was she bluffing everybody smoothly, steadily, uncaringly? Had she long since cunningly immured her daughter's soul in a beautiful apartment somewhere near the labyrinth's heart? Had she likewise confronted that daughter's father's spirit with that blue-eyed, pink and white china-faced directness of hers? Had she then – perhaps with a smile in honour of sexual passion enjoyed together – perhaps too with a smile for spiritual love and its mortal decay – immured him in charming quarters in another wing of the same palatial prison, let herself out of a side-door into the open countryside, into freedom, and sauntered whistling away? Her eyes still darkened, her fingers still tautly bunched, Laura's lips let forth a low moan of urgency. There in their solitary confinements Angelica's soul and Dario's soul would dwindle until they were extinguished unless . . . unless somehow someone could . . . unless she could think of – what? do – what? Anyway she must remember it was not a fight, she had been wrong about that. (Anna's footsteps on the terrace made her intensify her haranguing of herself.) Because if Imogen were allowed to think it was a fight she would not let herself appear to win it with considerate slowness and difficulty. She would harry her godmother off the field of battle with a violence of scorn which would leave her shaky and tearful. If she failed to be seamlessly loyal, not a flicker of mercy would she be shown. Laura was not confident that Dario, even supposing he were permitted to try a duel with Imogen, would be shown much gentleness either. And then the next day he would go away and that would be that.

But there was, Laura just had time to reassure her apprehensive nerves as her daughter entered with the tea tray, a sanctum. There existed, however shadowily, something in her which you might call that. There had to. Because where else could it have been that Dario De Corvaro for an hour after lunch had spread out the things he had dreamed? Where else but on the floor of the sanctum to which she had invited him had he laid out first this tightly woven and involutedly patterned and richly hued dream and then that one for her inspection – just like the trader in Varanasi who years back had offered Alexis and her rug after rug, unrolling them, holding them up, laying them out? So that now the floor of Laura's mind was most magnificently carpeted. She would have liked to linger there indefinitely alone, bending her gaze to this detail and that, standing back to encompass a whole design, stooping closer again. But in all decency she must usher Anna in, must try to point out the few subtleties she herself had so far had the time more or less to comprehend. She hoped the new arrival would not stump about on the dreams too heavy-footedly, not exclaim too volubly. It was her floor; they were Dario's weaves; she felt protective. But Anna had already guessed a little – so . . .

If Dario and she had elucidated anything during that hour of theirs, Laura now began softly to her daughter who had poured the tea and sat down, it had been thanks to their confessing to one another that they had been afraid. At first he had assailed her with a welter of apologies for his duplicity, she explained. He had – it had been unpleasant to witness – almost grovelled. She had cut him short. Like any paid priest boxed in a confessional in a side-aisle, it had been the so-called truth and the opportunity to be wise and just and forgiving that, contemptibly she feared, she had been there for.

"It seems to me that both our honours have, quite

accidentally, been saved by the telephone," she had said. "Or by your lack of adroitness. Anyway, luckily, back to the tussle we go. We might as well go together, don't you think?"

It was all very fine, Laura realised as she spoke, to keep reminding herself that today she was faced with what was probably her last opportunity of doing some new good. It was all very admirable to berate herself, to know starkly that she must not let her last adventure slither into turpitude, she must concentrate, must do more than just go on dying amiably enough. But the snag was that it was concentration which she found impossible except in snatched instants too ephemeral to help much. Now, for instance, her gaze had fallen on the school of Zoffany picture. How murky! she had thought. And then she had recollected once apologising to Natasha Schomberg, saying she absolutely promised she'd get it cleaned. (Natasha's aeroplane must be over the Alps by now. And those four daughters with their long legs and their golden locks would cause riots all over the island, naturally they would, and it would be Sophia above all whom they would take to their pitter-pattering hearts and who would show them how most pleasantly to go astray – and how old was the youngest Schomberg girl, fifteen? the eldest was at Oriel, or somewhere.) Have it *cleaned*? Natasha had snorted. It was a most pernicious business, the so-called restoration of pictures, she would have Laura know. It was big business these days and no mistake; but pernicious, and insolent. It was a sewer of pretentiousness and snobbery. It was pompous foundations, it was hireling scholars, it was people who couldn't paint ruining great artists' veneers and redaubing. Natasha had strode about, had blasphemed. The dog-days of the whisky and the ice in her glass had become a maelstrom. It was talentless people who simply had to have something to do with the arts, that was what it was. Like hangers-on who couldn't write but insisted on writing the biographies of those who could – that was another vulgarity which appeared to know no end. Anyhow, there the picture it was a shame was not by Zoffany still hung dimly, and Laura was not making much headway in her attempt to tell Anna what a relief it had been that Dario had not indulged in self-pity and had not hectored either.

If he were Angelica's father, why did not Imogen admit the game was up, bring parent and child into some kind of relation with one another which even if it were never to be close might at least be decent, at least be minimally sane? If he were not Angelica's father, why didn't Imogen say so? Dario might have been longing to agonise over these conundrums. He might have wanted to enrol his listener as a fellow tactician, pore with her over plans to surprise the truth where Imogen believed it most ingeniously fortified. He might dourly have demanded to know where his tormentress was. Could the estate please immediately be scoured for her? If he were to remain for a day, if there were to be a reckoning, let it be here, let it be now.

But no, Dario had told stories, Anna would be relieved to hear. Even one or two amusing stories. Yes, almost at once he had made her smile.

"It was just before lunch, Laura. We were all standing around the fire with glasses of wine in our hands, waiting for the fish to be ready. And I suddenly realised I hadn't a clue about babies, about children. Maybe Angelica was only just one year old, or wasn't yet one. Maybe she was three, and for some reason Imogen had never told me about her. The usual childless man's hopeless ignorance about infants. I must find out at once, I decided, and I set off toward the kitchen hut to ask Maria or Daphne. I thought it was the sort of thing they'd know about. But then it occurred to me it might seem a bit odd to barge in on them and demand: That baby out there, how old is she? So I turned back to the fire. I pulled myself together. I'd make myself ask Imogen, I decided. She was being a touch more civil to me by midday. So I did. She flicked her cigarette into the embers, she looked at me, she hesitated. Fifteen months, she said, and went on looking into my eyes, and then began to smile, and then turned away."

Eduardo De Corvaro was drowned in a fishing accident in the Moluccas.

God will forgive him his sins, his widow told the friends who came to the Umbrian castle to offer their condolences. To her son Dario she said, You must pray for your father's soul; and she added, The peace of God passes our understanding.

He was the most delightful of men, his old friend Laura Rodostamo, whose husband had died a few years before, wrote in her letter to the woman whom darling Eduardo had been an idiot to marry, honestly it had been the one tasteless action of a graceful life; and in another letter she told Dario that he was to invite himself to stay whenever he pleased.

Eduardo always liked Malay girls, his Roman friends reminded one another. And they smiled – because how could you mope over the exit of a man who lived so vividly? And anyway, none of them had known him well. Good Lord yes, Malay girls, Philippine girls, Chinese girls.

We must decide what to do with that end of the *piano nobile*, his cousins deliberated – who did not forsee any hitches in restricting an impoverished widow to a couple of rooms, and did not even discuss bestowing the father's apartment on the son. No wonder he died in debt, they concluded, what with all those voyages in the East.

I do not believe in this fishing accident, Dario surprised himself by hearing his own voice assert silently. (Aloud it was delivering a lecture on different stagings of Chekhov's plays.)

He did not believe. He did not disbelieve with conviction.

73

There were, in a quite exemplary fashion, no facts. The haze inside his head, the haze outside, their interminglings. The report of a consul in Ternate, a local businessman who represented the faint local interests of more than one European power. Dario had never been out of Europe – but it wasn't that. He could imagine the fishing-boat, the Indonesian crew, the first squalls which were the advance guard of the typhoon, the reef, the combers. It was not that he could wholly convince himself that his father had committed suicide either . . . Though the consul's account was so perforated with obscurities and uncertainties, that if an Italian gentleman with a known fancy for far-flung archipelagoes and deep-sea fishing had wished to disappear in circumstances which would seem to be those of an accident he could hardly have died more eloquently.

Yes, that *was* remarkable: the vagueness. The lack of apparent reasons to consider it a suicide, and the vagueness. For although the consular report had been one lacuna after another, the gaps had been stitched together with verve, albeit in the clichés of international English. The man must read a lot of spy stories, it occurred to Dario, marvelling at the predictable paragraph about how well known his father had been in the little ports of the islands, how well liked for his invariable cheerfulness, and pausing over the other paragraph about how alas typhoons were to be expected in those seas at that time of year, how the respected Mr Edward had never been a man to be daunted by foul weather, and had always voyaged in the local craft with their limited or sometimes non-existent navigational equipment.

The vagueness . . . Had the writer known that Eduardo De Corvaro and his crew were robbed and murdered, was he one of the politicians who protected and profited by the piracy in the Halmahera Sea? Was that why he pointed out that although most regretably nothing was known about exactly where or exactly when Dario's father set sail for the last time, he was known to have been offshore when the wind turned the straits to cauldrons? Or did he know it had been suicide, know that the rest of the crew survived? Did consideration for the dead man's family explain the stuff about invariable cheerfulness, about voyaging in the most fearless way? Had the consul and the fisherman perhaps been friends, drunk whisky together on Ternate evenings on verandahs and decks? It was even possible, Dario mused, that his father had dictated the report, or roughed it out. He was well up to that, the son thought; and smiled to think of it; and heard his father's voice: "Oh, you know, something to keep my wife happy. She's rather religious, you see. Happy? Yes, I think happy is the right word. You'll know the kind of nonsense to stick in. Anything to stop my relations feeling guilty that none of us ever became friends, and stop them feeling ashamed that I turned out to be a coward. Shove in something about a typhoon . . ."

Dario checked up on the typhoon. It had indeed passed through the Moluccas that week. Houses had been strewn, vessels sunk, people killed; the islands had been threshed, had been winnowed. But then he realised he had no reason to believe his father's death had not fallen the week before or the week after. Or indeed the month before or the month after, he reflected, reading the consul's account again, concluding that he must have known Eduardo, why else had he written a long letter rather than merely sending the doubtless brief police report of the disappearance, the presumed drowning? He was sorry about the delay, the consul wrote. News of the tragedy had been slow to reach him. Communications in the archipelago were still, he regretted to say, little better than they had ever been. He had wished to make the most exhaustive enquiries before coming sadly to the only possible conclusion, which . . .

My father is alive, he is earning his living as a fisherman, he has a house and a local girl, at last he is free and he is happy, Dario thought; and he tore up the letter to the consul in Ternate which he had just written, because if his father had wished to go missing, to vanish over a far horizon, to become haze, he should be allowed to do so. No, he was dead. Eduardo De Corvaro had come to the end of his tether, had he not? His marriage for many years a distasteful formality only. His son grown up. No money left, and no prospect of making any. The good times gone, he had waited till the fishing-boat was slipping gently through the equatorial sea one night; he had watched the helmsman drowse; had dived; had floated on his back after the vessel had left him; had drifted, looked up at the stars . . . No, not that. But in the last few years he would have welcomed a fatal accident. He had conducted his life in a spirited manner, had lived so that accidents might occur, had in the face of impending gales put to sea in small primitive craft again and again until . . .

A man still active in his sixties had been unlucky with the weather or with his equipment; or he had been killed with his crew or by them; or he had indeed come to the end of his tether and had hated to be thus tied and had despaired; or he had cut the tether . . . This was just the perhaps fortuitous beginning of Dario's wanderings among uncertainties. It reminded him, he had said, Laura told her daughter, of once when he was a boy and he went skating and the ice broke. Floundering in the water he had begun to heave himself onto the unbroken ice, he had got his elbows onto that smooth hard safety and had heaved and again the ice had broken. In the cold water he had fought with the cracked sliding raft of ice, a raft off which his grip slithered, a raft which had broken away but which he could not break in pieces and cast behind him. He had fought his way to the firm edge where the ice had not broken, where it stretched solid and white to the shore of the pond. Once more he had started to heave himself up onto it, cold and heavy and frightened and tired in his sodden icy clothes and his skates. The smooth hard safety had seemed to bear his weight and he had got his panting chest on it and it had broken. Again and again. On and on. Fighting with the slippery cracked rafts, in the end weeping with cold and

76

exhaustion and fright, heaving himself up onto ice that broke, again and again. Fortunately he had fallen in near the bank. But twenty-five years later, he had told Laura, there had been no shore in sight.

Dario had moved about the drawing-room as if in communion with shadowy portents. He had told his variations on the theme of drowning in an Eastern sea. He had sat down, had stood up, had seemed fretfully to speculate. He had told the fable of the boy fallen through the ice. He had again meditated for a moment. "It wasn't just that I missed my father," he had said, "though I did, of course. We used to talk about books a lot, and I missed that. It wasn't even that I particularly wished to feel certain about things. I despised people who went in for certainties, and I was too arrogant to want to be one of them. No, it was more . . ." He had lodged his shoulder against Laura's mantelpiece. "More like this . . ."

She had listened to unease, and had begun to feel calm. For in Dario, in her restless story-teller starting to whet her appetite and to concentrate her attention, in the man who had run away but tripped and gone sprawling and had therefore had to get up, stand steadfast, look into the vortex of the besetting turmoil – in him, Laura had seen an Indian of great professional detachment, of unruffled serenity, a connoisseur rich in baled stuffs who was picking first this piece and then that from his collection, who if one waited humbly and with patience might come to his most intricate designs, who displayed his fabrics with some appropriate commentary on each, some elucidation, for every one had a story. Or each weave and each shimmer was a story, the bright threads turned and met and divided, patterns appeared and disappeared, it took time to read the whorls. Yes, from the moment of Dario being wry about his ignorance of babies, Laura had begun to return to tranquillity, begun a little to cheer up. In some sense they were standing shoulder to shoulder – was that it? She had felt less alone.

77

After Eduardo De Corvaro's death, if death it was, in his stony town in Umbria the market was still held on Saturdays; the smallholders with their cloth caps and their three-wheelers and their plump wives and their old communist partisan loyalties still came to the square with the church portico and the nine lime trees; they still set up their trestle tables and sold eggs, honey, the different mushrooms that grew in the surrounding hills, every green thing their gardens grew. There came a tinker who sold pans. There came a man who sold clothes which the shops had given up trying to sell. There came a man who spitted a pig and roasted it, he would sell you a hunk of bread with a slice of peppery pork. There came a provincial sylviculturist who sold sapling olive trees; who if you asked him for a young magnolia would bring it the following Saturday with its roots in a clod bound with sackcloth; who one bitter day in Advent, when all morning sub-zero dusk seemed to have been falling, sold Dario an armful of mistletoe, took him to the café for a glass of scalding red wine with a lump of sugar and a stick of cinnamon in it, and as they stood sipping and burning their mouths spoke in a reverent murmur of exotic pear trees he was growing out in the country which one day – ah, one day! – he would take Dario to see; who described a curious medlar never known in Umbria before; and who recalled graftings of a sophistication that only he and one other man in all Italy could master, graftings laborious, graftings perverse, successes already mythical, fruits miraculous.

There was no cathedral, no ducal palace, it was not a town to which visitors often came, although in one of the three churches there hung sacred images, pictures of the archangels done on wood in the fourteenth century that no one knew who had painted but which had dignity. The bridge over the little river was Roman and was handsome in a grey rugged way, and the gardens down by the chuckling water were feathery with willows and swagged with vines, and all in all Dario had never disliked the place, and anyhow if your name was De Corvaro you were at home there, you couldn't not be. It was not enrapturing to buy your newspaper beneath the same arcade every morning and glance at the front page as you crossed the square, but it was pleasant enough – like going to have your hair cut by the barber who had cut it since you were a boy and who kept goldfinches in a cage and between clients played the mandolin. Likewise it was not disagreeable to drink your coffee with the lawyer or his secretary or the taxi-driver or the schoolmaster or the woman who kept the grocery or the farmer who sold you draught wine.

Far from disagreeable . . . But sometimes Dario reached evening with nothing but black water under his feebly kicking feet, nothing but ice all around stretching away, nothing but tiredness and futility as he heaved himself up onto the ice and it broke.

The click, click, click of his shoes as he strolled the twenty-odd streets which never altered and which he would be patrolling at evening till he died. A tenebrous alley. The cobbler's lit door. Still his own footfalls. In turn the three churches, locked now. At least in summer people set kitchen chairs outside their doors, but the winter after Eduardo was reported missing the only soul out and about apart from the ghost's son was the glittering hunter Orion with his hound Sirius and his sword stalking the dark coverts of the skies, so when Dario passed one of the three bars and noticed the schoolmaster he went in. When he was not striving to imbue the local Romeos and Giuliettas with the rudiments of Italian literature, he wrote children's stories. He had invented a gardener who, in a garden which bore a brotherly likeness to the De Corvaro garden which hung craggily over the town, performed feats of topiary so prodigious that princes and potentates from far countries would come to admire his creations and to tempt him with offers of fabulous wealth to stock their gardens too with his peacocks, horses, boys and girls, ships, camels, sphinxes and dragons, unicorns and what-have-you – all of which only appeared to be creatures of clipped yew and clipped box, and in fact, after nightfall, came to life. Their nocturnal adventures were what the schoolmaster and the lecturer would plot together in the café. But the genius of the topiarist was not an infallible panacea for melancholy.

It was not that Dario longed to solve some pantocratic riddle or other. He found it difficult to phrase a question worth racking his brains to answer. Of course there was all the resounding vanity like: Who are you? Who is speaking? Why? But such sonority was depressing, he found – and it left him sharpening his scepticism like the old fellow who still came round the neighbourhood to sharpen blades, who came through the cramped mediaeval lanes calling "Bring out your knives!" and pushing a contraption which had started life as a mere bicycle but was now far grander, had one wheel that was a whetstone which when you pedalled was by cunning gearing caused to spin round, so that with much grinding and much sparking and much admiring conversation everybody's knives, hatchets, choppers and scythes could inexpensively be honed. No – it was more that there had once been a cinema but it had lost money and had shut down. It was – Laura had laughed when he announced this – that food was a depressant, at least on his doubtless contemptible system it had this unfortunate effect. It was that the university did not pay him enough to let him rent a flat in the centre of Rome; and the outskirts he abhorred; and the colleague who regularly put him up in a spare bedroom could not be expected to have him live there thirty days a month. And anyhow although he loved Rome and had amusing evenings with his Roman friends he was a provincial at heart; he had been born in the family castle and reckoned to die there even if as a pauper in the stable block which was a kind of oubliette.

In a sense he was contented enough to haunt the town, on freezing nights to be out alone except for Orion in his heavenly panoply, to lean on the bridge and look at the moonlight on the leafless willows and on the stream which was boisterous after the winter rain and would cascade still more foamingly and palaver more exuberantly when the snow on the heights melted. He was not, perhaps, discontented. Certainly melancholy was not to be confused with depression. But it was as if – would Laura understand? he had wondered, and had rubbed his chin in a nervous way she had not recollected from his boyhood – as if the music and the voices in his head had been dying down, were nearly inaudible these days, nearly hushed. She thought she might comprehend a little, his hostess had hesitantly claimed; and had mentioned to him how occasionally alone at the butterfly chapel in her head time slowed down, it slowed, nearly stopped, truly you could not be sure if the rhythm had faded away or was still whisperingly there. How extraordinary! Dario had cried, and had wanted to know more. He had questioned her. Their cases were similar, he concluded. And what strange feelings to half have in common! Yes – curious echoes and dyings to half share.

In his head there was almost no more noise, almost no more resonance. An absence of judgements and opinions certainly. A few snatches of Dante and Shakespeare. Sometimes a thrumming as of stringed instruments as the last note quivers to obliteration. Dario carried this quietness around on his shoulders all winter. What else could he do? And pandemonium would have been worse. No, he assured Laura, his head did not ache, thank you very much. And neither was it a question of urging actors to speak up, singers to trill more lustily, musicians to play with reinforced brio. You could not alter things. Even to try to would be ugly and fanatical and ludicrous, like brooding on torture till the stigmata flowered obscenely on your feet and your hands. There had been a dying away. So be it. He would train his inner ear to follow the subtlest cadences. From an overture to death there would be things to learn.

He could not read all evening every evening. He could not invariably listen to music, either – if only because he discovered he only ever wanted to hear late Beethoven, he listened again and again to the quartets that were almost silence, and quite soon it became unnecessary to put them on the record-player because like the echoes from the *Inferno* and *Coriolanus* and *Three Sisters* they never entirely left him, if he harked attentively enough they were forever reverberating. He could not ceaselessly haunt the town, it made him feel like a pariah. He could pass an hour with his mother, that was a dutiful thing to do; but the family tyranny had decreed that her husband's library should be the widow's sitting-room – none of the reigning cousins were notable readers of books – and it disheartened Dario to sit encased by his father's replete shelves of history and philosophy and verse which his mother did not read either. Often he resorted to the garden. The gravel would crunch under his regular tread. Even on a winter night the cedars held out their ragged boughs with grandeur; when there was a moon, from the parapet you could see how the fall of the dark land had magnificence. There was a loftiness in being among the bay trees and lemon trees of the eyrie, there was a mightiness in the black void that was the valley.

It was then as if Dario's father were the familiar spirit with whom as he tramped he conversed. Eduardo De Corvaro was the Other who might understand things better, who might perhaps in death have hearing acute enough to pick up rumours of brass or woodwind or whisperings of voices or strings in the brain which he and his son had in common now; might be sensitive to vibrations which the man still living, strain his attention as he might, could not discern. It was not difficult to bring Eduardo's figure and face to mind; he came willingly. It was not difficult to hear his voice; he spoke freely. It was natural that the dead had speech for things which during life they had lacked the concentration or the clarity or the courage to declare. The dead, being refined a little beyond the living, being a shade more abstract, were more in tune – so Dario found it natural to suppose, and equally natural to remind himself that this was all mere fantasy – might be in tune, in his father's case, with the music and rhetoric in the circumambient echo-chamber of the world, or in the universal echo-chamber which was his mind.

Often after these pacings up and down and these listenings and these colloquies, when Dario slept he dreamed of his father – but these dreams, though sometimes they had charm, were all inconsequential. Once he dreamed that Eduardo took him down to the cellar, because in one of the chests there was a silver tankard with a coat-of-arms engraved on it which all of a sudden he had recollected and had wished his son to see. Dario followed his father down the cellar steps. They opened the chest, they rummaged, they remarked upon this and that, they unearthed several tankards, identified the right one. It was wrapped in tissue paper. Eduardo unwrapped it, he held it up to the glimmer of the single dust-smeared bulb, and in that instant Dario realised something. "Hang on a minute, Father," he said. "You're dead, aren't you? Didn't you die last year?" The older man turned from the engraved shield, met his son's eyes for a moment. "Yes, that's right," he said, slightly surprised to be asked. "Now, my dear lad – if you look closely you'll see that our arms are crossed with those of the Morosini. A wedding present, very possibly. Oreste De Corvaro married Benedetta Morosini in . . ." "What's it like, being dead?" "Oh, not very different, you know. Not very different. Yes, they were married at the Frari in the spring of 1746. Rather a stylish affair it must have been. There's a painting of it by . . ."

That was one of the least wispy of Dario's dreams – but his dreams were mere side-shows, he had insisted to Laura. Mere fairground stalls. The core of the mystery was that the Other had finer hearing than he had. The core of it was that often the next day when he was trudging muddy tracks up hill and down dale – yes, he had done a fair amount of that – his father was walking beside him. The core was that accompanying all the fresh air and exercise, of the self-same material as the solitude and hauntedness, was a hearing of flutterings of rhythms and softnesses of suggestions and rhymings of notions which before he had been too coarse to catch.

"Like dogs have sharper hearing than we have," Laura had suggested. She had a special dog-whistle, she had related to him, which when she blew it made no sound audible to human ears but which her spaniels could hear, bless their hearts. They would come galloping toward her as soon as she blew that whistle, she had enthused – exaggerating her dogs' obedience slightly perhaps, did Anna say? Well, yes, she supposed so. But it was an admirable whistle, Natasha had given it to her a few birthdays ago. And Dario had been amused by how she lost no opportunity to refer to her spaniels' virtues.

Even after a week's snow in January the oaks on the hillsides still bore their last year's leaves, on bright mornings they held their dark immovable branches and their curling tawny frills against the cold hard blue with a valour Dario liked. In February, storms came. Buffeted by a blizzard as he tramped a muddy path, he noticed how the oaks which stood exposed on ridges were beginning to be stripped of their gold-work on their upper limbs, but when the flailing rain blew over and it was easier to look at things he was pleased to see the lower boughs of the oaks were still decorated. In March when the chestnuts and beeches had been naked for months and in their boles the sap was rising which in April would put forth fresh leaf, still the oaks gave no sign, they stood in their thinning tatters. Often the valleys brimmed with mist, they were white lakes. You could walk down into the sopping pale stillness; you could wend your way through the skeletal woods where the birds were singing; and you could find, if you were Dario De Corvaro, in the cussed stolidity of the oaks and in the wood's opacity mirrorings of your own slownesses and mistinesses – for the Other, when he cared to interpret recherché echoings, spoke of the vanity and uncertainty of all things. "And what good even are mirrorings?" he would add. And what were signs for, but that the dim universal emptiness should be cluttered with distractions, that there should be sciences and philosophies and arts, innumerable shadows to furnish the void, and that thus the way to the truth be blocked, our only hope be dashed? The oak for steadfastness, did Dario insist upon citing, and the mist for our incomprehensions? Possibly, his familiar spirit conceded – for it could not be proved that to make images and to use them to think with was impossible, under no circumstances made sense. But if there were signs only that we should be led here and there? Philosophies so that we should not despair until we were capable of doing so profoundly? Revelations, that we should gape?

Was that what the dead muttered in their off-hand way? Dario sat on a fallen tree in the birdsong fog. But, then – what objectivity had the dead? They were more shadows. Doubtless one peopled the void with whatever phantasmagoria one's society and one's genetic coding prompted one to take seriously. Could Laura see any way of concluding otherwise? Could she imagine the laconic way the drowned sailor and fisherman advised him to listen not to the bewitching echoes but to the silence which encompassed them and was endless? "If you're man enough to do it," his father had a habit of ending. Till Dario found that what he thought depended on where he was, on what he had been reading, on nothing but contingencies. The truth suspected among the garden cedars by night when you had been reading Confucius and the truth glimpsed in the foggy valley by day when you had been reading Heraclitus were of equal charm – that was one advantage. But you were not – Dario had laughed helplessly, had appealed in mock dismay to his frail grey listener – meant to assess truths by their charm or lack of it, were you? It was not, he understood, thought well of, generally. Not in temples, not in academies, not in laboratories – nowhere was it the done thing.

But if there existed no more weighty criterion than charm or the lack of it? Let Laura imagine for a minute, he had besought her, that it so chanced that all the more respectable criteria were rubbish invented by people without the steadiness of heart and clairvoyance of intellect to take ravishing Charm with the smiling seriousness she deserved. Well, for himself he knew that if he stood up from his log and climbed the hillside till he came out above the white lapping lake of mist; if he climbed higher and came to the airy sheep-walk where on a knoll there stood a lonely clump of cypresses and in a dell was the ruin of a shepherd's cottage; if he strode over the cropped sward and noticed the violets were coming out and listened to the sheep-bells and saw a buzzard stoop – Laura had guessed, had she not? If he had been reading Vico then one kind of world had some reality, if Augustine a second, if Blake a third. So much for having been brought up by a father with a good library. "How well did you know him, Laura? You must tell me about him." Anyhow the upshot was – again Dario had laughed – that for a while he had thought he had solved the problem by only ever reading Proust.

"Did falling in love with my goddaughter change things?" I asked him, Laura recounted to Anna. And she realised that for the last minute or two she had not been looking at her listener but at the stuffed tanager that had perched on the weather-glass ever since she could remember, that little dead bird with its red and green plumage had been a fixed brightness in the gloom.

"Is it that obvious?" Dario had been wry.

"And having her fall in love with you . . . ?"

White lilac and purple lilac which came into flower and after rain would scent a whole hillside. Imogen cut sprays and brought them into his flat in the stable-yard and stuck them into every jug he had. Then the acacias which all winter wandering the woodland you hardly noticed were there, so nondescript were they – such meagre trunks, such a lack of handsomeness, they were just sticks with thorns . . . But then they flowered. Acres of them all flowered filmily together. Imogen and he discovered whole acacia copses which canopied them palely as they strolled. Was this, Dario had asked, the kind of twitter Laura wished to hear? Ah, romantic as all hell, no two ways about it – and they had both perhaps had enough love affairs to know how to carry the thing off with panache. They had gone to his friend who ran the local riding school, had borrowed two horses. They had cantered over the green uplands beneath a blue sky and scared the rabbits. Through the scattered stands of cypress and oak they had walked the horses, walked them side by side and held hands. They had gone to his other friend who ran the local trout farm. Imogen had listened to the explanation of how the dams and sluices worked, she had taken an interest in the breeding programme, she had watched the mottled fish poise quivering in the dappled glittering flow and watched them flicker and be gone. His friend had given them two trout, they had taken them back to the flat that smelled of lilac and had cooked them and eaten them with bread and wine.

He did not even pretend that she did not fall in love with him, Laura had thought. He did not pretend to doubt it with so much as a startled look or a shake of his head. "And the echoes?" she had enquired.

Dario had shrugged, had laughed. Nothing had changed, he had been quite clear about that, and everything had changed. What did he care now for the waning of philosophies? he whose mount forded the stream beside Imogen's, and they reined in and let the water babble round the horses' fetlocks and she smiled and he leaned and kissed her. Let philosophies wane: truths did: so, therefore, naturally should they. He was glad he had read the brilliant books; to be ignorant was dull; he would go on reading; the minor goddess Charm and he had a friendship he delighted in. Let the Other pace beside him still. (When Imogen was engaged with the fashion company in Milan, or when the university required his presence in Rome, Eduardo De Corvaro resumed his shadowing.) Let there in the echo-chamber sound whispers of Beethoven and Chekhov, they were exquisite amusements for father and son to share. And what did Dario care if the clear light of eternal nothingness was stained with a religion here or there? They would pass: all faiths always had: the dead told him that.

Meanwhile, that fallen tree would make a splendid fence for their horses to jump side by side. Up on the bitten sheep-walk they could canter for miles in the May sunshine and the soughing silence, and Imogen's hair blew like the triumphant pennant of melancholy itself; it fluttered with a gaiety he loved when she bowed over her horse's withers and the canter became a gallop and they raced neck and neck. For it was an honour as you galloped beside that pennant to be a witness to how ineluctable was mutability, how majestic was transience, how vain were faiths and clutchings. It was awe-inspiring to behold the beauty of the arts and sciences that were haze in the infinite meaninglessness. And it was fine in the soft twilight to hack back along the path hedged with hawthorn in white sweet flower, fine to unsaddle in his friend's farmyard, groom the sweaty horses, feed and water them, hear Imogen singing and watch the stars begin to show. There was a song – did Laura know it? – called *The Lullaby of Broadway* which Imogen was forever singing.

"Yes, she's mad about tap-dance," Laura had annoyed herself by burbling. Would her wits *never* stop divagating? But Dario had smiled, momentarily had seemed happy, seemed to have forgotten the – the whatever it was that had gone so atrociously wrong – the sadness that had come into things, or was always already there – what did they use to call it? – *lacrimae rerum* . . .

Yes, he had said, he had continually come upon her practising her tap-dance. In his kitchen, with bunches of lilac in her hands. In his bedroom, naked. Sometimes on the motorway when she was in the outside lane and driving fast, which she invariably was, she would start tapping out her dance steps on her clutch and accelerator.

"Tell me, Dario . . . What went wrong?"

He had regarded her, Laura told Anna, as if at an instant she had flung him far out into the middle of a thinly frozen lake where he would fight with the cold water and the cracking ice in vain.

"She . . . She shone a light on me."

"Like Psyche . . . ?"

"Like Psyche . . . ?" Dario had echoed her musingly. Well, yes, now he thought of it . . . There Imogen and he had been, in his castle, and she had wanted – he could not at the moment come up with a more apt image for it – she had wanted to see him. "To *see* me, Laura. A thing which, in a sense, she had not yet done. Or to see into me . . ." But, he had added, and he had laughed though without amusement, Imogen might be Psyche but he certainly could not imagine himself to be Eros.

That was not what she had heard, Laura had declared. All the length and breadth of Europe – Anna knew her habit of exaggeration and would please forgive this instance of it – the number of darling Eduardo's son's love affairs was murmured to be prodigious. Dario's tendency as he went meandering through life, his hostess had thought but had not said, to have attractive women lose their hearts to him and strew themselves in his way and very often get what they wanted was doubtless inherited from the dilettante scholar and keen fisherman who had presumably lost his useless but decorative life in precisely the circumstances reported – Dario might fantasticate, might do it most fetchingly, but why should the consul in Ternate? What she said aloud and peremptorily to the man standing before her with his hands in the pockets of his khaki shorts and a gloomy puzzled expression on his handsome face was, "Turn round."

Bewildered, he had obeyed. "Yes, absolutely. Just as I thought. They're beginning to grow."

"What are?"

"Your wings. They're starting to sprout along your shoulder-blades very promisingly."

Well, Laura told her daughter, at least she had made him laugh. At least she had made him for a minute discuss with her how the emergence of powerful and glamorous wings fit for Eros would necessitate alterations to his shirts – she had praised the one he was wearing – and to his jerseys and coats. Then they had returned to their myth. He was Eros all right, Laura had assured him. She might be old, but she was not witless yet, some acuity remained to her, while he had been talking she had mulled things over and had come to a tentative conclusion or two which it was heartening that he had begun to confirm. Oh, he was to tell her if she were wrong. But she did not believe she were far wrong – not far out, no. "And I know my Imogen," she had dared to boast.

At that, her own temerity had brought her up short. In fear, she had glanced at the telephone, had prayed that it would not ring. She had begged the curled quiescent scorpion not to sting. Let there not sound the voice of Imogen – whom suddenly she had been abysmally afraid she did not know at all, would forever piously adore but would fathom about as accurately as a theologian could plumb the Holy Ghost. Let that cool voice not sound . . . That voice so collected it would not even bother to sound victorious . . . That voice which might from the airport announce its unexpected departure, its most regrettable but suddenly unavoidable and irrevocable decision to depart . . . That voice which might not even take the trouble to sound – for Imogen was capable, if she felt her freedom threatened, of triumphing in so swiftly cruel a manner that her lost lover and her godmother would be left no hopes to entertain, no possibilities to cosset till they seemed to become probabilities. Yes, Imogen might arm herself with

Angelica and thus made impregnable take flight. She was well up to relying – relying utterly immorally, Laura had made herself acknowledge – upon the fact that Dario De Corvaro was of infinite gentleness, was undoubtedly a gentleman in the old sense and constitutionally unable to bully or corner or nag.

Laura had calmed the fluttering gasps of her confidence; she had contrived to have it breathe more decorously. With any luck the fact that Dario would never conceivably give chase would ensure that Imogen, whose vanity it was never wise to underestimate, would feel she might spare herself the humiliation of bolting.

She had seen too many paintings of that delectable moment in the story, Laura with her recovered steadiness had claimed to Dario, not to be able to bring the scene vividly to mind. Could he too not see the palatial bed-chamber; see Eros asleep; see Psyche – she too in a pleasing state of undress – with a candle in her hand lean over her lover who had always insisted she visit his castle at night, who had invariably received her in a room where no light burned, remorselessly each time sent her away before dawn? "Naturally she wanted to see you, to see into you. Why did you always have her in the dark? I cherish my own ideas, but I'd love to hear yours." What were her ideas? No doubt his sat more plainly on the table of fact, were more undeniably supported by four legs and a board; but hers . . .

He was pagan, Laura had informed him – and he would kindly do nothing so idiotic as to deny it, she was not in the mood to wade through sloughs of polite evasion. He was pagan through and through, and ancient, admirably ancient. If he were a god – and who had not some spark for the divine? – he was a god of love from before the blight of monotheism fell upon mankind. Yes, she agreed with him about religions, as it happened. She had always thought monotheism a blight, just like potato blight but fortunately not so serious. She had always thought that you only had to walk forth into the world and make use of your eyes and your ears to assure yourself that there were many gods, most of them evil, but a few such as Eros likeable. He came from the Hellenic Mediterranean, the golden age before Judaeo-Christianity was shipped from the Near East along with more serviceable things like opium and more glorious things like scimitars. By the way, she must show him the lovely one that hung on the back of the gun-room door. Yes, his scepticism and his sensuality reeked of the Hellenic past. His father had been a resounding pagan in much the same style, she had thought of tossing at him, but had refrained. Whereas Imogen . . . Dario could scarcely have failed to notice that her goddaughter was pure spirit, could he? She was sheer unadulterated spirit. In a sense Imogen had never had any need to believe in God because – Laura had laughed proudly, recklessly – she was sublime already, did Dario not agree? She recalled how astonishing the sight of her pregnant had been, Laura had warbled – and for an instant had dreaded that he was going to remark bitterly that he had been denied the privilege of that comely sight, but luckily he had more tact. Yes, the sight of that ballerina's body swollen had astounded her. That slight grace was the outward semblance of an intense spirituality – how could it do something so earthly as to bear a child? Imogen was terribly abstract – that was where she got her rather unfortunate ruthlessness from, and also her love of freedom which was easier to admire even if equally easy to be alarmed by. Imogen was all psyche. Like a mountaineer who had scaled a longed-for crest and now saw her vista stretching away, Laura had allowed herself her moment of success and a flourish of laughter to go with it. "Imogen is all psyche, naturally she plays the rôle of Psyche very well."

My mother is happy, Anna thought. She thinks she is teasing out a tangled skein, but she is not. She is happy because she is walking in solemn procession and bearing aloft her icon with the golden face of Imogen, just like at

Easter in the village the priest with his long beard and his long hair knotted at the back of his head and the faithful, and I too for I am faithful, walk through the white-washed streets and carry the tatty banners and the damaged icons and the big candles. But in my mother's case now it is a charade, all a charade. As soon as she lets me go, I shall find Dario and give him some friendly advice, sensible advice he will be grateful for.

"You still haven't told me," Dario had nudged Laura's attention, "why I would only have her in the dark."

"But you yourself said she shone a light on you." She had begun to intrigue him, she had been confident of it. She had begun to convince him with her picture of Imogen who was a mere breath, who was light as air, who danced divinely, who was the soul itself for abstraction and for delicacy, who with a light in her hand leaned and looked. "The question becomes: what darkness? and what light?"

"And what wax? Didn't a drop of wax from the candle fall on Eros and wake him up?"

"So the story goes. He woke up, he was angry to be seen, he banished her." She had laughed. "You'll have to tell me what the wax was – if you *did* banish her."

She had begun to transmit to him – she did not think she was flattering herself too shamelessly – something of the excitement she had felt when for the first time in that maze of a day she had thought the cards in her arthritic fingers made some glimmery sense, had started to look like a hand she might play, oh not confidently, not optimistically, but play. What was the rôle of Psyche, did he ask? What was the part acted so naturally by her goddaughter who was breath, life, soul . . . ? Why, in the darkness in which she found herself whelmed to love fearlessly. And then to disobey all injunctions – this was Imogen, all right! – to wait for her moment, to light a lamp, to raise it, to look, to take her fill of seeing . . . Or perhaps not be allowed to take her fill . . . When he had said, "She shone a light on me," at an instant she had seen Psyche raise her light, but as for what had happened next . . . If he did not feel like talking about the light and how absurdly offended he had been, she would, with his permission or indeed for that matter without it, go and ask Imogen. But first, to show him that she did not entirely lack cards in her hand and that she was ready to start flinging one or two down, she would tell him what he had asked.

"Why did you have her only and always in the dark? Why did you keep her in the dark, why wrap her in blindness? Because you are a pagan. Because for you a love affair has no before and after, is an end in itself, is a law unto itself, is sufficient unto itself." Yes, for a minute she had become downright eloquent, Laura promised Anna. "You took her galloping over the hills, you came back to the castle and you feasted on fish and wine and you made love, and all the time she was in the dark. Blindly she was feeling her way. You asked no questions. You offered no answers. You were happy. Am I wrong? You thought that thoroughbred horses and hawthorn hedges in blossom were what love affairs were made of. And they *are*, the good ones. But not only of these things. You strolled in the garden on May nights, I expect, didn't you? On May nights and then on June nights and July nights. And I dare say you sat on the parapet and I dare say the syringa smelled sweet and . . . I dare say I talk too much. But you're not going to claim it wasn't like that, are you?"

Why all this obfuscation? Anna wondered. The matter is perfectly plain. There are two possibilities only. Either Imogen was cynical all along – she enjoyed her passion, her fling – she made damned sure she got pregnant – then she vanished into thin air, or she thought she did. That is what I always believed. But I may have been wrong. Mother *has* discovered new things – though one can never trust her not to misunderstand the plainest evidence, the baldest statement, and never trust her not to invent. But there *is* the alternative, which is that Imogen fell in love with Dario, or at least fancied him like crazy – he broke the affair off – she compensated herself in her perverted way, or she is taking a slow, vicious revenge.

"Was I wrong to take her riding?" Dario had sounded prepared to defend his way of loving promptly, sturdily. "I don't think I understand why to sit on a parapet and to smell the syringa constitutes keeping someone in the dark."

"You weren't wrong to do any of the things you did. But perhaps you shouldn't have stopped at them, shouldn't have treated them as the essence, which I'm sure, being a disgraceful pagan, you did. I don't see Imogen standing in the sunshine by a trout stream wearing a pretty hat. I see her in pitch blackness taking a step at a time, I see her like a sleepwalker with her eyes open and her hands out feeling her way, slowly feeling her way round and round in an endless darkness."

"We shouldn't have stopped at what we did . . . ? We should have gone on . . ." He had begun his thought wryly; but he finished it as near to aggression as he would ever come. "Gone on to higher things? If you think Imogen was waiting for a proposal of marriage from me, you're wrong. And anyway – aren't you as pagan as I am?"

"I'm just as pagan as you are." She had had to listen to him declare her goddaughter's aversion to the idea of marrying him. Was he right? wrong? deceiving her? She had been forced to decide that she could not know for a while yet. But when Imogen came . . . Ah, she *must* come, mustn't she? Come, my darling! she had prayed. She breathed the same prayer again now, balefully conscious that Anna had stepped to the door of her sanctum but no further, was eyeing the rugs critically, was not enchanted by them. For tenacity too she had prayed. She would play only moves she was well-nigh certain of; but she must keep playing. So – "Imogen hasn't got much time for revealed religion either. But she's more metaphysical than we are. She'll have been looking for some kind of transcendence, don't you think? Looking in what ways she could. Perhaps scarcely knowing what she was looking for."

95

"It was a dreadful light."

What Imogen will never transcend is her selfishness, Anna thought. What she'll never rise above is her I, I, I . . .

"Did he explain what he meant by a dreadful light?"

"He tried a bit."

To answer her daughter's question, Laura stood up. She opened a shutter because that side of the house was in shade now, looked down over her olive groves to the sea which appeared innocent enough, lay still and blue in the sun of the late afternoon, but which was a graveyard, she remembered, thinking of Dario's father, thinking of how the souls of drowned sailors are unquiet because their bones are washed hither and thither by deep cold black tides perpetually, how it takes ritual to lay a ghost, spirits do not cross to the land of the dead without burial and obsequy, they remain to haunt us, they are wailing gulls. And her father, she now could not help recalling, had not been recovered from Keppel Harbour and given Christian burial. Perhaps if it was a direct hit there was not much to recover. Or did the Japanese when they had time burn the pestilent British and Chinese corpses that washed ashore? No, that was all nonsense about unquiet souls. Captain Salthouse's daughter gave herself a shake.

"For that matter, did you explain what you meant by darkness?"

"I tried!" The old lady gave a snort of exasperation. "It wasn't that we didn't try! That Imogen will have felt swathed in darkness, that the sensuality of things can have that effect . . . That to forgo the visionary may make the sensual world more piercing, it may indeed, but Imogen will have longed to sense her visions too . . . Oh, I reasoned like mad. I explained, or I tried to. That she will have ached to be as visionary as it is natural for her to be, ached to see things brilliantly, to have her eyes bright with light, have her mind bright with light. Dario said he thought maybe he was beginning to grasp what I meant. I nearly wept to hear it, but then when he started talking I suddenly felt so old and weary I couldn't work out whether his image of her bore any resemblance to mine. Imogen would have wanted to see where she was going, Dario suggested, was that it? See things lit with the lustre that having a future gives? See things in the perspective of time? Because I was right, he confessed I was right, he'd lived and loved from day to day. Didn't know how else to live except from day to day. But Imogen – yes – he'd caught a whiff of what I meant. And did I know about the old Orphic belief in the psyche as divine? He'd read a terrifically interesting book about the Orphic cults a few years before, he'd send it to me if I liked. Ah have mercy on me! I cried. Do not, I entreat you, lend me learned works. Help me solve this problem of ours now."

"You're just an old match-maker," Anna told her mother equably.

"Ah no! But," she could not help adding, "if only . . ."

"Mind you, to offer to marry him is the least Imogen could do."

"I very much doubt that the kind of match they'll make will be of the kind Jim and Margaret Scottow would approve of, or even, very likely, recognise as having been made. Yes . . ." Laura warmed to her notion. "If a match is made at all, which it probably won't be because I don't trust that girl an inch, it'll be invisible to the Scottows. It may be invisible to us. It'll be of an abstraction . . ." Laura regained the sofa. Exhausted, she sat down. She closed her eyes. She saw a darkened bedroom, she saw Imogen who tirelessly ran her fingers over a man she had never seen, Imogen who patiently and passionately caressed and learned and caressed and learned but was not satisfied. She saw Imogen wait till she was sure he slept, saw her fetch a candle, light it . . . To be banished for that! Enchanting damsel in dishabille bundled unceremoniously out of a castle gate, what an inane hullabaloo, truly men were ridiculous. Or . . . Or it must have been a light . . . ! Dario had used the word dreadful. "I think perhaps the light was too abstract for him," she said.

"Did he say it hurt his eyes?" enquired Anna, who was now inclining toward the second of her two hypotheses; was not unrelievedly distressed that Imogen had it seemed been rejected; was concerned with how the traitress's revenge might be stymied. It was a dilemma. So far as she could make out, Imogen could go on savaging Dario's feelings till he died. "I bet he was just being modest when he told you she didn't want to marry him. I bet she shone a glare in his eyes as if he were a prisoner and she were interrogating him. She wanted to winkle out every secret in his heart."

"Yes, he said it hurt his eyes." It was important to acknowledge Anna's accuracies. But if only she would not imagine things so brutally! Her daughter would never hit the bull's eye in her life, Laura had no intention of suspecting she might. But her arrows hit the outer rings of the target quite often, hit with the thud of a barbed shaft plunging into straw. "And he said it was a glare. You're right about that. A glare, a blindness, he called it."

"Well, there you are." Anna was all serene lucidity. "She wanted him. She wanted him for hers. She wanted to gaze into every nook of his soul, she wanted to possess him through and through. There are women like that. And it's not uncommon for men to be appalled to have that kind of searchlight played on them. Not uncommon," she had the air of knowing what she was talking about, "at all."

"I think you may be partly right," Laura said to Anna; and silently her soul cried: Imogen! "He said it was a blinding light." Where are you? Somewhere on this dusty land of mine you are dragging the ball and chain of your freedom. Somewhere you are limping and hauling, and that convict's hobble is jerking leadenly after you in the dust. "He said it was intolerable," Laura heard her voice say aloud. "She wanted to know everything, he felt ransacked." Here we are travestying you, Imogen. Dario and Anna and I in our different ways have all got you wrong. Oh I half believe in all three of us. But I believe only in you. "Question after question, he said. Advance into him after advance into him. Glare always brightening. More than a man could endure. Light after light." I believe in your self-knowledge, Imogen; you must lead me into it; I will follow; I will believe. I do not think I believe in this talk of a glare, of ransacking and pillaging, it is a travesty. I believe in you naked in the darkness holding up a light so that you can see. In that, yes, I have faith. In a young woman who hardly knows it is transcendence she is searching for but to whom it is natural to raise a light and to look. And if there is any smattering of justice in this dung-heap world, you will not forever be hounded from your happiness because you have the courage to make a light and to look. If your foolish godmother has even a little of her way – and I am a stubborn old creature, I am a mule – my darling you shall take your fill of looking one day. "Oh, I don't know," she wound up. "I need Imogen."

"To ask her point-blank whether Angelica is Dario's daughter?"

"No!" Laura was flustered. Her voice quavered in the way she hated. "Under no circumstances. Do you think Imogen would have a moment's tolerance if one of us came blundering at her like that? And for Angelica it would be all over. No . . . I want to know more about this strange light." She saw a girlish figure with a lamp held aloft advancing into a cavernous labyrinth. "When I have a clearer idea of what she might say to Dario, I shall find out if I have the guts to beg her to talk to him. Of course she may have decided already. She may have taken action already."

"I'm going to look for Dario." And from the door Anna asked, "What will you do with Imogen? Bring her here?"

"No, I've been in this room long enough for one day. If there's a wind we might sail. I don't know. I'll think of something. Pistol practice! Anything! It doesn't matter what we do. But everything," Laura pursued the falterings of her last idea, "Angelica's happiness one day, *everything* will depend on the calls. Because they've been calling to one another, those two."

"Yelling from country to country, do you mean? Hollering across the sea? Or do you mean they've been ringing each other up?"

"They've been calling silently. Stilly too, I imagine. With great stillness. But certainly silently. Dario from his castle. Imogen from her exile in London, from her office where it says *Imogen Scottow Limited* over the door. Everything will depend on those silent calls, on what they whisper – if I can hear the whisperings and understand what I hear. Now you go and be sweet to Dario, my dear, and remember not to hit him over the head with too much good advice. I shall die if I do not have a moment's peace and quiet."

Then it was as if in the wrecked ship of Laura's mind strange waters lapped and strange shadows danced. Did she sleep for a minute or two? She was weary; she was almost certain she drowsed. On a reef a few miles down the coast lay a broken-backed merchant ship. A scruffy tramp steamer she had been, lading freight between the mainland and the islands, but one stormy night the skipper had been drunk so there she lay with her back broken and her derricks like gibbets and rust pitting her from her keel to her bridge and below the waterline seaweed growing and sea anemones and limpets and mussels and barnacles. Often in *Nineveh* Alexis and Laura had sailed by, they had seen the sad way an angry sea would crash in through the rent the reef had made, and the other way, also sad, in which a tranquil sea would loll in the iron carcass and flicker its blues and silvers and greens and waver its shadows of blue and silver and green.

And was there honestly much difference between waking and sleeping? The question sounded as if it were asked in Eduardo De Corvaro's voice. Clearly the echo-chamber of reality was a mind one shared with others, a reverberating dimness where spirits apparently living and spirits less apparent might meet and talk. The unfleshed – were they unsouled? – came back to us with a splendid vengeance, Laura was prompted to note. Time passed and the self mercifully died with the dead, and then with the dead came back, a self momently reborn. And now – between waking and sleeping, any decisive differences? The passages between one form of lack of control and the other could have their excitements and terrors, indeed they could. Her tired head was tilted against the back of the sofa; her eyes were closed; her mind was that wrecked steamer. In a year or two the gale would blow which would thunder such combers into the wounded hold and obscure with such a blizzard of spindrift the deck and over-tower with such columns of spume the bridge that it would be her death, when calm came again it would be a different calm, she would have been transfigured, she would be a greyish thread, a twist, a turn, in a more nebulous pattern. But now it was a warm, easy sea that washed. Easy . . . Uneasy . . .

Eduardo and she had been lovers. Yes, she had gulled Alexis. Anna, praise God, did not know. A casual, delightful lover he had been. A casual, indifferent voice he came now lapping into the wrecked ship. His son's voice lapped there too. A school of minnows made a foray over the reef, vanished into a jungle of bladderwrack, swam out into sunlit glassiness again, headed in through the gash in the ship's side. Here reddish rust made a shadowy pool that might have been blood, might have seeped from the bosun or the mate. (No image so lurid corresponded to the facts of the disaster twenty years before – as a more wakeful Laura Rodostamo would have reminded herself. The crew had got away in the two lifeboats. One was lost with all hands. The other came safe to shore.) There in a gloomy crevice of what had been the engine room an octopus waited for prey. Laura remembered how you had to stab them between their eyes, stab the soft bulgy sack of the brute's brain. Then she remembered how year after year Maria and Daphne and she had taken the octopuses Achilles caught and had flogged them against rocks, had stood in the shallows and gripped the tentacled arms and swung the corpses against rocks for what felt like hours, flogged them till the flesh frothed pinkish white and when cooked would be tender. The echoes of all that Dario had said were fading. In a while the echoes of the unsaid would die to nothing too. But still there were hummings in the air. A seventeenth-century etching that his father had given him, something by Ribera, that was right. She had not recounted everything to Anna. Eduardo before his last voyage had walked across the courtyard carrying Ribera's *Poet* which had always hung over his desk. How did the scene go? Eduardo coming to the stable block, climbing the stair to his son's flat, telling him the picture was to hang over his desk now, he'd be lucky if he ever inherited much so here was a present to be getting on with . . . And a noble image too . . . The robed poet with his elbow propped on a great block of stone, with a wreath of laurel on his head, bowed in thought . . . Not a large picture, but one of a concentrated, sombre strength . . .

A wrecked mind. Washings and eddies of an uneasy calm. Strange waters slid, strange shadows fell. Images broke, they reformed. Dario the winter after his love affair took a horse and rode off into the snow. That rational, bookish young man had a streak of mysticism in him it seemed. Young? Nearer forty than thirty these days. No, it was the next winter. Last winter, he had said. After more than a year of calling, then. Well, the snow was right, anyway. Snow was falling. No wind, not a snow-storm. Pale air burdened with flakes falling. A track through trees burdened with snow. His horse walking. Muffled hoof-falls. When snow packed frozen hard in horses' hooves they could slip, they could slip and come down, it was best to walk. Imogen was in the air, in the snow sifting softly down through the trees, in his mind, he didn't know. He had been searching for her and he was near now. He had ridden many miles, and now in the quietness and stillness and whiteness she was very near. Her face, her form, her very life! Creak of the saddle, clink of the snaffle, soft hoof-falls. He had half known her, had half loved her, where were the other knowledge and the other love? Still forever white trees and hoof-falls and cold and quietness. Snow alighted on his horse's mane; on his hands, his knees. Snow brushed his face. Where was she, almost forming? He would give all that he had known and all that he had loved for that other knowledge and that other love. He would surrender – ah, but how? He had already lost all. He had half forgotten. He half remembered. Nearly he remade, or nearly refound. Her eyes open, her lips beginning to smile, almost she was here, almost now. Snowy trees. Snowy quietness. Snowy hoof-falls. Ah, come! Quick! Now, always . . .

"Coz!" Clear, low, a whisper. "Laura!"

THREE

"I guess you could say I've a call."

LADY LAZARUS, Sylvia Plath

The sun is waning, thought Imogen as she walked Xenophon through the olive groves and he swished his tail and chucked his head because the flies were annoying. High over my head the sun glints on the aeroplane which may be the Schombergs' aeroplane dipping now toward the town; but it is beginning to wane.

I have been riding for an hour, the air is not quite so dazzling and not so fervidly hot as when I started. The sun is laying the shadows of the trees at greater length upon the short dusty grass of the terraces. Olives and cypresses, mulberries and walnuts, they are being softened all of them, their depths made hospitable to more tones of dimness and brightness, more every minute it seems now. Look at this fig tree, its greens are increasing in number and richness even as I watch. Yes, in the moments it takes a horse to walk past a tree I find new gleamings on boughs and foliage now the sun is more subtle, infiltrates itself in between single leaves and into the heart, where the wings of sparrows flitter, with rays more horizontal and because more gentle more penetrating. Was that a bee-eater that flew off? It went so quickly. I hope it was a bee-eater. And this hay rick too, how palely gold! I like the way they plant a tall pole in the earth, and at hay harvest build the rick around the pole till it resembles a conical house, and then all winter as the animals need hay to eat the rick is depleted and the house loses shapeliness, it is eaten away on all sides, is gnawed to the bare bones and by spring the pole alone remains, naked, upright, gaunt. But now it is high summer, the very pitch of summer. They reaped the meadows last month. The rick is symmetrical and compact, it glows in the dwindling sun. At the end of summer they will cut the aftermath.

Xenophon's hooves clip-clop down the village street. I halt outside the one grimy little café, I pass the reins over my horse's head and hitch them to the trunk of the wistaria. I step into the gloom where the men drink ouzo and play backgammon and play cards, where the women almost never enter except to leave messages. We say how nice it is to see each other. They ask, how is Mrs Rodostamo? how are her dogs? how is that little rascal Adonis, that imp? He is thirteen this summer, I say. As unreliable as ever about washing and about meal-times, I say; and roguish, yes, when it comes to hurling other children off the quay into the bay; but the dearest boy. I drink a cup of coffee – bitter, grainy, sweet, hot. I drink a glass of water that has been drawn from the well and I think how stony it tastes, how superbly it tastes of cold fresh stone. And, I think, it was stupid of Demitri to go on having children with that vulgar suburban wife of his when it was as clear as the moon sliding out through cloud-rack that the marriage was a flop . . . But what is that to me? And Adonis among imps is the most adorable. What is more, he has character, I reflect, and the idea makes me smile as I remount and ride away. Look at the way, when he has decided that he will be a man among men, that he heaves at a fishing net, the way he drags at it steadily with all his might minute after minute till you can watch the sweat rinsing down his small scrawny brown back and watch the small muscles in his scrawny brown arms and legs fluttering and still he will not rest, he will heave like a man, will not give up, no, will not.

A mistake, however, to bring to mind a net. Because

although looking at the sunlight in the trees I was happy, although musing on the goldenness of hay ricks and the quickness of bee-eaters and the stoniness of water I had forgotten nets, there is a net in all things. Today I see the net of things. I am netted, I see it.

At daybreak at sea aboard the fishing-smack I was free. I saw the pilgrim spread his brilliant prayer-mat on the wrinkled grey desert of the Ionian, I saw him kneel to make his orisons, then I saw him ablaze in the resurgent light. I hauled at the net and I saw the black cormorants on bluffs stretch their wings to dry in the first sea-level beams of warmth, they looked as if they were opening their ragged black arms to embrace the coming light, and my heart was high, it was all over the sky. I took a swig of Achilles' wine and it tasted of earth and grape and sunlight, it tasted good. I dived and the sea was jocund as it played with me, and I felt cleansed and at liberty and I rejoiced. Then I came ashore and I saw the net of all things.

Now I ride out of the village in the late afternoon sun. I walk Xenophon toward the valley we must cross to reach Laura's estate and I say: We exist only by virtue of what we possess, we possess only what is really present to us, and many of our memories, our moods, our ideas and desires sail away on voyages of their own till they are lost to sight. But they know of ways across the sea, unseen by other eyes, by which to return to us. Time may be freedom, I conclude, and time may be servitude. Time can carry away old realities, it can consign to oblivion old selves, it can make free. But it can also tangle you in such a web that you will never fight your way clear. And when I came round the corner of the kitchen hut carrying my bucket of fish and I saw Dario, memory netted me. I was a wild creature for whom hunters had prepared an ambush, at an instant the net was flung over me, down I went kicking in the dust.

Now I am riding across the river valley where herds of goats and sheep graze. Sometimes here I have seen hoopoes, they like the wet low-lying land. Egret too. The white egret

106

come to feed in the swamps, in the shallow pools, in the water-meadows. At evening I have seen a flock of them fly back to the wooded hills to roost, fly trailing their skinny shanks and their silvery plumes. The river meanders. No, rather now it is the river-bed which meanders. It has not rained for weeks, the river is cracked mud with a puddle here and a trickle there. In spring the valley will be ankle-deep in flowers. I have a hat which Laura gave me which has an egret's plume, an aigrette, a panache. It is an old hat from the twenties. I would not buy or make a hat for which an egret had to be killed. Now my featherless straw hat still shades my eyes but I can feel the sun on my chin. The heat is softer. The light that was sheer blue is shot with more and more hazy golds, the woods will be green garments slashed with gold. You would not think the wide empty air of the valley were a net, but it is. Now I am alone I have the self-discipline to be tranquil – to be intermittently fairly tranquil. But if they come at me with nets I shall fight. Let Anna not come at me, or I shall hear myself snarl such things as shall in five minutes undo our cool cousinly friendship, our alliance of longstanding and of superficiality. She is innocent, but I shall hear myself utter such bladed things that she, aghast, cut to the quick, will never wish to speak to me again. The following day she may beg me: Say you did not mean those maddened things, Imogen, say you are sorry, let us patch our friendship up. I shall refuse. I am not a Christian, I do not believe in forgiveness, in its possibility. One may make light of injuries and ills: that is another matter, a matter of gallantry, of pride. But while time runs all actions performed in time will endure, they may signify less and less but until memory is dissolved they will not be dissolved, while there is history there is guilt, to say evil can be expunged is cant, to say the evil-doer can be restored to innocence is cant. Why should I pretend otherwise? And why invite others to pretend, to speak falsehoods, perjure themselves?

I gather up my reins. The valley is flat, the land soft,

a good place to gallop. I kick in my heels. Xenophon has mettle, he starts forward impulsively, breaks straight into a canter. With pounding hooves, with my hat blown off but caught by the riband around my throat, with the rushing wind in my hair, I shall cleanse my mind of savage thoughts. I am galloping, they shall not net me. Alone and galloping I can think the net to tatters, it is nothing.

Time may be freedom as well as servitude, I said, it has two abilities. It takes our selves from us, that is its blessing. But when carrying my fish-bucket I walked round the kitchen hut it was servitude which memory cast over me, a mesh more delicate than a spider's web, a mesh abstract, a mesh as enslaving as a point of view, as a way of feeling things. In the lightless depths no fish snagged by its gills struggles more futilely than I jerk now. They have taken from me the carefree way I used to come and go in the world. They? Or is it that I have ensnared myself? The gallop comes to an end, I walk Xenophon along a path into Laura's hills. Is it that all our gallops of freedom pass, we end up waking back into our old captivities? I am the past which is unforgiving and unforgiveable, suddenly I stand there to confront myself, I raise my arm, I cast my net. It is also I who fall, I who lie trussed on the dirt.

Here is the burned chapel with its spring. The water comes splashing out of a cleft in the rock, it gathers in the stone trough, it brims. Xenophon lowers his head, he drinks. It is a sad place. Earlier in the summer the grass in the ruin grew chest-high and now it is still that height but brittle and sere. I ride on. There is the path that branches off to the butterfly chapel. I do not take it. Up at the house they are waiting for me. Down by the shore they are waiting for me. Yes, but also I am waiting for myself, am I not? I was the merciless and unpitied past who stood before me among the huts in the morning sun. This time I advance forewarned, cautiously. "Come!" I call. "I am coming!" I call back. I go slowly, Xenophon's hooves sounding dully on the hard dust, sharply when a steel horse-shoe rings against stone. Basking lizards cock their green and red and silver heads as we come, they scuttle off into the gorse and prickly pear. I like this sound of slow hooves, it is a natural tempo, I approach myself at a rhythm that pleases me.

Anna has already convinced herself that Dario is Angelica's father. All morning I only had to hear the woman cough to be deafened by her mind going on ringing the same chimes, ding dong ding dong. When Dario asked me how old Angelica was I told him the truth, so he knows – what? That she was either conceived right at the end of our love affair or very soon after it was over. My freedom was so vital to achieve, shall I lose it now? Or had I not truly achieved it? Was it not mine? Was it not itself? Warily I approach myself, at the slow tempo of hooves. Shall I obsequiously renounce the liberty I have staked out, go back to respecting the customs of the tribe? Ah, never! Not I. I shall ride behind the house to the stables, I shall unsaddle Xenophon, I shall groom him. In his loose-box he shall have fresh water and a bucket of feed and a hay-net. Often I have felt free, aboard fishing-smacks on radiant mornings, galloping horses on hot afternoons, I have been free, the feeling is the thing itself.

To make the rhythm of time steadily the rhythm of freedom – but how? As if it were the beat of one's horse's hooves. To fall into step with freedom so that henceforth we walk together all the days of my life, so that no I shall ever again confound me at the corner of a hut, no net suddenly shimmer in the air and enfold me like a blindness, nor ever again shall I look into people's faces and see criss-cross netting, look at woods and scarps and horizons and see only the nets in them. That time should take my selves from me – that is my prayer. I pray: Let this self pass from me. Here are the yard, the carob tree, the stables. Let this self pass from me. Let another come. Let freedom and I fall into step and so journey on together until – oh I don't know. I wonder where Laura is.

Thus praying, Imogen dismounted. She had escaped on horseback in order to be alone, but now in all decency she must allow her godmother to talk to her. At lunch she had been on tenterhooks, Imogen had observed. Generally Laura delighted to entertain people. Her library where friends might read, her bay where they might swim, her table where they might feast – to offer these things gave her pleasure. But not today. Imogen had seen through her merry hospitality under the arbour. A crème brûlée which Laura had cooked herself because Ben Thurne had a weakness for the stuff, and of course she had hoped a little treat might cheer him up momentarily, and Alexis and Adonis could be relied upon to have second helpings – but Imogen had seen how near to panic the old lady had wobbled. "The trouble with that castle of yours is, it's not on the sea," she had said to Dario, she recalled, and by the agitation hopping and skipping and jumping in her godmother's eyes you would have thought she had produced a gun and aimed it at the poor fellow's chest.

She would tell Laura the sort of things that had been singing in her head while she rode. Imogen carried her saddle and bridle into the tack-room, she hung them up. She would be happy to talk with Laura. She stood a moment quite still apart from one hand that kept flicking her whip against her boot. Naturally she would talk happily with Laura – why, then, did she have to reassure herself of the fact? Had something between them altered since their conversation in Kensington Gardens? Had something altered today? Silence, apart from the light nervous whipping of her booted leg. As for Dario, he had had the better of her a couple of years ago, but she reckoned she had the advantage over him now and she reckoned to keep it, to keep the whip hand, she thought, and irritably chucked her whip onto the tack-room table and came out into the yard. But Laura . . . ? No, nonsense! They had always been loyal to one another, they would be so still.

She must be as gentle as possible with Laura, Imogen reminded herself. Even if the old darling ventured upon some intrusion, she must use just enough firmness to defend herself but no more, use the necessary minimum of unkindness but no more. She could on occasion be too hard, she was aware of it. Let this self pass from me, she prayed as she groomed Xenophon, but prayed idly, frivolously now, for she was mercurial and her mood had changed. Let freedom and I walk together all the days of my life, she prayed, but distractedly now, not discontented in the sunny yard to be drawing the brush down the horse's bay flank, whistling lightly through her teeth. Let me not be netted, she prayed as she led the gelding into his loose-box, but she prayed it without passion because she did not feel netted now. All the same, it was not a bad idea to remind oneself that trappers were afield, one should go warily, be ready to fight with fury.

Angelica would be fine with Maria, no need to worry about her. Maria would be happy to keep her all afternoon. Good. Imogen went into the house. At the gun-room basin she washed her hands, splashed her face, combed her hair. She hung her hat on a hook. Where would Laura be? There was no one in the library. Perhaps she was up at the butterfly chapel, perhaps she was down in her hut. From upstairs came the faint sad music of Demitri's flute. His gout tortured him, it was humiliating. Imogen glanced into the drawing-room. Ah, there she was. So old, she looked, with her head tipped back, her eyes shut, her mouth slightly open. Poor old Laura, she did not like her age. But it was wonderful to see her.

Imogen smiled as she walked toward her godmother. "Coz!" she said softly. "Laura!"

"You've come!" breathed Laura Rodostamo in happy wonder, for when she opened her rheumy eyes the sight of Imogen's smile bending toward her for an instant struck her as a miracle, as revealed truth, as naked power wilfully showing itself off. "And high time too," she rapidly adjoined with that prissy strictness which old ladies may, if they are loved and tolerated, on occasion permit themselves – because already she was off on the wrong footing, it was painfully obvious, and alas she might totter feebly this way and that a long while before getting her footing right.

Yes, she was off balance because already Imogen had started charming her. She seduces me shamelessly, her godmother inwardly moaned. Often without saying a word. Just by standing before me. Some people are like that. Damnable Imogen would dedicate a blithe and really not all that dishonest hour to charming her into submission, into acquiescence with whatever she had been pleased to decide it would be most convenient she should acquiesce in, and that hour passed she would go swimming or give Angelica her bath. Yes, in the evening Laura would see her strolling on the quay wearing a flattering dress of her own fashioning and holding a drink in her hand and chatting to Nick about Princeton, or to Tasso about fishing, or to Natasha – had she arrived yet? – about charity balls, or bloodstock, or whether the exhilaration of skiing compensated for the ghastliness of resorts, or the latest anecdote at her brother's expense. Dressed and scented for dinner she would stroll and she would sip and she would chatter, and she would have compromised nowhere, disclosed nothing, ceded nothing, and the next day Dario De Corvaro would depart on the ferry, and she would enjoy the rest of the summer very much.

"Didn't you expect me to come?" A voice that gay and that affectionate could make anything mean next to nothing. It was a voice that might very likely tell silly stories till midnight, might lightly touch on Angelica's fate and her own labyrinthine self-knowledge but without confessing them to be the mortal riddle they were, without the disentanglement of this knot being any more important than the mockery of Mark Scottow's habit, each time a painting by Ingres

112

went to an American or Japanese collection, of buying a new Mercedes Benz.

"Of course I knew you'd come," Laura lied determinedly, because it was essential not to be bewitched, and because now she was already falling into bewitchment it was suddenly impossible that she should ever have doubted that her Imogen, when the serious joys of equitation relinquished her (boots, breeches: Laura focused on them) would hasten to her side. And because it was a familiar delight to be thus spellbound, the uneasy waters of a minute before no longer lapped in her head. Dario was no longer riding into the falling snow. *My head thou dost with oil anoint*, Laura thought. Aloud she exclaimed with the gaiety Imogen infected her with, "I was just wondering *how* you'd come." Her voice lilted, already she believed in her trust, believed in her new happiness. She was as summarily converted as the man who was hacking along the road to Damascus when his steed shied and he was thrown, a man to be mildly despised as a singular perverter of what might otherwise have been a humane enough doctrine, and to be more profoundly despised because it is a poor horseman who falls without his mount falling. "Oh I was fairly singing," she cried. "*She'll be riding six white horses when she comes.* That kind of thing. *She'll be wearing silk pyjamas when she comes.* I'm sorry I only have one bay horse to offer you. There'll be half-a-dozen greys in the stable when you next visit I promise."

For was it not a great good thing to have beautiful Imogen stand before her with laughter and love in her eyes? It was a grand thing. That was why it was simplicity itself now to go straight ahead, to say smilingly and mischievously and fearlessly, "I've been having a *fascinating* time with Dario, sweetheart. He told me the most glorious love story I've heard for years. And I'm sure I don't have to tell you what he thinks about our darling Angelica."

Laura scarcely had time to recall that in fact Dario had merely joked about asking the child's age, she was already listening to her goddaughter's response. It came with merriment. "Oh!" Her blue eyes were uplifted. "The things men think! Now I *must* tell you, I've had the most magnificent ride. I went all the way to the village, came back across the valley. Xenophon was in terrific fettle, and I thought a whole lot of things I want to tell you. What do you feel like doing? What shall we do that will be fun, you and I? Do you fancy a swim?"

They stood at the window, looked out to where Alexis' father had been shot. "I'd love to take *Nineveh* for a sail, but . . ." Laura scrutinised the cedar. "There isn't a breath of wind. Would pistol practice amuse you?"

"I'll be wildly erratic, I haven't fired a shot since last year." Imogen was buoyant. "Or maybe I'll be lethal. What do you think?" She held out an imaginary weapon, sighted along her fingers, fired at a chimney. "Does my hand look steady to you? Do I look deadly today?"

It was an honoured ceremony of theirs, pistol shooting. (Anna hated gunshots, they frightened her, as a girl Imogen had delighted in making her jump.) In the gun-room to light upon the old Colt revolver that had seen service in Alexis Rodostamo's hand among the partisans when the Germans and Italians overran the lowlands and the hills, and only on desolate mountains was freedom kept gutteringly aflame, only from caves and hovels fortified by inaccessible crags and defended by trackless woods was justice visited on the weak sinful world below. To rummage in the chest-of-drawers, sort through shot-gun cartridges of various calibres, at last find the box of pistol bullets, put a couple of handfuls in your pockets or in your bag or fit them into a cartridge belt and buckle it on. (Imogen certainly looked marvellously dangerous, her godmother fondly told her. With her breeches, with her bristling belt, she was some bride on safari between the wars.) To stroll then companionably side by side to a particular olive grove where one terrace was so wide that it made an excellent range, you could prop whatever your makeshift target was against the bank and get far enough back from it to miss more often than you hit, and the bullets buried themselves harmlessly in the bank with a little spurt of dust which was useful when you were adjusting your aim for your next shot. To take turns. To tease each other about their inaccuracy. It was a ceremony, a way of love.

But today they did not go to the olive grove. "The west headland!" It was Imogen's commandment, not her plea. Did Laura feel up to walking so far? She must think of how overjoyed her spaniels would be to make an expedition to such a far-flung promontory. And yes, Imogen allowed as she buckled on Alexis' holster with a hand on which gleamed his Egyptian ring with a scarab cut in cornelian, she might strip off her clothes and swim. But the chief thing was, she wanted to watch the sun sink into the sea. If they didn't dawdle they would, she calculated, be on the headland by sunset. What? Like Eros and Psyche? Laura was to explain what she meant, please. No doubt it was an absolutely brilliant perception, but it was unclear to her. They could talk as they strolled. Well no, as a matter of fact if it was all the same to Laura they would tramp along reasonably briskly, on account of her desire to witness the sun, which that morning she had seen rise, go down.

Subjection to Imogen's charm had the effect upon Laura that she resolved to make a virtue of necessity. So be it, she found herself constrained to reason. Of course it would always have been a mistake to stand up to this dashingly booted and armed mistress of destinies. To cause her even the smallest annoyance would always have been a frightful blunder. Better to let oneself fall helplessly under her sway. My last adventure, Laura admonished herself, must not only not appear to Imogen to be a fight, it must not be one, must not be allowed to come to that. Better docilely to adore. Better that her goddaughter should thoughtlessly hold her in her habitual position close to her heart. Thus embraced, thus familiar with the heart, she might by inoffensive watching and listening discover what she wished to know – and the list of these things was growing like Jack's beanstalk. No, it was more like Jacob's ladder, every time she dreamily blinked it had grown a few more puzzling rungs, it ascended higher into the incomprehensible heavens, had more perches for angels, revealed more possibilities – cherubic? demonic? seraphic? – climbing up and down. For instance, when Laura had told Anna that Dario and Imogen had been in love, she had heard a voice add silently that they still were. But that had been immediately after her talk with Dario. His account of his ride through the snowy woodland had left her in little doubt that his passion for Imogen was of a different order to his other doubtless numerous and doubtless enjoyable liaisons. But now after five minutes with the object of his passion . . .

Could a young woman who after the lapse of a couple of years was waking to the realisation that by happy chance her love was here, was now, had not forgotten her, be quite so carelessly blithe? A young woman surprised one day, surprised between terror and joy, by her own most shaking passion? A Psyche whom Eros forgave? Laura was no longer so confident that the uncharacteristic agitation she had displayed that morning – the tremor in her voice, her swings between affability with Dario and iciness – was to be explained by the rediscovery of love as well as by fierce protectiveness of Angelica's and her independence. Very likely it was the latter alone. Or if Dario had indeed rejected her perhaps her awkwardnesses sprang from humiliation remembered, from hatred revived. And was she blithe now because she knew she could scare Dario away, knew she could inflict a wound on him that would ache a long time, felt the sweetness of it, knew herself the victress and felt free? Or did she not know that he was still in love with her? It all depends, Laura rehearsed to herself dourly, upon the calls.

Dismissed from the castle of Eros in disgrace for having broken the rules of the amorous game, did Psyche sit down desolately on a rock and gaze at the castle now forever forbidden to her and mourn with a faithful heart, as she was painted doing by Turner or was it Claude Lorraine? Dear God, some days she could *feel* her memory rotting, she would swear she could – though now she recalled that the girl in the picture was a sturdy wench, bore no resemblance to wasp-waisted Imogen. Or did the twentieth-century Psyche shrug, remind herself that some games of chess you win and some you lose, go her way in peace, possibly with some irreverent commentary on male selfishness and vanity and curious erotic fancies? And if – but this scenario was utterly hypothetical – before her banishment from the castle she insisted on one last night, if she deliberately conceived a child, was that an act of love or of hatred? The idea that Angelica might have been conceived in hatred was abhorrent, but Laura made herself stare at it. Did Imogen, rejected, want Dario's child, want something of his, resort to theft? Or did she want a child irrespective of its father, as in Kensington Gardens she had claimed? Did she want a fatherless child, and in sudden hatred of her heartless lover grab her opportunity of getting one and getting her revenge too?

There was nothing for it, Laura realised, but humility and obedience. There was nothing for it but to follow Imogen into her self-knowledge, hoping to be so loyal she hardly existed and so would hardly be noticed, would not incite the anger of the adventuress who was undoubtedly proud enough to prefer to think herself alone. No – nothing else for it at all. What other hope was there that Angelica would ever be able to answer the question: Who am I? Not that it mattered who anybody's father or for that matter mother was. Descent was one of the least interesting aspects of a person, roughly on the same low level as people's creed or their race. Nor that it much mattered whether anybody's beliefs as to their parentage corresponded to fact or not. No – but in this case it was indicative of a more awesome cloud of unknowing. That Angelica should not live to breathe only the gas of uncertainties, that she be saved from that – ah that mattered all right. Well, perhaps Imogen would tell her – what? That she had been madly in love with a French mountaineer and he with her, that they had been about to get married, she had been pregnant, he had gone to scale some infamous coll in the Atlas mountains and . . . Imogen would tell a stirring tale. And it might be the best thing to do. And it might be true.

In the meantime there was nothing for it but to tiptoe behind Imogen with her raised lamp. She must hope to be there when the light fell on whatever mystery the labyrinth contained. She must at all costs be there at the kill – if there were a minotaur, if at the centre of things there proved to be a monster whose death would bring freedom to the innocent. Laura just hoped grimly that the adventure actually was taking place. Imogen might lazily be bluffing, she might easily. Still, the story of her musings while riding Xenophon, a story now being told as they took the path toward the western headland, gave grounds for some cautious optimism on this score, Laura felt – and tried not to suspect that her goddaughter had become so arrogant she reckoned self-knowledge was something she had achieved years ago.

Ah, the light! the old lady exhorted herself. She must follow the light. She must perforce doggedly believe that there were a light to follow. Alas too it was certain – and it was a thought to downcast the most besotted and loyal of followers – that if Imogen had exhausted her love for Dario, if he had killed it in her or it had spent itself, there was a blank end to all good possibilities. Then if Dario were Angelica's father or if he were not, the only decent thing to do would be to try to convince him that he were childless, or anyway convince him that the sensible thing for him to do was to pretend to be convinced. For Imogen would never share her daughter with a man she was not in love with. Dario indeed would not insist, with sadness would renounce. Odd stuff, courtesy. No, Imogen would not renege on her solitary journey, her pursuit of happiness with only a babe for company, would she? Laura wondered how solitary you could be with the air resonant with voices. Well, Imogen chose to appear to believe in her solitude. And she would not renege – would she? – unless . . . It wasn't much of a possibility, but unless . . . Unless this accidental meeting on a Greek island might shed an illumination in her which had not been shed before, which her first raising of a light, her first venture in seeing, had not revealed. That had been a looking outward, after all. And if this were inward . . . ? Laura would tiptoe into the labyrinth at her heels. Well, in a manner of speaking. The path to the headland was rugged, Imogen was setting a fair pace. Panting after her, Laura snorted with laughter.

Arrested by a thought, she checked, she stood stock-still on the hillside that was dappled because the hollows were acres of shade now and only the ridges were still swathes of golden haze with trees' shadows lengthening. Just supposing – just audaciously and hopefully supposing – that Imogen today was urgently debating her fate between love half forgotten, now agonisingly remembered, love for Dario De Corvaro lost, now discovered far deeper than before, and freedom hitherto never forgotten, never betrayed. If Imogen, who had halted too and was smiling her patience with her elderly cousin's puffing need for a breather, was right now precipitating, calculating head over booted heels, into the dreamy gulf of self-knowledge which the morning's chance confrontation with her past had opened yawning beneath her previously hard-headed raffish progress . . . If involuntary memory – which could come like an Eastern caravan to a European market with jewels, silks, spices, miraculous wares – had brought reappraisal . . . If her high flying had hurled her into this emptiness where now she had yanked the cord which unfurled her parachute, her free fall had been steadied, under some control she was drifting down through what was turning out to be not void but a breathable, blue, sunlit air where images appeared which might be focused on, where soughings were audible which

119

if you listened were sometimes voices you might understand
. . . Just high-handedly supposing all these fine things, did
Laura's own experience justify advice to choose this or
choose that? She had, she feared – she had never regretted
it more piercingly than now – only ever loved temperately,
been free only ever in moderation.

In one pan of the scales, love of a person. In the
other pan, independence, solitary adventurings. Or was it
perhaps that Laura agreed with the conventional wisdom
according to which love and freedom, or at least enough
of each commodity to satisfy most palates (greed being
frowned on) might be partaken of simultaneously? You
scarcely even had to sacrifice much of each – it was
enough to wait while both naturally declined. Was that
historic compromise a valid one, or at any rate adequate
to satisfy the gentle longings of souls likely to be socially
acceptable and successful and happy? Devotion to a person
and devotion to freedom were sworn antagonists since the
fount of time. Since bending over an inky copy of *Antony and
Cleopatra* in a Maltese schoolroom Laura had never sharply
doubted it any more than she had sharply suffered it. And
now she wondered – how was the fight going these days?

"It was I myself that I saw at the corner of the kitchen
hut," Imogen had just said. "It was I who chucked the
damned net, I who fell, do you understand?" It looked as if
freedom were not exactly triumphing, reflected Laura. And
to Imogen, who was impatient for her burning western sea,
she said, "Yes, you lead on. I can keep up. I'm not dead
yet." And to herself, as she set off again along the path which
never ran smoothly for more than thirty paces of trodden
dust without then requiring you to scramble up a slope of
slithering stones or climb over a boulder and jump down the
other side, she thought: Thank God, a fact at last, a veritable
fact. For Imogen must suddenly have comprehended her
godmother's confusion, her embarrassment which stemmed
from her London undertaking never to pry. Either that, or
she had decided this was the version of events Laura was

to be fobbed off with – but the wheezing, stumbling old lady was not in her perennial enchantment able to keep a constant watch on this latter possibility. Anyhow Imogen, tramping briskly toward her appointment with the sun, had half-turned her head, over her shoulder laughingly had exclaimed, "Good Lord, you don't have any doubts about it, do you? Oh I *am* sorry, darling. I ought to have put you out of your misery right away. Of *course* Angelica is Dario's. That's why this morning's meeting has left me so ludicrously perplexed. And it's all your fault, damn you. Why in hell do you never remember to tell your guests who else is likely to be of the party?"

Where on her property Laura wondered, were Dario's reflections upon the Orphic cults, on the psyche as vital strength, the psyche as the breath of the divine, being interrupted by Anna soberly advising him – would she have the gall? and the coarseness? yes, she would – by her earnestly counselling him to see his lawyer, to have blood tests done, perform all the ponderous insufferable common moves. Well, his father's mistress of a feckless and unforgettable week in Avignon reckoned Dario could look after himself. Bad luck, though, when you were meditating on mortal breath as mortal soul to be told to go and see a lawyer. Still, still, the great thing is I am getting somewhere, Laura congratulated herself. Imogen didn't tell me about her affair with Dario while it was going on because she was in Italy and I was in Greece, for those three or four months we didn't see each other. And afterward . . . ? I suppose she didn't tell me about it in order to keep Angelica seemingly fatherless. But now some certainties I begin to sense under my dusty sandals. Scrambling after this huntress has its rewards, scraps are chucked behind her for my nourishment. And for Angelica this news is good. Dario is a marvellous man, the girl is fortunate to have him for her father. Now if we can only fix things so she is allowed to have him . . .

Was Laura betraying Imogen? It did not seem so to

her – perhaps because self-congratulation had the effect of putting her off her subtler guard – perhaps because her goddaughter was not a bit like her daughter, did not stand in the doorway of her sanctum and regard the rugs and tapestries and saris with philistine disapproval. Imogen walked straight in – smiling, affectionate, interested. Acting out of self-interest? But it was natural, surely, for her to be interested in all that her lost lover had said, and it was this that Laura, now the narration of the ride and its attendant notions had been concluded, would begin to relate. Was it not of the first importance for Angelica that her estranged parents should know of one another's feelings? Laura would make a start. Yes, yes, she was as conventional as Margaret Scottow, she supposed she had to confess that to herself . . . But she could not bring herself to wish to see Imogen humiliate Dario with silence, drive him away into lostness . . . while she with her daughter injured in spirit, and her grace not quite wholesome, and her freedom not quite hers and not quite the real thing – while she was charming on quays summer after summer with glasses of whisky in her hand. Not after an hour in which Dario had shown the magnanimity to offer her his dearest treasures, had unrolled this rare weave and then that for her pleasure – no, Laura could not wish to see him hounded out to dwell in a greater sadness than any he had yet known. And Anna, blast her, had been right to accuse her of just being a match-maker, an ancient busybody. An unattractive aspect of her sex, Laura had always believed – but did not remind herself of this now, because suddenly the idea of taking her revenge upon Imogen for years and years of slavish adoration of her was not unattractive. And it would not really be revenge. Naturally not. It would be help. Yes, she would perhaps deceive this oh so commanding young lady now a little, and later it would have been she who had helped to save her, helped her to cut and wriggle her way out of the net of deception which was her past. For that was how inconstant Laura beheld the thing now. Alas Anna had been yet again

122

the one to see things plainly. Imogen had indeed raped Dario's heart. By telling her godmother who the baby's father was, she had convinced her of that.

Had Imogen not said she was ensnared, lay right now trussed on the dirt? Might not love be a way of raising her to her feet? Might not love be liberation? Laura ignored the fact that she herself had never particularly found it to be so. Was it not Imogen's deception of Dario two years ago which now – was this perhaps justice? – had enmeshed her? Well, then, the answers were openness, honesty, knowing. Was it not the past, was it not memory which had flung the fatal net? Well, then, freedom lay in the future, in imagination, in risks. And Imogen did not appear to feel that her godmother was betraying her. She moved cheerfully about the sanctum, she examined this pattern and that. Would Laura please fulfil her promise to explain what she had meant by Dario and she being like Eros and Psyche? "I expect I butted in," she apologised, "never gave you a chance the first time." They had come over the crest. They stood side by side, looked out where the hillside fell steeply away and you could see the sun would not set for another five minutes, even ten. "And I want to know what he was wearing, how he seemed to you, every single thing without exception and without misquotation that he said, whether his mood altered in the course of the conversation, whether he laughed, whether he cried, how the various mentionings of my name affected him, whether he made any sense at all, how often you repeated yourself, whether you entertained him with stories of your dogs, how often you forgot what you were going to say next, whether you let yourself become enraptured by him and if not how you prevented this – all right now in one word please."

"If you will let me rest."

The weariness of Laura's legs had transferred itself to her head. She sat down on a rock. The air smelled of thyme, of resinous pine. She smiled at Imogen who stood smiling back at her, her hand on the revolver at her hip. To Anna, Laura

123

had declared that they would see no match made that Jim and Margaret Scottow would ever recognise, if anything a match perhaps no one but the protagonists would know they had made – but had she been too despondent, too inventive, wrong? It was essential not to be carried away by hope. Probably Imogen was toying with her. Whatever game she was playing was clearly amusing her.

"And if you will then tell me if you have been calling to one another. He has been calling to you, I can assure you of that. Marvellous things. I'll tell you. I imagine him – oh, strolling in his castle garden in the evening, shall we say? – and in his mind talking to you. Silently calling his half of a dialogue into the vague airs which drift around the world and might waft his calls to you in London. And I imagine you . . . I think I imagine you lying down. At night on your bed. By day on that chaise-longue you've got in the room where you work. Lying on your back, your mind calling . . . I want to know what you have been calling, whether your calls at all answer his."

On the western horizon my pilgrim has spread his prayer-mat, Imogen said to herself as they made their way down to the shore, her godmother hardly puffing at all now their path lay downhill. His gorgeous mat laid on the sea, he kneels, her inner voice said – because this acute presentness of things to her, with today's confrontations and revelations, had endured, if anything it was thickening. The presentness even loured, had something of danger in it. And still it was day, and what would night bring? Her voice had never whispered more articulately, with such incisiveness, it would wound her she was afraid, wound others too. She had never felt so vulnerable.

This morning my nerves were fretted. (It was soothing

to put it into the past. Narrative gave distance, safety. So long as from the arena of the past the gladiator, the Fisher with trident and net, did not step.) There were too many people around, I was fenced in by people, I liked none of them. What is there to admire in men and women who are posts and rails? Why should I like souls who are restraint made visible? Never shall I make any attempt to like them, it is not desirable. By midday I was more calm. Posts and rails could be vaulted, I remembered as a girl in Wiltshire vaulting paddock fence after paddock fence. Nets were things which might be cut. When Laura's father was a lieutenant during the First World War, his was the first submarine to get into the Sea of Marmara. The Turks had strung anti-submarine nets across the Dardanelles, but he swam out of a torpedo tube with cutters strapped to his chest and he started cutting the mesh, swimming up to the surface to breathe and swimming down again and going on cutting. He swam up and breathed and swam down and cut until the submarine could pass through the gap he had made, and in the Sea of Marmara the Turks were not expecting them and they sank a lot of shipping and that was Salthouse's first D.S.O. From him I shall learn, I told myself, and I was more calm. He fought his way through his net and he lived victorious and he lived with honour to die with honour in a later war. So shall I do too. I shall make sure I have a sharp blade always at my side.

Most of the shore is rock, but there is this shingle cove. The spaniels trot along the beach with their heads down sniffing, Laura regards them fondly. I look out to sea. The pilgrim's mat is a small patch of flamy colours floating on the blue immensity. I was a girl on holiday here when I first imagined him – eight years old, maybe, or nine. At dawn he summoned the sun, his is the human intellect that makes the cosmos whirl its suns and solar systems and burn with light and life. Now he is praying the sun down onto his head. In the blue evening the blood-orange orb descends. There are no clouds. There is no shipping. I see it all. He does not cower, he kneels with dignity, my scaler of tempests and saunterer of calms. The sun is very near his head now. Upon him the light shines, it falls, now it touches! He is on fire. He is made light, he is made flamy ripples, he is made red and orange and gold and pink which burn along the blue, he is made great loveliness, in him there is no impurity now. He has gone into the sun. Now the sun is going. How fast it sinks! Already the horizon cuts it in half. Up the sun the sea rises. What blazing battleship ever went down so fast? Now nothing is left. We are in shade, Laura and her dogs and I. There is still sunlight high above our heads, there the last rays still play, up there for that reason the day's last midges have climbed and are jigging now and the swifts who feed on them have towered up there too, at a great height in the blue I can see their dark swoopings and harryings, from a great height come their shrill cries. I imagine my pilgrim shriven now, in a state of grace. Like Prometheus, again and ever again he suffers for us. He rolls up his mat, he slings it over his shoulder. All evening, then all night he will walk the sea. In summer, twilight is long. After it, the stars will come out. My philosopher the lighthouse will wake, will open the eye of his mind. "All right," I say to Laura, "I'll shoot first."

I walk along the tide-line with my eyes lowered, I am a beach-comber. Seaweed that has blown ashore lies in brown hummocks, flies crawl over them. There are sticks which were in the sea a long time, they are bone-white, bone-dry, light, salt-imbued, they would make excellent kindling. There are the rotting fruit of the prickly pear, flies crawl on them too. There are shells. Ah, here is what will do fine. Scavenger, I stoop, I pick up the plastic bottle which will be our target. I love the blue and the rose and the stillness of this time when the sun has just set. The sea is glassy, it is a good hour to go water-skiing, as you rush dancing over the gleams and shadows you can look down beside your careering skis and beside the spray, you can see down into the silky blues and the blue transparencies.

Sheep-bells sound from the hill, it is a peaceful music. The cypresses are sentinels, motionless. If the ripples touching the shingle lapped any more softly they would be still; the next thing after such a soft sound is silence, it is the immediate, the closest thing.

Laura talks, she brings it all back. Even so, not everything she says convinces me. Her attempt to deceive me is pathetic. Has she forgotten that I know the man of whom she speaks, forgotten it even as she speaks about my knowing him? I who know his reticence and his obliquity – how could I give credence to a Dario De Corvaro who would betray his suspicion that he had suddenly met a daughter he did not know he had conceived? He might not be able to conceal his turmoil – but speak of his hopes and doubts and fears? Never! With no one but me would he discuss these things. It is because Laura desires a rapprochement between him and me, it is her clumsy paving of a way to that. It was enough to tell her that Angelica is his child, it was enough for one minute to talk like a girl in love, and away Laura's thoughts went haring. So – I learn the measure of her loyalty to me. Two or three times she has lamented to me that she has never loved intemperately, never loved irrevocably, and once she added that I was the exception, I was her one reasonless and unwavering love – but it has its limits, her loyalty. Never mind. It is of no importance. Anyway I have sent her haring off, she has gone, I am alone, that is good. But has she forgotten that if, as Dario and she appear to have agreed, he is Eros and I am Psyche, I was kept in darkness, I was kept a prisoner of passion, of ignorance, and most shamefully of all of caprice? Sight was taken from me, knowledge was taken from me. With imagination alone you quickly go mad. Endless darkness or endless blindfolding is the kind of torment they inflict on prisoners to break their resistance. Has she forgotten what happened when I showed some spirit, when I rebelled, when I tried to redeem the vision which is the most precious gift we have? Has she forgotten

127

how I was punished for my revolt, my courage? Has she forgotten the anger I was shown and the coldness I was shown, how my heart-strings were jerked to snap them? I am a mystic, she says, it is my nature, and Dario is a pagan, that is his. I do not disagree. But if light is what I desire above all, sunlight and moonlight and starlight and lighthouse-light and in my mind light, has she forgotten how I was first kept in inner darkness and then flung into outer darkness? Ah, they would pitch me back into the prison of passionate love, would they? I have known happiness, it was a blindfold.

Laura talks, she brings it all back. Can I be sorry that Dario and I have met today? Can I be sorry his escape was cut off by Laura? No doubt the mystic and the pagan have from eternity fallen in love with each other, to eternity it will fail. I set the plastic bottle up against a slope of stones and dirt, I walk thirty or thirty-five paces back from it, I turn. I load six bullets into Alexis' revolver. Laura stands just behind me, with some difficulty she calls her spaniels to her and makes them sit, but I have sent her off, I am alone as I stand straight and raise my gun. It is not a large plastic bottle. It only ever held one litre of whatever it was. The slope is greyish brown, the bottle greyish white. It is distasteful to me to think of Laura and Anna in the drawing-room mouthing Dario and me. He will have been embarrassed by the collapse of his stratagem of the phoney telephone call. He will have been dismayed by the failure of his attempt quietly to absent himself. It could so smoothly have worked. To his credit, yes enormously to his credit, that his instinct was to let me go my ill-gotten way unhindered. That is not cowardice, that is greatness of heart. To his credit also – Laura seems to have transfigured him into an Indian dealer in sumptuous stuffs – that he showed her his dreams. How Laura marshalled the vulgarity to treat them as tittle-tattle for Anna beats me. Now I take aim, the barrel wavers, I steady it, today I wish to be deadly, I remember the recoil, I fire. A couple of feet from the bottle, the dust puffs. "Damn," I say. Laura says, "You'll have to let me stand a bit closer, my love."

Laura talks, she brings it all back. In what, taking aim a second time, do I believe? The sylviculturist I never met, but the schoolmaster I knew, he was delightful. And Dario prowling the town on winter nights – in him I believe. In his solitude too I believe, despite the great number of girls, and in his melancholy deeper since I left, though he will have been too modest and too mannerly to make a song and dance about that. Dario half drowning in a thinly frozen lake, fighting with ice that always breaks – in him I believe. And in Dario who has a flirtatious friendship with the extremely minor goddess Charm, and in Dario in whose mind echoes die away – in these two I have faith. And the man who walks down into a valley of brown oaks and white mist, who finds the oaks mirror his slownesses and the mist his opacities – it is him, it is him! And I believe in him to whom his father returns, I remember him in whose echo-chamber the Other's voice whispers. She brings it back, she brings it back.

Now I have missed the plastic bottle for the third time. My shots fall close, but they miss. I shall think it is I myself who am the target, perhaps then I shall hit it. I bring myself to mind as in photographs I see myself whole, as in a tall looking-glass I see myself trying on a new dress, I stand that image against the slope of stones and crumbling earth and roots and weeds. I close my left eye, sight along the stubby barrel with my right. I take aim at my own breast. I notice the contrast between the gold of my bracelet and the gun-metal of the Colt. I fire. The pistol jerks in my hand however hard I try to hold it firm. Missed again, but closer, three inches maybe. My breast is larger than the bottle, if I had been standing there I would be down on the dust now with a bullet in my lung. Good. I raise my gun a fifth time and I think this is a strange hour to have for my destiny, this hour of standing at evening on shingle where a summer sea laps and shooting a pistol and thinking it is myself that I shoot. I listen to Laura talking with great sympathy about Dario, about how Eduardo's death was a great calamity because he was not only his father but also his best friend, and I think that it feels as if it were predestined, this hour of mine . . . And yet who could have forseen that, after thirty-odd years in this world and with maybe thirty-something to go, the fatal minutes should be these of the Ionian at evening turning a darker richer blue and a pistol cracking and swifts skirling and a dog that is gun-shy, poor wretched brute, and whines? Of all hours this hour. I did not intend to meet my lover again. So lately as this morning I was carefree. I did not intend to remember. Now I cannot help remembering. I had half forgotten. Now I remember with a wholeness I had not felt before. I squeeze the trigger. Down I fall – ah, fine shot! Blood on my shirt, moaning, gasping, writhing, I am hard hit, not dead quite yet but that bitch has got no fight left in her, no spirit, she'll be no more trouble, the last lying breath is seeping from her lips. I fire again. The bottle jumps. There's pleasure in this. Again I pull the trigger. Click. No shots left. Laura says "Well done" as we walk up to the bottle, proudly I inspect the ragged hole in its ugly form.

When I was a little girl one day out riding my pony shied and I came off, but I cannot have been wearing proper boots, my foot caught in the stirrup. The pony was alarmed, he trotted off down the lane quite fast. Snagged by one foot I dragged along beneath him, I remember the back of my head banging on the lane and the pony's grey belly above me and the sky above that, I remember the glint of shod trotting hooves as they missed my face, how fast the steel flashed close to my eyes and my nose and my mouth again and again, and then my hat was knocked over my face, I was blinded, and still my arms trailed and my head banged on the lane, in my darkness I imagined the flash flash flash of the steel, and then my foot came free and I lay still and the hooves died away. My world is as topsy-turvy now as then.

I am Hector, the myrmidons have by treachery triumphed over me, the only difference is that there is still life in me as with my feet roped to my arch-rival's chariot I am dragged in the dust around Troy and once more hooves flash in my sight and my head jolts along the ground – and there is this further difference, I now apprehend, that the champion and the defeated are two halves of one idea, they are one.

I lean against a rock, I pat the spaniels, I watch Laura shoot. The unlucky creature which is gun-shy holds its trembling head to my knee. What use is a gun-shy spaniel? But perhaps it would be kind if we did not shoot long. Laura is not concentrating, she is thinking in a flustered manner about Dario and Angelica and me, even at twenty paces she will miss. For a minute or two now she will be quiet. What has she brought me?

In an acacia grove Dario and I sat on the grass, we ate bread and cheese and cherries, we drank from our bottle of wine, it was Arcadian enough all right, and I was in darkness, that woman with grey hair taking shaky aim with her dead husband's revolver is right about that, but the darkness was sweet. Were we not there in it together? It was early summer, the acacias were in flower. The darkness was a game, but it was a game to make the blood beat. Without the visionary, the sensual world has more piquancy; it is all there is. That gives it magnificence and gives it sadness and that, yes, has piquancy. That May and June it was good to get away from Milan for a few days now and then, good not always to breathe noxious Milanese air, good to breathe Dario's hills. Once I drove all night, reached the castle just before sunrise. It was a solid joy to get out of the car in his stableyard where the birds were fifing their dawn chorus; it was a solid joy to stand in the grey violet air, as this morning it was a solid joy to step out of my hut into the dawn; it was a solid joy to breathe the lime trees and the honeysuckle and the jasmine, as this morning it was to breathe the sea. Then I lost the solidity of joys, as today I have lost it again. Or was it the solidity I was trapped in, had to break out of? I was a sleepwalker, Laura says, who knows me well. She sees me with my eyes open but seeing nothing, she says. I stretched out my arms, my hands fumbled with the black air of a dream. Solid, the darkness of sensual things! And as for days, they are of a solidity . . . ! The tissue of time so densely woven, it must be impenetrable to vision always. Dario only knows how to live from day to day, he told Laura that apparently. It is true. But for me it is to live from one Black Hole of Calcutta to the next. Dario was not to blame for my claustrophobia. He was not guilty, though with me he was responsible. But what could I do among all those densities, those oppressions? When each day is an overcrowded prison cell where there is no light and people die because there is not enough water and not enough air, and at midnight the survivors are herded from that Black Hole which is now called Yesterday and along with some new prisoners are packed at gun-point into an equally foetid stifling Black Hole called Today . . .

Dario is at his ease in time. It is important to be fair about this. Each day takes a self from him, each tomorrow brings a new self he will be, the rhythm is a steady one. His days are not Black Holes, it is I who dream bad dreams, his days are days. It is he who has fallen into step with freedom, it is I who stumble, go too fast, too slow, never get the pace right. They journey on in harmony. I long to travel with them, but all I can do is hang on the skirts of their expedition, I run and then I lag, I tag along, I complain, I am a nuisance, pitiable. He has his solid joys. I remember his delight in horsemanship, his delight in melancholy which is his most vibrant joy. He is solid. Was it from him that I had to break out, in him that I longed to shed light? When I looked into him he was dark.

Dario has promised to stay until tomorrow, Laura says. After that he will go. Will I see him, will I speak with him? she asks with the most phlegmatic voice she can command, but her mind is tremulous. I think of Dario, his aquiline face, his brown eyes. There are questions I must resolve before I can know if I have anything to say to him, whether I wish to listen to him. Perhaps it is most fitting that our salute should be silent, that at dinner in the cheerful hubbub we should catch each other's eyes and for three or four seconds hold that reciprocity in celebration of all things known and all things imagined, but that then we should again turn to the chatter and the clatter and tomorrow go our ways. It is fitting that the past should be commemorated – but briefly, even lightheartedly, and without hope of going back. A long glance across a dinner table, half a smile, these are fitting. We are the dead – have we not been enjoined to bury one another? Around us the living speak amongst themselves, as is right. Spectrally with spades we set to work, up at the butterfly chapel he digs my grave, I his. I imagine it. Is it fitting?

After the darkness which was sweet, a tyrannous pleasure, the other darkness, inner, solid, eternal, of the tomb. Yes, as if the darkened bedroom of Eros and Psyche were a mausoleum, it was among spirits that I lit my candle. Was it not the spiritual I wished to see? the spirit, however splendidly pagan, of the man I loved? It was the spiritual that with anger he defended – for him it was private, an inner essence, a feeling not to be lit up, not revealed, betrayed. Then the outer darkness, in which for two years I have made my vagabondish freedom, gone my defiant way. And now the shingle crunches under Laura's feet and the revolver cracks and the ripples lick the pebbles with their soft lips and kiss with their tongues which were silvery but are shadowy now.

I shall lean against this rock, I shall think about time. For it is as if I too have been a pilgrim, or at last I begin to learn from my walker of the seas, I have not conceived him in vain. It is now as if, though any wandering in the world may be effective, mine has brought me to this evening, to my hour. I feel less cut off from myself than I have often felt, have more in common with myself now. If time were freedom I might have something to tell Dario, something worthy to be given him, might I not? I should go to him. I should say to him: Here, now, this. I should say: Take, look, what do you think? Time is different now, it is no longer one Black Hole of Calcutta after another, it is no longer a tissue so densely woven it is impregnable to thought – so I should tell him, if I knew how to conceive it true, demonstrate it true, make it true. He would smile, he would say the light of day has never been a Black Hole, he would tell me the heavens at night have never been a Black Hole either, open your eyes Imogen he would say. I never kept you in the dark. It would have been impossible to do so. There is no dark. You imagined it. You imagine it still, Imogen. You are one of the weak who to satisfy their absurd psychological needs live wrapped in a created darkness and talk of visions hysterically. And how should I reply?

Shingle that shelves. A dog that whimpers, will not be comforted. What answer can I make? I am the gladiator who lost, I am the swordsman over whom the cunning Fisher cast his net, I lie entangled on the sand of many slaughters. The arena is in an uproar, the Fisher stands over me with his trident raised and the mob shout. Some on the tiers yell for me to be butchered. Others yell for me to be spared, I fought valiantly they cry, I may give entertaining sport another day, if not I can always be killed later when my valour is no longer of the finest quality. I shall not accept either fate, where is my knife? I need transcendence, with that I could cut my way free. I need a timeless moment, now and always. Then I should stand up free. With my elbow I shove away my rock. I stand upright. Here is a rusty tin. Now they are my riding boots which make the shingle shelve. I set the tin on a rock at the sea's edge, I take the revolver from Laura. "When I've shot that tin off the rock, I'm going for a swim," I say. And it is now, as I slip first one bullet and then another into the chamber, almost as if I could hear Dario call, "Are you there?" and hear my answering call. Almost it is as if I have come far enough, come this evening to the right time. Four bullets, five, six. I shut the chamber, spin it round. It is as if time were made of eternity, or partook of it – so it seems to me now. So that the past may no longer be a nightmare cast over me, a tangle in which I thrash my arms and legs without hope, from which I cannot wake and rise. So that now if my lost love and I met at the corner of a hut or on a beach or a quay, if I saw him and therefore saw myself I should no longer be confounded by that seeing but look peacefully, because time would be made of timeless moments, would be a pattern of them, a pattern of great fascination but not a net, never again a net while this rhythm of remembering and forgetting and remembering were mine. It is as if now to this island, this cove, this shore all time comes and stays.

"And the calls?" my grey old Laura would like to know. Ah, how shall I ever listen with sufficient attentiveness, imagine with proper accuracy? Perhaps to her I shall rehearse a few grace notes only. Something she must be rendered. She insists. "And the calls?"

"You changed, Imogen." The supposed Psyche rehearsed their parts silently. "In June you were happy when our horses forded the stream, in July you were not. I no longer delighted you. The real world no longer delighted you, you gave yourself to shadows and they maddened you."

"Yes, I changed. I am fickle, I am capricious, you say. I say I grow. That month I began to wake up. There was no threshold which I crossed and then could say, I am awake. I was a dolphin who had been swimming deep down where the sea is dark, and now I began to rise, the black water began to be grey."

"So quickly you were altered from one person to another! In the kitchen the gay tattoo of your tap-dancing feet was cut off, you stood with both shoes firmly planted, you accused

135

me: Why do you never unmask yourself? Who are you, that you should not be known? Do you have no within, you whose being is sufficient to him, whose world is natural to him? I did not know how to answer."

"You had often been sad, I knew it. Particularly since your father's death – solitary, sad. But the way your solitude was natural to you even when you were in love with me – that I could not endure. How should I ever approach close to you? You turned my love to futility, how could I help beginning to hate it? And the way your melancholy was natural to you, the way you knew it was right, you dismissed all longings that smacked of faith as self-deception – that I could not endure."

"I was as I was, I had no other way of being, and all that I was I gave to you. I gave, and still you asked for more. I rejoiced in the hawthorn hedges in flower and at once they were for you, those white sweet-scented thickets of may were yours – and you turned in the saddle and your voice asked sometimes and your eyes asked always: How can you live only in sensual things? how can you sense even ideas? There is something cloying in it. It is a blindness, a wanton blindness, your eyes said. At the riding-school at dusk you dismounted. You carried saddle and bridle indoors and your eyes were hard. It is you who are unseeing, I thought. Your eyes never relented, they wanted to know everything, they would not accept that there was little to know, I was as I seemed, all else would be fantasy. The warm summer night fell and in the lamplit stable you turned with a curry-comb in your hand and your blue eyes demanded facts, certainties. There are none – why should there be any? – I suggested, loving the smells of the fouled litter being carted away and the clean litter being pitch-forked down in the stalls, loving the smells of hay and of saddle-soap and wishing you would dispel the convictions or truths which only existed in your head and did you little credit and illuminated nothing, loving the shadowy bulks of the horses, the sounds of their tired feet moving and their teeth pulling hay from their hay-nets, and someone filling buckets of water at the standpipe and someone calling goodbye. Information! you demanded. Looking up, I pointed. That is Vega, I said. That is Cassiopeia. Those are the Pleiades."

"I was waking up, it no longer sufficed me on summer nights to look at stars. I ached for you to wake with me, to show some discontent with forever swimming in the gloom that weighs on the sea-bed, I longed for us to swim upward side by side. Was it love on your part, always to assume I must be contented with the moment, the sensation? They became my prison cells, those moments of delight."

"Was it love on your part, to barge trampling into the pleasant rooms of my soul like a squad of military policemen? What state had I suborned, that my cupboards should be snatched open, my drawers tipped out on the floor, my letters read, my panelling wrenched from the walls in case it concealed a safe, my shelves scanned for subversive works, my notebooks confiscated? What did I think about this? you ceaselessly required to be informed, and what was my view of that? and why? What did I do in such-and-such a year in such-and-such a city? and the next year? I was like a suspect into whose frightened eyes they shine a blinding glare and order him to speak. You are positive that you voyage in realms of the spirit; but you have the nature of an interrogator or a psychoanalyst or a priest. I swim deep, you complain? It is a womb as well as a graveyard, the depths are the source of life. And perhaps I like the dark. Perhaps I like crepuscular notions and feelings, for obscurity is not only the refuge of the defeated, it is also the privilege of young growing things. Maybe one day I shall swim higher, but if I do it will be of my own free will."

"Why did you tell Laura that there was no question of my having wished to marry you? Why did you lie?"

"So that you need never feel vulnerable on that score. To protect you."

"Protect my honour, were you about to say? Your

honourable behaviour will have me in the madhouse, just wait. Still, at least you do not deny that you knew I longed for you to ask me, and I had just determined that I would ask you when – how shall we phrase it? – when the candle dripped, the hot wax fell."

"I woke up. It was not the waking together which you dreamed of, but I woke. I woke to how I was being ransacked, how I felt ravaged, how love defiled. Tell me something: Was it out of revenge that you conceived Angelica?"

"You say that I ravaged you, my love defiled you – I do not think that I feel like answering your demand right now. Angelica as yours or not yours . . . ? Angelica as my revenge or my freedom or my prize . . . ? I told Laura one thing, sent her haring off in one direction. I shall deliberate, take my time. What shall I tell you, where shall I send your emotions scampering? Do not underestimate my power of self-defence. Am I not free to say what I please? The words are air. I draw a breath, I think, I part my lips. My breath comes forth, my words ripple for a few moments in the air, die away, are irrevocable – for what I shall say you will never forget, the knot I shall tie you will never untie, do not cherish the presumption to think you will. Though now it appears to me of little consequence what you and I did or what we felt. This evening I have discovered the nature of action: it is to shoot at a tin on a rock, no more than that. See, my shot ricochets off the rock, flies away to spend its force in the air and fall into the sea. This evening I have shot myself dead, I have called to time and it has come to me, I am inclined to be serene, to overlook old wrongs. Yes, you are correct, I am capricious, it pleases me to be so, and it is a tactic. Those days when I could see you were rejoicing in our love and yet again and again you perhaps unconsciously rebuffed me when I came to the pleasant rooms which are your soul, rooms I swear I never wanted to violate, peaceful charming rooms where I thought to set up my happiness – those days I will put by, not take into account. Nor the later days when your repulse was quiveringly conscious, all that dust-blown August when you stormed at me for an invader, for a befouler of the integrity which is any man's right – those days too let us decide not to weigh in the balance, let us remove them from the scales, chuck them aside. This evening I am inclined to be magnanimous – so I say. Do you be so too. You are capable of it, I know. Today did you not try to leave me in peace, let me be? It was the merest accident that you failed, like the accident of our meeting here."

So Imogen Scottow remembered, so she imagined. These last two years Dario in his apartment in the converted stable-block of the Umbrian castle must often have read late into the night and then put aside his book and gone on sitting quietly and listened to her voice and called to her. Often, often she had conceived of him. The chimes of the castle clock. Over his desk Ribera's wreathed and bowed *Poet*, a figure of such concentrated thought and such gentle melancholy that she had seen it as a likeness of Dario's alter-ego – as if he had a doppelgänger which was his wraith, his double, not as he appeared but as he most essentially was. And certainly Laura had been right, she herself had called to him, time and again had stood up from her drawing-board, had stood a moment at the window looking out to the London street, crossed to the chaise-longue and lain down and dreamed.

"Do you see the tin balanced on that rock?" she now called to him, called gaily because she felt herself to be strong, in command. "It is the past. Soon I shall dispatch it. Crack! Missed. Crack! Look, it has gone spinning away, there is nothing there. Why must you still be angry, still despair? How shall I amuse you? I shall take a box at the theatre, I shall wear an evening dress, we will see *Annie Get Your Gun* or *The Importance of Being Earnest*, anything to make my saturnine Dario smile, *Private Lives*, something like that. I will be imperious, I will be lavish, I shall have a bottle of the most expensive champagne brought to our box. I have in mind the evening dress I shall wear, it shows my figure off more audaciously than nakedness, I do not consider that you will resist me in that dress. When I am combed, when I am painted, when I am jewelled, when I am scented, you will no longer feel it is in your interest to withstand me.

"Agreeable – no? – the whang as my pistol bullet struck the tin. Ransacked, you say, ravaged, you say, defiled, you say – oh la la! Interrogator you name me, and befouler, you do not spare your words. Fortunate, my serenity this evening. Let us hope you do not succeed in fracturing it. Do I convict myself of any guilt? Not at the moment – it is their fleetingness I like – because the rusty vacancy of the past has most frivolously and satisfactorily been sent flying off the rock of the eternal present, so I unbuckle my belt, lay it with its holster on the pebbles beside Laura who has sat down to rest her seventy-year-old legs and to comfort the animal which was afraid and whinged. I begin to undress. Look, I pull off my riding boots, does this entertain you, do I please you? I strip off my breeches, my shirt, my knickers, everything. White, I walk into the shallows. I notice the softness of the water, its contrast with the hardness of the stones which bruise my feet. I proceed carefully. Sometimes I have lost my balance, flailed my arms, staggered, cut my feet. Also it is important to keep an eye out for sea-urchins, to tread on one is like grabbing a scorpion fish in your fist, there is the same need for a sharp knife used with firmness and for antiseptic ointment. The still sea against my legs and the still air against my breast and my face are of equal softness. I am up to my thighs, I make a flat dive, I swim. My hair is slicked to my head and floats behind me in a way I like, the slither of the water along my body I enjoy too. A hundred yards offshore I roll onto my back, I let all my muscles go slack. Are you listening to me? Am I imagining your thoughts anything like right or all haywire? Do not be alarmed, when I swim ashore I shall edit these airs for Laura with prudence. Come, a pale glimmer of light is not so appalling. Shall I promise not to shine it at you this time, not into you, but into myself? Here and now perhaps I shall make a start – why not? Yes, here awash among ripples, buoyant, unstrung, undulating, now when I call to you and I hear a gull call and hear that higher the swifts are calling still. Should we not trust our consonance, you and I?

"Around me and above me the blues are dimming. Far off, a ship has passed, the failing heave of its wake reaches me, I rise a few inches, I ripple, I fall. The warm calm laps on my breast, around my head. A riband of seaweed ties itself to my thigh like a garter. The night Eros banished Psyche was his night of power, but I think the night that is coming may be mine. The sea sustains me, the air gives me life and speech, all time laps around me. I forget this or that and I remember it; I give to this time life and to that death; this time or that comes to me and gives me life. We are equal, time and I. Unexpectedly we invite one another into being. In our dealings are richness, equity; there is nothing we do not give and take; even moments of everlastingness are in our gift. As time is made of timeless moments like this moment, is made of eternity, so am I; it laps around me; it washes in and out of my mind; it flows, it stays, now it has gone like a garter of seaweed or a minnow or a breath."

On the shingle, Laura Rodostamo lay back, she drowsed.

Up at the house, on the terrace her brother-in-law and Ben Thurne were drinking ouzo and playing backgammon. Carrying his own cloudy glass, Dario De Corvaro heard the rattle of their dice as he came out of the front door. He chose a wicker chair that was a little way from their game, he sat down, took a sip of his drink, lit a cigarette. The survivor of rather a lot of Anna Rodostamo's good sensible advice, for a minute he would simply admire the handsome cedar and try not to think of anything else at all. Hopeless, of course, he realised at once. The one impossible thing. How could he not fall back to composing the bitter address to Imogen which all day when he was left momentarily in peace his mind had been writing and rewriting? His hostess had informed him in the friendliest of manners that his attempt to depart had been cowardice. Firing at a tin, Imogen, though he could not know it, had attributed the same unsuccessful retreat to magnanimity. To himself his motive had appeared to be despair. With a heart in which neither love nor anger had withered, he had longed to get her out of his sight. Once to stop her savaging him he had banished her. Now in her iniquity it appeared she had equipped herself with a new way of torturing him. Tricked, humiliated, trapped, how should he not despair, resolve this time to send himself into exile? He was at her mercy. She could tell him anything she fancied, or nothing. He knew himself, dreaded how he had been brought up to pretend to believe, to accept. He would let her triumph, nefarious, unopposed. Still, although his thoughts on the terrace did not marry with Imogen's while she swam, it might be said that he called.

"You remember that after my father's death the echoes in my head were forever dying away? What I did not tell Laura is that after you went often I could hear nothing at all. I sharpened my inner attention, my inner hearing. Of course I could *make* words or notes sound – but if I waited, if I listened? Nothing! I was the echo-chamber of the world, but no note tremored in me, I thought I was going mad, where my mind had been there was nothing. The first time it happened was at night. I started up from my chair, my face slimy with cold sweat. The chair scraped on the floor, that was a noise, was something, I kicked the skirting-board just in order to hear something, I rapped my knuckles on the window. The horror, Imogen, can you imagine? I went out to walk the town. All my life I had walked in order to think. I told myself that if I could make my brain think in its normal way, if I could make it listen because for me thinking has always been listening, if I could listen and hear something I could not be mad. I walked fast. The few people still about must have suspected I had gone mad, the way I came charging along a street and swung round a corner and was away, but a few minutes later back I came charging along the same way again because you know that damned town has only got twenty-odd streets, and then maybe I'd get to the last lamp-post and swing round and retrace my strides, go striding back past some bewildered fellow walking his dog or a couple kissing who would stop kissing and stare and say something and laugh. The sound of my footfalls, their tempo, that was something. I winched my concentration tight, tight, tight. Silence! The horror of it! As if the world had nothing more to say, all the music had died. You are Psyche, according to your godmother. Fine. But the failure of our love unmade me, these last two years when I have raised a light in myself I have lit up a man who scarcely exists any more, an echo-chamber which used to reverberate with marvellous strains but no longer quivers to anything. I light up a man who haunts a little hill town at night, who wearies, who breathes woodsmoke and hears his footfalls and the stream purling and nothing else, who walks slower, ever more slowly, who wearies of listening in vain, a man to whom no voices come who drifts to a standstill and listens and walks slowly on and stops again.

"I stand, shall we say, on the Roman bridge at night. My ghostly father the Other comes to me. Shoulder to shoulder we stroll. To him I make my confession. He has no power of absolution, but it is not redemption I believe in or desire, it is resonance. Here are the stream with its twittering and the willows with their fluttering, they are better than nothing, that is good. She looked into me and she saw nothing, Father, I say. I was appearance only. Within, there was nothing for her to see. That is what she saw. Absence, Father. The emptiness of an echo-chamber, call it what you please, the soullessness of the sceptic if you ask a priest, incarnate clarity I used to dream, I still dream, the truest mirror, the right unmisted mirror for waste history and void rule, what you will, love of the world prepared for the world as a bride for her groom, yes I dream away. And it was this nothingness which I so ferociously defended, I confess as our patrol brings us past the church with the fourteenth century

143

archangels and then past the café where some evenings with the schoolmaster I discuss creatures of topiary but which is shut at this hour. We reach the square. Along the arcade we fall into a sentry-go, father and son, along and back, along and back. The clock strikes midnight or one or two. I defended what I should have opened, I lament in the vice of my remorse. What was shameful about the clarity of my mirror? And an echo-chamber has to be empty. She might have come in, might have listened to the echoes with me. But she made me see myself as nothingness, Father, I confess, that must have been it mustn't it, been the beginning of the horror which I cannot shake off? And because I was too proud to display my fear as itself I expressed it as anger. I cast her out.

"I told Laura a pretty story about a ride in the snow, she liked that, but shall I tell you about my ride a few days later in the thaw, Imogen?" Dario finished his drink, he crossed his legs which were clad in white now, again fished his cigarettes out of the pocket of his white jacket, put them back, heard Ben tell Demitri that if he didn't throw double fives or double sixes he'd be gammoned. "The same woodland, the same creak of the saddle and chink of the snaffle, the same soft hoof-falls. It had been a late snow-fall, the birds were singing, where the snow had melted off the trees you could see the blackthorn was in flower and the almond trees were blossoming, only you couldn't see much because after the snow had come mist and through the mist it was raining, mild vertical thaw rain. The track was dirty slush. Again I cried that I had half known you, I had half loved you, where were the other knowledge and the other love? Are you there among the sodden trees and the soft sound of snow falling from branches and the sound of slow hoof-falls? my heart cried – but no vestige of an answer came. No intimation of your presence could I feel. Not a line of your face, not a quiver of your voice. It was as if the world had forgotten how to imagine you. Come to me, I prayed, let us forget old unkindnesses. And

144

then, because your absence from the air was terrible, your withdrawal even from ethereal life was a grief more piercing than any I had yet known, I turned to the Other. Sometimes she has seemed to come to me, I cried, why will she not shadow me now, not murmur now? She has come, I heard his voice reply. It is you who have been unmade. She is here, she found no one, she found she was alone."

The heroine of this episode, the young lady who, if Dario's mental life was not remorselessly one delusion after another, had come when invited to the echo-chamber of his mind but had found it silent, void, lifeless, was slowly swimming, still back-stroke, along her godmother's shore. She was swimming because she had felt a shiver of cold, not because she wished to get anywhere.

Her brother Mark was engaged to be married. She must remember that evening to amuse the dinner party with his presumed enamouredness – but no, it wasn't that. She would wear her dark blue dress and her strand of pearls, no, perhaps not the pearls – but it was not that either. Something, though. Lazy kick of her legs. The voluptuousness of the slow upward and wide backward reach of her arms down which drops of water ran. Around her neck she might wear her gold chain. On her feet her red sandals, they had highish heels but they could be kicked off, night dust cool and dewy beneath her bare feet she had always liked. Laura was fretting about the difficulties of acquiring a marquee for Anna's wedding – God what a bore, would she have to stay for it? – she must remember to try to be helpful to the old darling about that. No, no. But still . . . And still . . . She was aware of a challenge to take up, Imogen decided as she swam, but was cloudy still as to what it might be. Could she in whose mind times and timelessnesses lapped respond to her silent offer to Dario to shine a light not in him but in herself? (The old lady whose most fervent wish it was that she should do so was asleep on the shingle, thin, grey, still. The infant in whose nebulous cause she had exhausted herself was in the kitchen hut being fed gruel by Maria.) Was it fatuous to think one could ever shine a light anywhere *but* in oneself? Might she go to him, might she declare – what? Here are all the stories, all the patterns of time. Here. Now. You. I. Take, if anything pleases you . . . Might she offer that? Ravel out the cadences, might she, and hear that, whisper that?

Would they speak tonight, Dario and she, alone? She was excited, she could no longer deny it. She was preparing herself for an encounter – but with him or with herself? Imogen had never bothered much about the truth. When she was a child, her high-handed way with versions of events had more than once caused a superficial ruffling of her parents' placidity and their profound embarrassment when this trait came to the attention of her schoolteachers or the mothers and fathers of her small friends. "She is so imaginative!" Margaret Scottow had found it behoved her to boast laughingly more often than was comfortable. And even when Imogen had grown up, the lighthouse as a black and white tower with a lantern at the top and the lighthouse as a nocturnal philosopher who would throw open his blazing mind and shine forth a great light were realities equally real. The pilgrim who spread his prayer-mat at sunrise and sunset was as true as the sea he sauntered – either that or they shared one falsity, the delusory was universal. So that now, languorously raising her arms down which droplets of water slid, looking up at the sky which was being scumbled so the blues were ever softer, she could contemplate her illumination of her inner self and her meeting with Dario – how devastatingly would he accuse her? – unafraid. She had played one ace, had trumped her godmother. But there were other aces, were there not? The world was various, she would take a glance at her hand of cards.

Alas for Laura who had been told what she wanted to hear, had been fed a titbit sopped in the wine of hopeful love which when we drink it has one effect only and one effect always: belief, illusion, ignorance. Now on the stones she lay troubled by uneasy dreams, no spaniel's devotion could save her. Alas for Dario who with a second glass sat exactly where in 1944 the then mistress of the house had knelt grey-haired over her grey-haired husband whose chest and stomach had a few instants before been riddled with German bullets and on whose slabbered shirt flies were gathering. Now his call to Imogen was bitter – "What right did you have to trick me into fatherhood? why did it please you to condemn me to a lifetime of not being able to love my daughter?" – no justice could save him, no eloquence could save him. Alas for Angelica whose existence had, a few days after her birth, been registered as that of Angelica Laura Scottow, and whose mother now was revelling so unconfinedly in the pleasures of swimming and of speculation – self-contemplation, Anna would have snorted – that she had entirely forgotten her, thus giving Maria the privilege of bathing her. (This was an honour which Maria enjoyed. But she would have enjoyed it more tranquilly had it not, on all Imogen's recent visits to the estate, been foisted on her so regularly that her heart ached because the baby only had one parent – ah, the poor angel! – and to be neglected by her . . . !) Unfortunately perhaps for all three – unless isolation as absolute as Imogen's might disclose itself an absolute morality – her call rang confidently.

"I shall come ashore, I shall take up the challenge, Dario. I used to be one voice and you another, but now I am many voices, I am a harmony or a cacophony. I do not know which, but out of this medley surely some revelation must sound its clear note, some new motif be born. I am called – by you? by myself? by some power I am beginning to apprehend? I have a calling now, time and I are at one, I too am of eternity, and my first duty and my first delight will be to offer this to you. Thank you, I shall say. Would it amuse you if I curtsied? For was it not the accident of our meeting here, was it not that morning moment at the corner of a hut when a net shimmered in the air – or rather, as I now feel, when for the first time I realised how I had always been bound, oh tied up like a fetishist's call-girl – was it not *you*, your sudden presence before my eyes and your unexpungeable presence in my thoughts, who caused me to reach for my knife, cut myself free, so that now I can stand up, brush the dirt from my clothes?

"What we actually decide to do – and may we not by accord silent or spoken decide to *do* nothing? – seems to me pretty insignificant. What do you think? If you were swimming beside me I should ask you straight away. If we were swimming stroke for stroke, if for once in a while we were dancing in time with one another . . . Has not our wretchedness been possibly that we have always danced out of step, wanted the same things sometimes but never at the same time? Often fluctuations of moods are all that I think exist. If you were swimming beside me and you suggested we do this or do that, you said you thought happiness might lie this way or lie that, I think I might find it in me to let you do the deciding. Right, I might say. Fine. That doesn't sound too awful. Let's play it your way.

"Yes, I am in a mood not to care much what is done, what transpires, what follows what. Swimming on my back, I gaze up, I remember Ptolemy's spheres, I forget them, remember again. Is this my calling, to call into being and to be called? Ptolemy's spheres, I say, are still turning up there although they have been disregarded for centuries. Were they any more real when people believed in them, that since Copernicus they should be less real? I too have some degree of reality for a while and then lose it. With this love of time's makings and unmakings, this love of remembering and forgetting in my heart, I shall swim ashore. Look, I roll over, I change direction, I swim more vigorously. There is the cove. I shall land. Dusk is falling. It will be the night of power. Whether it is best for you to be Angelica's father or not, it will be as if I set foot on that shingle for the first time, as if, though it was my shore of departure, I knew the place for the first time. Whether it is best for me to cut myself utterly free of you or not, best to turn toward a further solitude or not, when I feel the island under my feet I shall know myself for the first time, this bathe in this water has had that effect."

Like the loneliest Greek sailor after the longest voyage, naked Imogen waded ashore. The dogs came to meet her. Hearing footsteps on the stones, Laura sat up stiffly. Imogen had brought no towel. Patchily she dried herself with her clothes, put them on. "I've decided," she announced. "I'll talk with Dario. Do you think he'll be horribly harsh with me?"

Laura tried to speak; tried once more; buried her weeping eyes in her hands. Imogen stood looking down at her. She smiled. She buckled on her pistol.

So it was that the Rodostamo estate was crossed by unheard thoughts in which the reasonable and the fantastic were scrambled like eggs. Or it was as if Dario De Corvaro on the terrace brooding, Laura Rodostamo on the shingle dreaming fitful grotesqueries she forgot before she could understand but not before they had depressed her, and Imogen Scottow in the sea exulting were three Aeolian harps on which the same air breathed but which, because no harp was constructed precisely like another, moaned each its own tune. Other minds, dotted here and there about the estate as if a hostess more sophisticated than the present chatelaine had indeed thought to place one harp on this balustrade and another on that, a third in the branches of a favourite olive tree, a fourth in the wistaria arbour and a fifth in the rigging of the fishing-smack, thrummed to different breezes.

Ben always beats me at backgammon, Demitri Rodostamo complained to the stuffed tanager perched on the barometer as he put the set back in the tallboy.

I rang up Stephen yesterday, I must not ring up again so soon or he will think I am checking up on him, Ben Thurne ordered himself, and besides if it is that son of a bitch Pierre who picks up the telephone I shall be sick with anger and

149

sick with jealousy until I ring up again and find Stephen alone and even then I shall be only slightly consoled.

The place looks much the same as ever, Natasha Schomberg reflected as in the encampment down by the shore she got out of the car and thanked Yanni for driving them, but it is the first time in my life that Laura has not been here to welcome us.

Angels and ministers of grace defend us! prayed Yanni who had, as ordered by Maria, begun scrubbing and disinfecting dustbins, but had raised his head from this malodorous labour and seen the four Schomberg girls stroll giggling away, each with longer golden hair and longer golden thighs than the one before.

The summer nightfall was slow, Ptolemy's spheres, which according to Imogen still ghostlily turned – oh, not so indisputably as in the Middle Ages, but with a lingering shadow of their old ethereal splendour – took a long time to darken. Slowly Yanni took up his scrubbing brush once more, slowly bowed his head back into the dustbin. Slowly Laura's household gathered. (It was true that usually she was punctilious about being present to meet her guests when they arrived. Changing in her hut while Imogen changed in hers, Laura thought guiltily that Natasha *must* be here by now, she tidied herself for the evening with what haste she could. Honestly today, what with one fearful thing and another, she felt she would never catch up with life again. Life would get farther and farther ahead, she would pant pathetically after, and then life would go out of sight, she would no longer know which way to stumble and puff, she would sit down and die, that was what you did when life left you wasn't it, you died?)

Tasso, who had again watered the vegetable patch, now doused with water the scrub around the fireplace in case during the cooking of dinner sparks fell where the undergrowth was parched because for weeks there had been no rain. The fireplace was a low stone wall in the shape of a horse-shoe. In it now a fire was built on which, when it was a bed of red embers, the mighty gridiron would be balanced and the cuts of lamb and goat grilled. Between the kitchen hut and the arbour people came and went with crockery and cutlery, both round tables were laid. The driftwood crackled, it blazed up, around it people stood with glasses of wine in their hands.

While dressing she had heard the Scops owls in the eucalyptus clump calling, Laura told her goddaughter as they strolled toward where laughter suddenly pealed into the quietness – yes, with that shindy, that mirth, it could only be that Natasha and her troupe of maenads had arrived – and where woodsmoke steadily plumed into the dusk. Changing in her hut, Imogen had decided that she was possessed of the finest godmother in the wide world, she reported and put her hand through Laura's arm, because on their walk back from the headland the grace-notes she had rehearsed to her had indeed been few and this she wished to make up for. And was this not absolutely the most glorious of all hours? she cried, and gave the ancient elbow in her grasp a good hard squeeze – for Laura must on no account be allowed to suspect quite how coldly she had been weighed in the balance, found wanting, discarded. Was it not superb how just before nightfall sea and sky put on their most peacockish colours? And soon the first star would come out, Imogen rejoiced, any minute now they would see the evening star. And yes, she was glad Laura had noticed her red sandals, they were brand new, she was mad about them, quite quite mad. Right this minute she was mad about a lot of things, come to think of it. The way the headland beyond the bay was going shadowy. That yacht's sails. (*Odysseus' ships have not yet passed the islands*, her godmother remembered.) And the way the dimness collected beneath the maritime pines – did Laura not agree it was magical? And how the herbs one trod on released their pungency, but the underlying smell was always that of the sea ... What, Nick and Marina? Yes, they *were* rather beguiling, Laura was right. Indeed it had been a stroke of brilliance to have the place decorated this summer with such a good-looking pair of lovers, they graced the estate charmingly, kept an admirable tingle of the erotic in the air, did she think the affair would last? If not, a similarly enchanted and enchanting couple must be lined up for next summer. And what would Maria, she wondered gaily, have been up to all afternoon with Minoan Linear A?

For in the midst of the hither and thither of voices under the arbour was an almost silence, at spaniel-level walked a language in the first stages of being worked out. Even Nick Morston, whose good manners had so impressed Laura and who now not only had Marina to adore him and Sophia in whom coquetry was innate but also the Schomberg bevy of damsels flocking round him – even Nick was not the star of the party in the way that Angelica was. (It will be all right if Alexis falls in love with all four golden creatures, his aunt meditated nervously, coming into the cocktail party which had fizzed to life around the fire. But for pity's sake let him not fall for just one of them because they *are* maenads, Natasha's girls, and Alexis all sweet simplicity. Let him not be too enthralled by Caroline, for example – they were laughing into one another's eyes – though really it *was* rather delectable the swiftness with which a lad of fifteen and a nymph maybe a year older could tumble into rank flirtation.) In the midst of general adulation the child stumped to and fro, was petted by this grown-up and that. Her freedom from conventional family relationships or her unending misery might be being schemed by Imogen, but she surrendered and acquired bits of stick, tennis balls the dogs had chewed, biscuits. The anxieties of Dario and Laura and Anna might home in on her till she seemed to wear a halo of others' speculations, it appeared impossible that the aura could not be seen by every bystander, she was a child composed more of others' passionate concern than of flesh and blood . . . But she did not speculate; or, if she did, her wonder was for the contents of a kitchen cupboard, or what lay beyond a particularly enticing bush, or where she had dropped her ball. To hearings finely attuned by love the air might be quivering with calls, but Angelica's simple call, when Imogen joined the throng, was "Mummy!" Picked up and kissed and put down, she moved among people's legs, the cynosure.

Dario sipped his wine. When Tasso asked him if after dinner he would give him a hand to lay nets he said yes. He watched Angelica. One of the spaniels' wagging tails hit her, she cooed with laughter. Probably all this is a tissue of illusions, Dario thought with the weariness of despair. Probably she is not mine.

FOUR

"Unarm, Eros; the long day's task is done,
And we must sleep."

ANTONY AND CLEOPATRA, William Shakespeare

"My brother is engaged to be married!" Imogen's amusement rang clear. She had Demitri's attention, Natasha's, Nick's . . . Now all the table was listening. "To a merchant banker! Don't you think that's extraordinary? A woman who only ever thinks about interest . . . from morning till night souses her mind in usury – nothing but that . . . !"

"I had to ditch my second husband, but the first one, bless him, ditched me," Natasha explained blithely to Demitri, because her hostess, she knew, had placed her between the novelist and the one-time manager of a factory which had made plumbing equipment until it went bankrupt in order that she should rub some of her gaiety off onto them. So now she took her high spirits in one hand and Demitri Rodostamo in the other and smeared; she daubed, she polished, she infused. "Laura tells me you have had the same good fortune. Now confess to me with absolute frankness, don't you feel that at last again you can feel the wind in your hair?"

I warned you, Laura said with her eyes to her brother-in-law, and smiled her encouragement. Did I not remind you that her daughters and she galloped all over Somerset on five chestnut thoroughbreds, you were to expect cavalry attacks? And indeed he was rallying, she noticed with relief.

154

"I have almost no hair," she heard him say. But had it been a good idea to intersperse her three sad men with Natasha and herself? She never knew whether it was wise to place people or to let them sit where they pleased. Both tables were round – never for a second had she regretted having Tasso make them round – so the general effect was egalitarian and no one was ever far from anyone. (Not a gill of Tory blood befouled Mrs Rodostamo's veins; her democracy was an old Whig liberality.) At any rate this evening she had tried to introduce a little order into one side of one table. She had Dario on her left for the second meal running. Imogen she had let choose her seat – rightly, wrongly? She had hoped she might plump for the chair on Dario's left, but she was on Demitri's right. Dario on his other side had Maria, which was probably a good thing because before dinner Alexandra Schomberg had appeared to think him rather fascinating, which of course he was, just as his father had been – the same eagle's head and sunken shadowy eyes.

So here we all are, thought Laura between exhaustion after the day's phantasmagoria and thankfulness that at least a semblance of social decency was being maintained – for it lent an eerie doubleness to the party, this unblinkable fact that four people considered that a game of mortal – mortal what? destiny? – was being played out, while seventeen believed they were eating a dinner like a thousand dinners. It made her want to ask: How do you play Mortal? It's not a game I know. Will somebody teach me please, explain the rules? Still, a few ordered and most higgledy-piggledy, here all her people were, oh all the rank and fashion of the island, the Honourable Natasha and scratching Yanni, and beyond the arbour the headland was a promontory only of dusk and the bay was a bay of shadow now and the stars were out although the hurricane lanterns hung from the rafters made them difficult to see. The night comes, let it be merciful, the lady of the manor prayed. (The other side of the table, Imogen Scottow glanced over her bare shoulders into the gloaming. Look, it falls! her heart cried. It is the night of power.)

"Tell me something, please." Natasha Schomberg turned to Ben Thurne. "Have you ever noticed that in England there are two institutions, High Church Anglicanism and the opera, which have been almost entirely appropriated by homosexuals – male ones of course? They're a couple of armies of unalterable sodomy as far as I can see. Is it the same in Paris, in your experience?"

Dear God it was as if Natasha did it on purpose, Laura's mind squawked. But then immediately she reflected, Yes, perhaps she had indeed made her gaffe deliberately, for though for an instant Ben flinched he was not really offended she now saw. He was smiling. He was of that persuasion himself, he remarked. Yes, of that proclivity. And Stephen while he had been fit enough to work had been a designer of opera sets; and as for the English church in Paris he never went near the place, couldn't tell her in which street it stood. Natasha, he supposed in his turn with just enough malice to be delightful, was doubtless a pillar of her local church, contributed generously to the roofing fund, read the lesson occasionally, that kind of jazz? For himself he could not abide the English counties. "All those pigs, all those sheep, all those cows!"

"I do, I do!" Natasha bewailed. She was – she would be blunt – exactly the sort of county lady Ben so shrewdly, she suspected, despised, with the sole distinction that she was worse than all the others, she played the part dyed in hypocrisy, didn't believe in a damned thing, never had. "Never have, never will, just can't!" she mourned. "Ask Laura, she knows what a sinner I am." So that lady, appealed to, could confirm her friend's sinfulness, and could marvel yet again that the social graces were the most brimming with grace of all on earth. What had Ben and Natasha in common except for a smattering of wit and a dash of wickedness and the courtesy to use these talents to make the rivulet of the evening glint and shimmer as it splashed its way down the hillside to the sea of, presumably, oblivion? Now they had gone on to the moral superiority of sceptics. When had the agnostics ever persecuted the atheists? the Somerset horsewoman demanded to know – whereas you only had to go to the Near East to sample the justice and mercy of Hebrews and Christians and Muslims. Had the admirers of Shelley burned at the stake those of Hume? It was not recorded, that she knew. No, it was faith, faith of any kind Ben might care to name, faith in Allah or the Holy Ghost or communism or fascism, faith that turned charming children in a few years into swaggering murderers. And when, the expatriot novelist echoed her, had Unbelief plagued innocent communities with missionaries, or raised regiments to conquer Belief? So that one might with an easy heart, their hostess bethought herself, leave them to it. Civilization, in their playful hands, would come to a lot less harm than in sterner grasps. One might turn to Dario on one's other side.

To Dario who had probably urged Maria to be his dining companion – his good manners were quieter than Natasha's, perhaps more profound, and the old woman's homely talk would be a baffle against the winds of cruelty, would it not? To Dario whose laying out of intricate patterns in her sanctum Laura had betrayed to Imogen – but she had been intended to, surely she had . . . though it was queasy, the feeling that she had got carried away, had distorted things. To Dario behind whose chair Angelica on her circumnavigation of the table was now passing so that he fleetingly smiled and patted her small fair head. To Dario who so resembled his father that she felt now a silly rush of tenderness for him – the week in Avignon back in the fifties had been splendidly mad – and whom she had invited to be of the party this month, she recollected almost with a flush of shame, not unconscious that Imogen was going to be here too, thinking that maybe, possibly . . . I am a dotard! she wailed, and unlucky with it. But even now, breathing the oregano which Daphne had sprinkled over the platters of grilled meat, gazing round at her gallimaufry of household and guests, raising her glass of wine, hearing a moth beating its wings in futile self-destruction against the lantern over her head – even now she could not help thinking how marvellous it might have been if Dario De Corvaro and Imogen Scottow had never met before. She would have had them both stay right on until the end of summer (there would have been the convenient excuse of Anna's wedding). Right on until the sacrament and the jollification and the ghastly expense were over, and the man who one day would on her shore build villas had taken her daughter to the Windward Islands or the Leeward Islands or somewhere, and everybody else had left her in peace too, and the weather broke.

She loved the late summer days when the weather broke, she did not know why but she always had. Humidity such that your skull felt as if it were packed with wet wool. Of course, you had to have the tension, otherwise the release did not work. Haze thickening all day. Nerves tightening. Imogen who was highly strung could get snappy in such weather; lowly strung Anna always went her placid way. No wind. The growl of thunder far off. And then the storm would break, would machine-gun the earth with hailstones the size of bullets sometimes, afterward you would find the impressive perforations they had made in the broad sappy leaves of the Angel's Trumpet in the courtyard, and then the rain would bring mud sluicing down the hillside till every path was a brown cascade. Imogen and Dario and she would have flung oilskins around their shoulders – though truly what was the point? you were drenched whatever you wore – and hurried laughing and splashing down to the bay to check that *Nineveh* and the fishing-smack were all right. With the foul weather approaching, all warps would have been checked before. But it would have been a duty and a delight to check them again, with those seas breaking against the rocks so that warm spray exploded up the slope into the olive trees and the prickly pears, with the wind shrieking so passionately that the combers had their crests blown off, spindrift blew scudding from wave to wave so the sea in its violence was veiled in white, and when in your oldest clothes and bare feet and billowing oilskin and your hair in rats' tails you fought your way out along the quay the spume drubbed upon you welter after welter. Within the breakwater of the quay the seas would be humbled, sullenly they would mooch about, their turbulence without direction now. But during an inshore gale the waves even when broken would not be negligible, and it would be prudent to make certain that warps were not chafing; it would be awe-inspiring to hear the scream in the rigging; and since *Nineveh*'s mooring needed to be renewed and she was lying at anchor it would be an excellent idea to take the dinghy and, pitching on the tumultuous waters, put out a second anchor too, and it would then be the work of several careful minutes on the heaving foredeck to make sure she was lying to both lines equally and they would not cross and tangle whatever the squalls did.

Yes, it would have been fun, Laura lamented. And her last adventure might not have been today's wrestle with phantasms who would not even grip her and fight but dissolved in her ams. It might have been – now she knew how close to felicity she had unwittingly steered! – that bringing Dario and Imogen together she would have set a crown upon – she did not quite know upon what – upon thirty years of loving the girl? Her hillside and her valley would have been the site of their falling in love, of a happiness they would not forget till they were buried side by side. That would have been a worthy achievement for her old age. And when the storm abated and the blue days returned – often after the breaking of the summer the bright weather went on till Christmas – they would have helped her with *Nineveh*'s new mooring. Dario and Imogen with the cheerfulness of those who are in love would have dived with shackles and swivels and chains, and she would have stood on the quay with her chest so taut with love that it would have been difficult to breathe. She would have called, "Thank you! That's wonderful!" as together they swam back to shore, and it would have been good to know that the sloop could ride out any tempest now, was moored with bright thick new steel which would not wear thin till after she were dead.

Natasha and Ben were having a high old time; they had finished dilating upon the pope's dexterity with double standards, his layered hypocrisies; now she was telling him about the unctiousness and illiteracy of her Evangelical parson. "Why should he preach to us?" she enquired of the sultry darkness and the crickets and the Scops owls. "Perform the ceremony, yes, that is his function. But lecture us? Last Sunday there were about a dozen of us at church – average for Metton these days. The parson gave his usual simplistic, sentimental sermon. I glanced around at the congregation. The most insensitive and certainly the most ignorant person in the building was being paid to harangue the rest of us. Have we all lost our wits?"

Restlessly Laura assured herself that the gold and silver balls of civilization were still rising and falling merrily in the air, the two jugglers on her right hand had not let them drop and bounce and trundle ignominiously to a halt, they were tossing up and catching with spirit those two, in their distinct ways they had class, she need not fret, breeding would always show, no that was not the kind of thing you were meant to think these days. Turning her attention to Dario sitting at her left hand – and honestly she must not leave him to make polite conversation with Maria a minute longer, it was inhuman – was not proving altogether straightforward. She could conceive of him – but the simplest conception was a soap bubble that a child blows and makes swell, blows so it grows uncertainly, glistens with new sheens, wobbles, takes on lumpy transformations and then either flies unsteadily off to come to grief against the first solid fact or bursts and leaves nothing but an empty feeling behind.

160

Restlessly Laura assured herself that it was as she had predicted, Anna had indeed been annoyed by Imogen's mockery of Mark's engagement, she was ignoring her. As if Imogen would care! Thus piqued, she would take the first opportunity again to deride matrimony or the City. Still, Anna of course was as banally right as ever, Imogen should not make public mock of her brother's fiancée, Laura made herself think it. Truly she should not . . .

Restlessly she attended to Maria trying out the simple Italian she had picked up during the war, Dario fumbling to express himself in Greek. No two ways about it, thirty words of a language were not enough. In a moment she would intervene, she would detach him. In the lantern-light, the shadows of the jugs and bowls and bottles lay very black on the pale scrubbed planks. She glanced around at the gnarled mahogany face of Achilles, old guerrilla, old patriot, old killer; at the creamy china face of Imogen . . . Would she be able, if the voices around her rose to a crescendo, to murmur to Dario that the glazed figurine had parted her pink lips, had breathed onto the air that Angelica, now ensconced on Maria's capacious black cotton lap, was his child? That she had later declared that she would speak with him?

Time will run back and fetch the age of gold . . . Ah, if only! Laura had been half dreaming, automatically she reached her hand beneath the table, ruffled a spaniel's silken head. If time would run back, run back . . . Fleet of foot as the Faun when Nijinsky danced it, run lightly back and fetch – and fetch . . . ? *And speckled Vanity* – this was right, wasn't it? – *Will sicken soon and die* . . . But the fetch, she now recalled, meant a double, a wraith, the fetch was death itself; and she thought of her Angel of Death who might be pacing

161

the glade up at the butterfly chapel, might be waiting for her there; and her wits were wandering again, it was all very well to know oneself ridiculous but it was frightening too, because when all her notions wandered off in different directions and left her she would be void, she would be her death; and the table – she awoke to the fact – was in an uproar of mirth because Imogen was holding forth on the subject of – what? Of her!

Of her! Had the girl no mercy? Hers was a vanity which showed no signs of decently sickening and morally dying. Ah my darling, Laura breathed – never would her adoration of Imogen leave her for more than a few seconds, never! damn it – you are Vanity all right. (Imogen had still been pony-tailed and boy-chested when Laura had first had to moderate her birthday and Christmas generosity to her goddaughter, make sure she gave her daughter something sizeable.) You ought to have your image painted with the richest oils on the palette; you ought to be painted – who could we ask to do it? – with the glistering hues annealed into your cheeks, with your face a brilliant enamel and your eyes of diamond . . . Good God why must I sit here doting and raving while you entertain the table at my expense? For it was true. Even Dario could not help chuckling softly. Imogen's imitation of her godmother addressing the world on the subject of spaniels was having such a rampant success it could only just be heard above Adonis' hilarity – and he was still chewing his last mouthful, his aunt noticed and frowned, so that more than one person thought she disliked being the butt. Laura's wisdom on Springer spaniels and Clumber spaniels; the gravity of her discussion of the merits and demerits of the Irish Water Spaniel; her lordly rejection of the Cocker, except for one strain of working dog of which she had come upon a few examples in North Norfolk and South Lincolnshire and which had considerable virtues when it came to retrieving wounded wildfowl from the reedbeds along the margins of meres . . . The King Charles (she would have none of them), the Blenheim, the Picardy

162

. . . The word – might she be permitted to enlighten them? – came from mediaeval French, it meant the Spanish dog . . . Across the table, Vanity's diamond eyes blazed at her godmother.

Laura would lean toward Dario. She would speak to him in a low voice.

Time will run back and fetch the age of gold . . . Then were we happy. Then were our ills at an end. Send the Faun of time running back through the dappled glens to fetch – to fetch . . . ? But alas it does not please the Faun to run errands for mankind. ("See how I am treated!" Laura Rodostamo exclaimed to the aquiline man beside her. "And at my own table! That girl . . . !") There shines no lodestar to draw him. He canters here, he idles there. Now in a flash he is off galloping – where? Nowhere! Now he stands at gaze. Now prettily he lies down; the bracken is soft; he will sleep; he will forget his mission; he is above missions; he is free. It does not please the Faun that we should be redeemed, that we should be rescued from our follies and our cruelties and our chicaneries. Why should it? He does not care, being free, being of an absolute freedom, Laura mused. Or, if he cares, he likes justice, is not displeased that we should suffer one another, suffer ourselves; it seems reasonable to him, trotting through the forest, if he thinks about us at all, the Faun of time. So she was scarcely surprised to hear Dario, in response to her softly spoken confidence, reply that to be quite honest in his weariness and his despair this evening – she would forgive his directness, she knew it was not her hospitality which was responsible for his despondency – he was nearly beyond caring whether Angelica were his daughter or whether her mother had anything to say to him. "Anyhow, this is what she told me," Laura concluded. And you believed her, his brown eyes reflected. Well naturally, Laura thought, he would not say aloud that my goddaughter sometimes tells lies. And no, she was not much surprised to hear he was so sad. But she was grieved, so that she prayed: Faun, come onto the stage of my mind! Come and dance for me, Faun of time! Enchant me for an hour!

Such was the animation around the two tables under the wistaria arbour that Laura and Dario found they could exchange a few sentences without appearing discourteously to whisper and without being overheard. The spoken was one colour among the many colours of the unspoken in the tapestry; Laura followed that brightness as it wove its way through the design, saw it vanish, imagined it travelling hidden in the depths of the fabric, saw it reappear elsewhere; she deserted it to follow other richnesses, further complexities, for though to speak was a duty the unspoken was more to her taste, its metamorphoses were more dramatic, its sleights of mind more beguiling. Just enough dialogue with Dario she must sustain so that Ben on her right would not feel politeness required him to relinquish the far more witty double divorcée Natasha and make smalltalk with his hostess . . . Just enough – but not so much that Imogen would suspect they were plotting her capture . . . And yet sufficient encouragement she must offer her man of sorrows to be some recognition of his truly astonishing open-heartedness with her this afternoon . . .

Dario finished his cutlet, his aubergine, his bread, laid down his knife and fork, sipped his wine, gave her his sombrely smiling attention. With night now fallen, the arbour was a flickeringly lit deck in a black universe and they were the last twenty-one souls voyaging on the last Ship of Fools, no, twenty-two, Angelica had a small soul. And now it seemed as if she might, with what would be the last effort of a day of accumulating bewilderments, ups and downs, fatigues, imagine one last prospect . . . No, that was wrong. Doubtless before she slept, if tonight she succeeded in sleeping, the cement-mixer of her brain would go on churning over the slurry, go on churning, churning.

"Oh yes, please smoke if you'd like to," she answered Dario's question. "I won't disguise from you," she added,

164

admiring the sardonic way he could smile at the wretchedness he was trapped in, "that it's occurred to me – you mustn't mind my saying this – that it would be the best thing in the world for Angelica if you were by us all assumed to be her father."

"You mean . . . whether in fact I am or not?"

"I mean . . ." Laura glanced from his gloomily twisting lips to the laughing Vanity across the board; she brought her glance back. "I mean – heavens above, the immoral things I am thinking and saying today! I hope you don't consider I'm always like this. And I hope you will forgive me for what I'm about to say about your lover."

"My one-time lover."

"Ah . . . Yes. I mean . . ." It was a possibility Anna had stumbled on, at once shied away from. But Laura would not relate that to him. "Once, in Kensington Gardens, Imogen told me she reckoned she'd covered her traces pretty well. And we know how ruthless she can be. Have you ever wondered if, in despair at your rejection of her, in self-hatred and I dare say with a measure of hatred too, she deliberately went fairly wild? That she . . ." Laura Rodostamo was old-ladyish enough to blush at her own words. "That she not only deceived you, stopped using any contraception – what does she generally do? take the pill? – but then . . . I, er . . . So that she may honestly not know who the child's father is? May have secured her freedom like that – or tried to . . . ?"

"Yes. It has occurred to me. A lot of things have occurred to me."

"Let us assume that the truth does not matter. Let us assume – when you're my age you'll catch yourself thinking this more and more often, just you wait and see – that the truth does not exist. So . . . Whatever the facts may be or the miasma may be . . . Am I being absurdly optimistic, or do matters hinge on whether or not you *want* a daughter?"

"I could half believe in Imogen's self-hatred, I suppose

. . . Yes, about half. And I understand your concern for Angelica. But – are you in a position to offer her to me?"

Laura could only raise her widened eyes and hands, only whisperingly wail "I don't know!"

There fell a lull in the chatter, they had to break off. And anyway, Laura pondered, Dario and she could switch from question to question again and again, they were like a vessel tacking upwind, they could turn and turn and turn – but there was a gale against them and a flood-tide against them, were they making headway, getting anywhere? And this afternoon Dario had given her his all, it was with Imogen that soon he must speak, not with her, so therefore she must make her last faltering contributions right now, ah now now now! and soon dinner would be over, and she was tired. Probably the poor fellow was fed up with her interferences, wanted to conserve his alertness for the real set-to . . . And the congeries of dilemmas in her head! Soon the cement-mixer would start to ache.

Imogen has found me in her path, Dario thought. Startled, irritated, she will kick me aside. Why does Laura not understand? And I, who since she left the castle for the last time had been thinking of her more generously, I who had just about overcome my anger at her intrusiveness, I who riding in the snow called to her with love, now find it impossible to contemplate other than with bitterness how contemptuously she has exploited me. There she sits with her face golden in the light of the hurricane lanterns, with her bonny mien, with her tinkling laughter. She is a degrading cheat.

Sitting beside him, Laura clenched her attention. There was a farther possibility, was there not? There was one last hope. Had transformations never been wrought in the human heart by understanding, by pity, by love? Might not Imogen be so wrought upon by today's confrontation with herself that she changed? Might she not, by at last meeting her lover's eyes squarely, by recognising the three-fold limitations of her self-knowledge and her freedom and her love for her daughter, be moved by compassion, be precipitated into a love more innocent and more abundant than any she had dreamed before?

What does the naïve old darling imagine? Dario was dejected already, and now the night air brought him the far, faint yammering of frogs from the stream and obscurely that made it worse. That Imogen would let me visit the child at whatever fashionable English school she sends her to? That she might wish me to perform all the inadequate pieties of the father separated from the mother of their child? That at airports and railway stations the little *signorina* should be passed from hand to hand? That I should give her lunch in depressing London restaurants, diligently enquire about her friends at school, buy her new tennis rackets? Then take her back to Imogen's hall which will smell of polish, there unfortunately as I kiss the girl goodbye catch sight of the whole farce in the looking-glass, ask her whether she would like to stay with me in Umbria during her summer holiday and hear her mother answer that it might be a nice idea but they will have to see, she will let me know? Why does Laura want to condemn me to this? And how often does she think I can afford to go to England anyhow?

Might not her goddaughter's deceit of Dario be atoned for by renewed love, by bolder love? Already Laura had convinced herself that it might; she was almost ready to bet that it would be. Not for the first time that day, she overlooked the fact that her own experience of conjugal life had not been all that inspiring. Imogen's scepticism on the subject of forgiveness she overlooked also. Might not she discover in her hitherto rakish heart a love for Angelica so omnipotent that she would *want* to give her the happiness of knowing her father, of loving him and by him being loved? How could Imogen not *need* as an absolute imperative to bring father and daughter together? Her reward would be to smile at the great good she had achieved. Her reward would be that both would love her forever more. The meeting at the corner of the kitchen hut that morning had been, Laura knew, a fight to the death of I against I. (That Imogen was savage with herself did not jog her godmother into recollecting that she could be savage with those who stood in her path.) And now the spectacle of the child scrambling from Maria's knee to Dario's in order to assist him with the consumption of his lemon sorbet could scarcely fail to touch her – Daphne's lemon sorbets were her pride, she must not forget to tell her what a success these were – so was there no chance that Imogen might be transformed? There was gentleness in her as well as hardness . . . might not tonight be its hour?

These hopes Laura now, in the most off-hand manner she could command and beneath the providential fray of cheerful voices, murmured to Dario. (For a minute he hardly listened. Tasso was telling Imogen that after dinner they were going to lay nets. Would she like to come too? Without appearing to, Dario harked. Would she refuse categorically? Jump at the chance, offer to take Tasso's place? "Come with you . . . ? Oh . . . Can I tell you when the time comes?") Now at last, her godmother was suggesting, might Imogen not emerge into a love in whose service was perfect freedom? A freedom which required a tougher bravery than her so cherished independence but might crop with sweeter plenitude, a love to serve which would be an honour not won before . . . what did Dario think? (He suspected that such healing transformations only happened in novels by Dostoevsky, but kept his silence.) Was not love – she was possessed by clairvoyance, she would be dictatorial, arbitary – our last chance on earth? What else was there, when all was said and done, to keep us here? And had they not reached an end, and was there not before them the necessity of making a new beginning, and might not the unlooked-for mercy of this dispensation be fiddling whispery music on Imogen's heart-strings? She was a consummate actress, he was to remember, her ease and her exuberance before their eyes were not to fool him.

There was an artificiality about beginnings and an indubitability about ends, Dario reminded her.

Ah, she protested, but at this juncture could Imogen simply decide to behave as if today had never been, go selfishly dandering on as before?

What kinds of understandings were beginnings and ends? he soberly invited her to consider. You proclaimed the one, you bowed under the other. Up to rant, down to acknowledge, on and on. What else had ever occurred (this was the voice of the Other) since time dawdled and leap-frogged? On and on, for no discernible purpose, on, on . . .

He was not to distract her with philosophy right now please, Laura required of him. What she wanted was his response to her extremely plain hope. It seemed to her this evening – yes, she was pig-headed but was not quite ga-ga yet though it would not be long – that miraculous benedictions *did* befall even the most wayward of mankind. Oh, not often! But today . . . And she was shaken now by the hope that the snow-drift of Imogen's heart might feel the thaw, might suffer the first stirrings of spring . . . Was she mad? He was to answer briefly, please, yes or no.

But Dario was not to be bullied. He mused. Were miraculous benedictions observable? He was not certain he had ever seen one.

There was one sitting on his knee, Laura pointed out.

But even at that he did not let himself go, beyond a curt laugh. What would she have him say to Imogen if he were given the opportunity? If you want my life, come and take it – something like that? He too, according to her scheme of things, would have to feel the thaw, would he not, melt at the beginning of spring?

At which with glistening eyes his hostess laid her disfigured hand on his white sleeve. Be thawed! in a whisper she besought him. Have pity on Angelica! she entreated. He too had walked unsuspecting around the corner of the hut that morning, had he not? Had he too not at an instant confronted his lost love eye to eye? Had it not been in a

169

miraculous, a blessed sense to see himself? Was not that what it had meant?

Meaning . . . ? He wondered. He smiled. He had just felt the breath of a night breeze on his cheek – what did that mean?

After dinner there were those who volunteered to wash up. Natasha directed operations with such despotism and such ignorance of the dispositions of Maria's domain that scarcely a spoon was put away in its accustomed place. There were those who went down to the fishing-smack. There were those who stayed under the arbour and played backgammon, their dice rattling on the wooden board. Some yards from the arbour was a low flat rock which sometimes acted as a table and sometimes as a foot-stool and often as an umbilicus around which deckchairs were drawn. Anna placed a hurricane lantern upon it, pulled up a chair for her mother, herself sat down. Imogen with Angelica asleep in her arms sat down too for a few minutes on her way to put the baby to bed. And so it came about that Anna – with a quick glance at her mother which said, You see, I have the courage and the nous to go straight to the point – did the one thing the old lady had that afternoon insisted nobody ought to do. She turned to where her cousin in her dark blue dress and red sandals reclined. She asked, "Tell me something . . . Is Dario Angelica's father?"

For a moment silence fell. Then with a ripple of laughter Imogen leaned into the lantern-light with her daughter held at her breast and her gold necklace that gleamed.

You may cuddle the child now, Anna thought as she waited for the effect of her sally; but really, considering how steadily you consign her to others' care, I don't know why you with your so nominal maternal instincts ever went to the dramatic trouble of having her.

Damn your diamond eyes, Laura heard her aghast mind cry, finding herself face to face with a Head of Victory which would have no compassion for the defeated, no not an ounce. Damn your diamond eyes, damn them . . .

"Good heavens no!" Imogen's eyes might coldly stare their triumph into her godmother's, but her mouth as she addressed Anna was laughing. "After the way he treated me . . . Do you think I could want a child by him? For Christ's sake, Anna, have some imagination, or at least some sympathy. No, Angelica's father is . . . Well, when I was pregnant I told you that his name was going to remain a secret, and so it shall. But Dario De Corvaro? God no!"

Still that diamond gaze into Laura's eyes, into her poor soul which was cringing as an oyster will on occasion cringe when you squeeze lemon on the nervous pulp. Still that triumphing and that smiling mouth that lied . . . which this time was enjoying being known arrogantly, openly to lie . . . which would hide the truth among so many lies it would never be lit on.

"What happened, if you really insist on knowing, is this." Imogen had been transfigured; she had a new rôle; for a minute now, perhaps for five, to the cousin she had shared school dormitories with she would natter about love affairs, money, clothes. "After Dario threw me over, I went to stay with friends in Venice. Well, not precisely in Venice. On the Lido. The very first evening I was there, or maybe the second, at a party I met – I met Angelica's father. He's a . . . Well, he was there for the Biennale. Staying at the Des Bains. I'd arrived pretty bloody desperate; but . . . We had a glorious time. You can imagine, Anna, can't you? He hired boats. We got rid of quite a lot of money at the casino. I bought a dress, I bought shoes. We walked along the beach."

Before Laura Rodostamo could start to disentangle the knotted cruelties, she felt the pain. Up from her creaking deckchair it raised her. Away from the lantern on the rock she was harried. Away from light of any kind she longed to withdraw. Concealment she must have. Darkness would be her only solace now. The moon was not yet up. Starlight would be spectral. Good.

The idiotic thing was, that even with this overweaning pain which lorded it over all lesser feelings and should by all the rights of torture have commanded her absolute attention, Laura found it as difficult to concentrate as ever. To be glad that the moon was a young sliver and had not yet risen – what an unproductive thing to think! Had she no graver concerns? So her sufferings were to be dilatory, stretch themselves luxuriously out. And now she had remembered that she had forgotten to compliment Daphne on her sorbets, so although her feet were stumbling toward the track to the butterfly chapel she made herself turn back to the arbour where voices murmured and cigarettes glowed and dice skittered – they had uncorked another bottle of wine, Nick had his beauties clustered about him, quite a party was under way – and now why did she have to recollect that Stephen was dying? One should forget deaths and remember sorbets, that was the way to live, not the other way round. But suddenly she could not help hearing Ben's voice. A few evenings ago it had been. You know, Laura, I didn't give him that virus, he had said. I'm not killing him. It's someone else, or several other people.

What was the other thing which she had been trying to remember that soon she must make time for? Her roses needed pruning, that was right. That would be the day! Ah, let them straggle. Let the autumn winds tear them off the walls of the house. She would be dead not long after Stephen, perhaps before him, let Anna and her husband cope. Let them remember to have the leaves cleared out of the gargoyles each year because otherwise the gutters overflowed and the water seeped into the walls, as it was half the rooms had damp patches, and during the war the picture which was not by Zoffany had been allowed to get damp, perhaps if she never breathed a word to Natasha she

172

might ask a restorer to have a look at it. Let them build villas, turn her house into an hotel, dig in their venality and their vulgarity a swimming-pool, make their fortunes, what did she care? *And their houses shall be full of doleful creatures; and owls shall dwell there, and satyrs shall dance there.* No, she had forgotten, there was no justice, Anna and her doctor would make a mint of money, exploitation generally succeeded. They were not roses that were straggling, they were her thoughts. But perhaps there would be justice in the end. *And the wild beasts of the islands shall cry in their desolate houses* . . . Her spirit would see the ruin of Babylon and rejoice, the air would ring with her ghostly cry of triumph, would shiver with her laughter at her revenge. *And her time is near to come, and her days shall not be prolonged.*

Her efforts all evening, and now this! Laura's hurt mind wailed as a second time with her dogs she set off for the butterfly chapel. For a further idiotic thing was that, in the troupe of carnivalesque mockers deployed by Imogen's lie – a lie which just might, Laura instructed herself not to forget, be true – the first masked figure who capered before her rheumy vision was one who shrilled at her: See how your petty stratagems go awry! Yes, it was her mild pride as a hostess, of all nonsensical things, which was the first nerve jangled. Ah, the pleasure she had always taken in entertaining her friends was an innocent one, was it not? So why now was it chosen for especial humiliation? How stupid to dream that by seating X beside Y one might alleviate miseries! People arose from their appointed places; they went their own ways; they took action to satisfy their own desires (Anna, Imogen – but not Dario or she), reach their own ends and their own ends only.

Which Tiepolo was it who painted those mad maskers – Lorenzo, Domenico? Had he ever painted a crazier crew than this? With the effort of stumping uphill, Laura's sight blurred, but in the dimness grotesque faces leered, in her singing ears disembodied voices cackled, whispered, bellowed, whistled, pretended to sob. Harlequin? Pierrot?

Columbine? These were the demented, the damned. The masks of the lie jigged before Laura on the path that snaked between boulders, round a clump of arbutus, through juniper. The voices of the lie hissed at her from the olive grove which in the light of the stars lay silvery and silent and still. And in the midst of the incensed troupe, always the face of Imogen that had looked golden in the lantern-light – always her eyes of diamond . . . That was the cockatrice's true and mortal stare all right, this way of lying so the lie was known for what it was and you knew you were being fobbed off, cast aside unvalued, unpitied, unwept. Herself, then Anna – to each her appropriate lie, Imogen dealt them out lightly; and without even the wish for truth what could the future hold? After thirty years of loving her, this is how you are served! a mask spat. This is the gaze of the cockatrice: look back into it, if you dare. And indeed now the lie arrogant and victorious, the lie contemptuous and incisive, struck Laura, plodding through the warm darkness with her spaniels at her heels, as the one self-evident truth in the wide world. This was the look from which there was no honourable backing away, no turning aside.

Don't say you are surprised! a mask spluttered with hollow mirth. A skein of knotting cruelties – whatever do you mean? A defensive position like any other, the simplest in the book. And if this is a web, you old blue-bottle, why did you go buzzing into it? Buzz, buzz! Fly away! Oh, are you caught?

Was this the Imogen whom Laura had determined would not always be hounded from her happiness just because she had the guts, naked and passionate in the darkness, to raise a light and to look? Was this the so-called visionary – Laura blushed to recall her eulogies – who at any cost not excessively immoral she had sworn should take her fill of looking one day? Was she now maybe watching her goddaughter stand before a sacrifice of all compassion too fiendish to pay – yes, watching – but not seeing . . . ? Blinking, ducking, twisting her scared head this way and that way, ramming her knuckles into her oozing eyes – anything rather than behold Imogen calmly paying that price, be guilty of witnessing that, be a party to it?

For the second time that day Laura had been routed, was fleeing uphill. Her defeat was definitive now. There could be no more hopes. There would be no more speculations, no more plans. The butterfly chapel, she must reach the butterfly chapel. At her feet, a slab of quartz gleamed. On it, a glow-worm shone. She stooped to admire its green glimmer. She straightened up, felt dizzy, walked on.

The cost – the price – the coolness with which it was paid . . . Dario De Corvaro was one of the outward forms of the sacrifice. She her insignificant self was another. But the real sacrifice – she had been right, had she not? – was of compassion. That was the innocent Iphigenia who had to be butchered before the killing ships could set sail. Compassion was the virtue which Imogen had decided to sacrifice. Why, ah *why*? her godmother moaned. Was there after all no gentleness in her hardness? But no, she had herself received gentleness at Imogen's hands a thousand times, and you only had to see her with Angelica . . . ! Why, then? It seemed to Laura perverted. What was so irresistible about the lie, what did it reveal that nothing else had the power to clarify?

Power . . . Her mind had said power – was that it? Though honestly a mind so played upon by exhaustion and panic and desolation as hers was hardly to be depended on as a useful instrument. Or perhaps *in extremis* it might blurt out guesses of a lucidity for which all through her hidebound decades she had lacked the unhappiness? Was it the power of the lie which seduced Imogen, made of her the most adoring of slaves, almost the most enthralled of victims, so that her godmother now shocked herself by imagining her as an odalisque stripping off her silks and handing a whip to her master the lie? Did the truth, perhaps, not exist? She had murmured as much to Dario at dinner. Was that why the lie triumphed with a brutal ease that people became

175

slavishly obsessed by? People's natural servility was not to be underestimated. Was there no truth to triumph over? For sure when you tried to utter your modest truth it never amounted to much. When you muttered – what? – All I know is that I know nothing – something along those lines – what changed, what remained, what *was*?

Her defeat was definitive now. She had thought it; she was beginning to comprehend it. Her plan had been to tiptoe at Imogen's heels into the labyrinth of that swashbuckling young lady's putative self-knowledge, dog her progress into the inner tortuousness of her mind, hope not yet to have been shaken off or out-distanced when the raised light was shone on – on whatever at the centre there was or was not. Things had not commenced too inauspiciously. The maze existed – she had been correct about that, Imogen had not been bluffing her. And at first as she stole after those heels the leader of the expedition had appeared to tolerate her presence, had appeared almost to forget she was there. Laura's hopes had asininely risen. But then . . .

To find yourself alone, abandoned to your fears in a darkness of a thousand directions and no way out. (She recollected Dario as a boy in the Appenines going skating, falling through the thin ice, floundering where every certainty you heaved your weight onto broke.) With what disdain, impatience, casual unkindness, had Imogen given her the slip? To stand in the blackness and stare and see nothing, flap your invisible hand before your eyes like a madwoman. To stand at the mercy of every dread drifting by on the inconsequential, indifferent airs and to listen and hear nothing. She had dreamed she would be there at the kill, if at the heart of the maze there were a monster whose death would liberate the innocent – a monstrous selfishness the slaughter of which at Imogen's hand might free Dario and Angelica to come into one another's love. But if this labyrinth had no centre but an endless emptiness? Imogen had gone ahead alone somewhere – but where? She who, her godmother suspected, rejoiced in the delusory nature of all the fabrics of thought as in her rightful inheritance to be accepted with a clear mind and a light heart, had stepped into a pitchy alcove, had let her follower take a wrong turning, had stepped forth again another way, her true way. And now . . . ? Was she, perhaps, somewhere, taking her fill of looking at last? Had she arrived where she desired to be, lit a light, lifted it up? Was there a god of love – a god of wild loves and loves not invariably wholesome and loves remorselessly intemperate and loves which rarely if ever sketched a bow before any morality – a god Laura had quite simply never conceived of – a god to her appointment with whom Imogen would certainly not go accompanied by a respectable old widowed lady of doubtful loyalty and limited imagination – a god for whom Dario for all his charm would only ever be but the most paltry substitute . . . ?

Leaning against an olive tree to draw her breath, Laura was adamant about one thing only: she was not a person to whom questions as to these nebulous possibilities – and probably they did not so much as exist, was the cosmos nothing but nightmares? – could fruitfully be asked . . . though that, of course, did not stop the ferret of investigation twisting blindly on into the dark warren. A god of rejoicings in the infinite intricate beauties of the delusory . . . ? A god of love of the void, of passion for vanity and void; an odalisque who let her silks fall . . . ? The labyrinth was not a prison for her goddaughter, suddenly Laura emerged beyond all doubts on that score. The outer circles of her self-knowledge might offer convenient places where unwanted companions could be stranded (and who to love her god did not go alone, to love in this distasteful case the god of her self?) but Imogen's maze was for her a palace of untellable joys.

Burdened with this knowledge, leaning against the olive tree in the starlight, Laura Rodostamo began to weep.

Yes, her defeat was definitive now. Tomorrow Dario would leave. He would be delightful as he said goodbye;

but he would tell her no scrap of what she ached to know. Nor was it likely that Imogen would ever decide to inform her godmother as to whether or not Dario and she had spoken in the course of that short summer night and if so to what effect. No, it was not likely. Not now. Not any longer. Had she not decided that she had no more use for her grey-headed follower, no more tolerance for that shadow? Had she not tricked her as unscrupulously as she had tricked Dario a couple of years before, left her alone in this blackness to shed futile tears? I shall never – Laura made herself confront the likelihood – know whether my last adventure was a success or not, whether Dario and Imogen and Dario and Angelica will ever be united in love – but there is this that I can be assured of: that the last I knew of this most Quixotic of travails was that it could scarcely have been going worse. Well, henceforth I shall worry about the farm accounts, about Achilles' lameness and Demitri's. I shall mourn for shores sold, built, befouled, for an impoverished befouled sea.

Very probably Imogen would leave now too. With a fresh sob, with an undignified snuffle, Laura focused on the cold emptiness in which she would have to live until she succeeded in dying. For she had lost Imogen. Since the wretch was born she had loved her; that very morning she had delighted in their love fearlessly; but she had lost her now. Imogen had caught her out in her old-womanish bumbling, had not thought to forgive her wiles and her ploys because although they were pathetic they were well-intentioned. Ah why had she let herself forget that in Imogen's radius it was unwise to cultivate any intention beyond that of serving the advancement of hers? Why had she permitted herself her schemes, her disloyalties of thought if not of word or deed? In Kensington Gardens before Angelica was born, and then in the hospital where she passed her first few days, Laura had declared her unswerving loyalty to Imogen and to her planned trajectory in all its strangeness. (The old lady in her anguish neglected to recall that even at the start she had cherished secret hopes.) For that adhesion to her goddaughter's cause she had been rewarded with the reconfirmation and perhaps the deepening of the love which was the solitary inspiration of her old age. And to blunder now, throw it all away! Passing a tussock, Imogen had chanced to notice upon her shoe the clot of mud that was her godmother, automatically she had wiped it off, strode on her way. Ah, why had she been such a fool as to hope that the girl would not divine her manouevrings, see her for the mud she had revealed herself to be? If you loved you did not scheme, did not manoeuvre. You were loyal. You loved.

Yes, most probably in a day or two Imogen on the strength of some excuse or other would take Angelica and be away. And Laura would be unable to bear that – she knew it now, could forsee the hour, fortell all. She would have to shut herself in her bedroom up at the house or in her hut down by the sea, her tears would be uncontrollable, she knew they would. Who would go crawling over this sad earth alone? Imogen would visit the estate less frequently, perhaps not at all – why should she, with their old trust broken, their old flame out? Quite soon she herself would die, ignorant, loveless, alone. After that, Imogen would certainly never come back. Anna and her husband would build an hotel.

To lose so much in one day – but it had been the longest – to lose everything of worth! Of course it was all Anna's fault. It was Anna's crass question which had made Imogen step lightly back into a further lie.

Stiffened by a swig of the spirit of dislike, Laura pushed herself off from her olive tree; then half hamstrung by guilt she tottered as she took her steep way. Perhaps it was not entirely Anna's fault. I should never have burbled to Imogen about my talk with Dario, she berated herself. Of course she immediately decided I was untrustworthy, of course she did! As we sallied forth to go pistol shooting she must already have been deciding that she would let me trot

179

after her a little way but then would brush me off. Yes, as I went toiling after those riding boots, those breeches, that holster, and she looked back over her shoulder and laughing told me that Angelica was Dario's child, already she was lassoing me with a first rope of that confusion we call a clue, a certainty, a belief. Give the old creature something to believe – Laura's mind could hear her goddaughter's amused, affectionate dismissal. Tell her what she wants to hear – it's generally a winning move. Send her off to chase an *ignis fatuus*, you can always send her after others later on. Imogen knew her too savagely well, she lined up her telling sentences like a marksman lines up his sights.

Anna's question to Imogen had been her revenge. Laura could make out the small, white-washed, not quite straight bell-tower, she could make out the cypress which over-topped it, she was nearly there, but of a sudden her eyes swam, there came a film of despair between the butterfly chapel and her, between the world and her, and there was strife between she who loved her daughter and she who knew she was not wholly wrong to be tempted into hating her, no longer merely find her dull and unsympathetic, be clear-headed and clear-hearted at last, hate her. *Lacrimae rerum* – the words visited her for the second time that day. The tears of things. The tears of marriage, Laura thought; the tears of childbearing; the tears of bitterness as you come to death. Anna had wanted to drive a wedge between her mother and her cousin, the years of being found uninspiring had wired even her slack nerves tight enough for an assault. With her interrogation she had muscled in between them. She who early in the day had convinced herself there was no mystery whatsoever about Angelica's parentage had in spite put the matter to the crudest of tests, knowing that either Imogen would own herself beaten, own that the child was a De Corvaro, own that Anna's morality had triumphed over hers, or else when cornered she would lie. The questioner's glance toward her mother while they listened to the story of the love affair on the Lido had been eloquent. See, her eyes had declared, she lies to me, she lies to you, she is a lying bitch, what is so wonderful about her and where is your famous special intimacy with her now, what scrap of your grand alliance which has never invited my participation remains? Listen to her deceiving you, taste her lie in your heart. She may not be lying, you protest? Ah, Mother, how can you be so obtuse? But have it your own way. Let us say that on this occasion her every word is gospel. Then she is promiscuous to a degree . . . !

That Anna should weigh my ethereal Imogen in her so grossly material scales! That she should besmirch her with her pedestrian assessments! Arrived at her sanctuary, Laura flopped down on the stone bench that ran along its south side. Her own child had taken her great joy from her, her last delight, her Imogen. Thanks to her own daughter's coarseness, thanks to that probably inherited insensitivity, she would die without Imogen's comforting love. Assuming that she eked out a few more months, perhaps pegged about her house and her hillside and valley and shore for another pointless year or two, she would have leisure to savour all the desolation of which her limited soul were capable – and it was going to prove embarrassingly difficult to do so without hating Anna.

Faced with Anna's charge as by the charge of a rhinoceros – it gave Laura a flick of pleasure to compare her to an animal so bulky, so scaly, so heavily rough – Imogen had stood to it, a slight immobile huntress in breeches and bush-shirt, she had raised her rifle with its chamber of words . . . Not that her godmother found the story about a Venetian idyll incredible. Events might have fallen out that way. They might not have done. Laura vaguely hoped that the story had some substance to it. Why not? Once on the Lido she had played tennis on a court surrounded by laburnum trees, now she imagined Imogen and her lover in white playing in that enclave of yellow and green. She saw them saunter at dusk along the shore. Why should Psyche not console herself? She might allow herself a revenge which would harm Dario not at all since it would never come to his knowledge, but might satisfactorily harm that offending nerve in her which she might have resolved should be judiciously pained. Yes – might she not with new strong sensations punish her spirit for having loved too truly, reward her body for still being game for gallant and disinterested delights?

And the look, Imogen's diamond look? Laura stopped marvelling at how in one day she had learned more about how to be immoral than in all her preceding years, instead met again Imogen's gaze in the glimmer of the lantern set on the rock. The cold, bright hardness had meant she was going where her godmother should not for an instant delude herself that she might accompany her – but the laughter? For there had been laughter – Laura got a grip on this aspect of things for the first time – and it had been laughter not only at Anna's question and her own reply but also . . . also *at* nothing . . . but laughter as a signal, maybe? Her eyes were sapphires of the iciest brilliance, but in their derision of her godmother's fumbling with the problem of Dario and Angelica, in their mockery of her impertinence and her incompetence, had there been hidden a promise, a promise of a return? Of course I'm ditching you now, what on earth do you expect, but I'll come back . . . Something like that? So that sitting on the chapel bench under the stars Laura discovered that she could not even despair, even that last tribute to the world was beyond her decrepit abilities. She had told herself scarcely half an hour before that there could be no more hopes – but that had been as untrue as everything else, as indeed a more collected intelligence might at the time have surmised. I'll come back – Laura could not resist letting the imagined promise beat through her brain. You silly old darling, to think that you could interfere with Angelica and me! But why should I be annoyed, how could I be irritated with the finest godmother there ever was? What should I care? You were never going to have succeeded in doing any harm.

Yes, I'm off on this adventure now, but I'll come back. Just wait. Your bunglings are at an end. Wait at the butterfly chapel, wait in peace. How should I not love you as before? I'll come back, we'll talk. All will be as it was before.

And the look which in the lantern-light Imogen had cast at Anna? The scorn behind the friendliness, veiled by the chatter about the garden at the Des Bains? Laura's pride in her goddaughter might take a battering but it could never fail, and here she felt her skates on thicker ice. You don't know what it is to have been loved and broken with, Imogen's arrogant soul had cried to her cousin. You haven't been broken with. What in your dowdy engagement to be married, in your fireless heart, is there, worth speaking of, to break? But Dario's and mine was everything a love could be, filled to the brim with the wine of consciousness. And do you now think, though I talk with you – oh, I talk, I talk! – that it had a meaning so poor that I would let you breathe your blight on it? I was exploited, I was betrayed – but was it so that you should be confirmed in your righteousness, believe more sturdily yet that your blinkers are field-glasses? Was it for the edification of any of your breed that I was condemned after a few months of summer to find the golden flame a grate of ashes?

On the terrace of the house where he had been born, the house to which after his years in an Italian prison camp he had returned to find his mother alive and his father dead, the house where practically as his sister-in-law's pensioner he still prolonged an existence which gave slight pleasure to several people but not to him, Demitri Rodostamo played his flute. Beside him, Ben Thurne listened, a glass of brandy in his hand. From the orchard, an owl called.

A couple of miles offshore, Tasso lit a cigarette, passed

the bottle of wine to Dario, watched him drink from it, accepted it back from him, drank. So far were they from any city with its lights and its foul air that the stars blazed with a brilliance rare in Europe at the close of this dirtiest of centuries. The fishing-smack carried lanterns, but they had not lit them. The white masthead light gleamed palely. There ought to have been a red light in the port shrouds and a green one to starboard, but nobody had remembered to rig them, and in these seas who came to complain that fishermen were remiss about navigation lights? The young moon was rising in the eastern sky. The lighthouse cast down a swathe of radiance upon the gulf, for a moment left it glittering on the calm water, then snatched it away into blackness. They had paid one net out over the gunwale. Now its polystyrene floats were a chain of white dots. In a minute they would chug a short distance, lay the second net. But now – for a moment . . . Dario straightened his back. He looked around into the immense night. A school of tunny were rumpling the grey.

Who was it in which Chekhov play who said that in a hundred or two hundred years life on this old earth of ours was going to become marvellously beautiful? that we should work to prepare the way for that civilization . . . Dario's bitterness had him by the throat tonight, now it choked a snort of laughter out of him that caused Tasso to throw him a puzzled glance, hand him back the wine. Dario said "Thanks," he raised the bottle to his lips. But, then . . . He lived in a country in which every man in the government was corrupt and every stream was polluted, *ought* he to be cheerful? He lived in a world grossly overpopulated, a world which halfway through the next century would it seemed pullulate with double the present swarm of mankind, would be a noisome barbarism, uninhabitable . . . As lately as that morning he had been cheerful enough, in his quiet, solitary fashion. To lean on the rail as the ferry nudged in toward the wharf, to think how pretty the houses rimming the bay looked in the early sun, to look forward to a few weeks at

184

Laura's farm, to carry his suitcase down the gangplank . . .
All cheerful enough – but now . . .

Dario did not know that Anna had made a passionate speech to her mother on the subject of the tragic love which today – to her it stood clear, a mountainous fact – was being born in his heart; he did not know how she had raised a corner of her red and blue silk to dab her eyes. His distress was a less elevated one. Could he love Angelica? Supposing that Imogen decided to establish that the child and he had no splash of blood in common, would it ever be anything but faintly distasteful to him to be aware that there was a girl growing up in this world who might possibly be his daughter? Supposing that Imogen decided that he was to be saddled with fatherhood, had he in his melancholy and his distantness got it in him to love the child at all effectively? And supposing – most far-fetched, most unanswerable and most dreadful of hopes – that there was that in Imogen which the thaw of self-knowledge might melt, that there was in himself that which Laura's plea for forgiveness and for love might touch . . . ?

No, no, it was saner not even to contemplate it. It would be better, if Imogen offered him fatherhood, to refuse. She would not insist.

Tomorrow he would take the ferry, soon he would be back in Umbria. Things would go on as before, only more sadly still, with an unquietness, a hauntedness. Again he would take up his lonely station in the silence in his mind. With no magnificent voices any longer sounding in his head, naturally sooner or later he would let his feelings carry him away, if he could find any feelings in him, find or fabricate. (For an instant he could not stop his heart suggesting that if ever he were to let himself be carried away again tonight was the night, but that idea was a slug through which a spade could be jabbed.) Who was he, that he should not increasingly be degraded by futile love affairs? Winter would come, at evening he would go down to the café, seek out the schoolmaster. Spring would come, evenings would fall cloudy and cool, he would see the apple trees in blossom in the castle garden and hear the birds singing and his hauntedness would be more than he could bear, no it wouldn't, one bore everything, how, short of suicide, not? Only now, as Tasso shoved the diesel engine into gear and he stooped over the crate to check that the second net was not tangled, would feed out without twisting and snagging, it appeared to him that his life was over as if he had never lived. Not as if this evening his life were drawing to an end; but as if it were beginning never to have been, so sheerly meaningless, after today's confrontations with his arrayed hopelessnesses, was he having to perceive himself to be. The flarings of happiness, the instants, the mad embrace at the corner of a field between one exalted clod and another, the leaning from your horse to kiss the other rider – they were not gone, they had never been. It was as if the man who existed had deserted the man who did not – were we not all such doubles? – had left him alone.

What nonsense was this, that the instants never were? Of course they were. He must not give way to exaggeration, to thinking things because they sounded dramatic. Oblivion was inevitable, he was leading the most insignificant of lives, but he was leading it. Dario turned from the net. He gazed across the sea to where the new moon had laid a silver path. With the vibration of the engine, the deck under his bare feet was quivering, but what he trod were the cold depths of a lake in Italy, what he felt against his chest and his arms were not the balmy brushings of the wind of their passage but cracking panes of ice, what he saw was not the majesty of the Ionian in the moonlight but bare trees along a bank of muddy snow, a shore toward which he fought but automatically now, because it was what you were meant to do.

On the bench along the wall of the butterfly chapel, Laura Rodostamo lay down.

For a while, indifference had held off from her, had done no worse than lour in the interstices between her thoughts, hiss its judgements through the chinks. She had sat, she had admired the sweep of the hillside in the light of the stars, had admired the crescent moon when it rose, how it spangled the olive grove. Whether Angelica would grow up to hate Imogen for selfishly depriving her of her father's love and for treating her father with contempt, as a sexual machine, nothing more; whether Imogen had been lying when she had undertaken to speak with Dario; whether he would be moved by nascent love of the child to confess to his tormentress that forgiveness was greater than abhorrence, to posit a love that would vanquish solitudes without impingeing upon freedoms, to invite her to abandon herself to the intoxication of hurtling beside him down that incomparably steep and eternally dazzling *piste* . . . These hopes and fears had still troubled her, but less forcibly – she had been constrained to acknowledge it – less forcibly with the passage of the night, less, less. And then she had realised that she was even being tortured less energetically by her belief that by her day's fumbling she had lost Imogen. It was with the humiliation of this recognition in her brain feeling like the cangue around a Chinese convict's neck that she had let her body tip sideways, had hauled her rickety legs up onto the bench, had laid her defeat wearily down.

The fire came back to her. What was it that she had learned? You could pray for every creature to be spared and at the same time be glad that the world's meaninglessness was not going to be tampered with just because of human hopes and fears. Yes, you could be inconsequential like that. In her first fire the snakes had slithered and the rabbits and the weasels had bolted neck and neck and the bats in a shed roof had been made cinders and whether the pine marten had gone free she did not know and the birds had flown up shrieking from the burning trees. Through the abandoned house the Angel of Death had paced, taking from the table in the hall the Byzantine dagger with its chased blade, jade hilt, garnets set in its sheath, sticking it into his belt. In that fire her ghostliness had begun, she had begun to be refined, the making a spirit of her had begun. She had rejoiced in the Angel's coldness when he glanced into the gun-room, when upstairs he fingered her bracelets and rings. Her house's fate had depended on the veerings of the wind, on whether this copse or that caught fire when the sparks were whirled that way, on chance; and that had been good, that had been as things ought to be, she had kissed Adonis as he was lifted aboard the sloop and she had known that it was good. Her goddaughter might plan the most dashingly Icarian flight, might upward through her thoughtscape indeed soar nobly in her solitude, her pride, her freedom and her contempt for the society that lay below. But Laura Rodostamo, floundering in the sea down into which Imogen would plummet, betrayed her human nature by clutching at the first straw that might indicate an ordered universe. She looked at the wretched sodden stalk her fingers were clutching, saw that it was the randomness of things, it was chance. A fine universal order to be buoyed up by! Her arm lolling over the bench, her fingers uncurled. Her head on the stone, her mouth smiled.

And her second fire? All day she had been burning in it. Her mortality was on the wane. Her first fire had half consumed her physical world; her second had half destroyed her mental sphere. All day it had raged – how had she not burned in Angelica's cause! It was still smouldering. Only smouldering. She had been constrained to admit that already she cared less desperately about losing Imogen. Her brain was a glowing coal. Slowly it would shrink, slowly it would cool. You are being made spirit, made abstract, a voice remarked. It was the voice of the Angel of Death, how could she doubt that? It had to be. Of course he had come to meet her. He was here. If she sat up and looked around she would see him pacing the glade among the olive trees and the moths and the bats. Or perhaps he had checked in his strolling. Perhaps he was standing still, regarding her where she lay. She must sit up, she must look. But her mind was half burnt away, she went on lying and gazing up, she could see a bit of dark cypress and a bit of pale chapel wall and a bit of eave and stars, stars, stars.

Yes, you are being made a spirit, the Angel went on, and laughed softly. You had not got one before, but it is being made for you, fire by fire, made out of you and for you. The complete fire – the third fire, shall we say, in your case – will be death. You will be almost all soul, then in an instant nothingness, unmade utterly. Do not be afraid, this world is punishment enough, hell-fire was only ever the self-excitation of sadists. This world is also heaven enough, do you not agree? There are the butterfly chapel and the cypress, both good things. There are the buff and russet colours of the moth which has alighted on your sleeve, there are its tremulous antennae and its tremulous wings now it takes to the air and its dancing flight and its vanishing, all good things. There are the glimmering bay and the fireflies in the orchard and a child asleep. You call me the Angel of Death, but I am your capacity to become spiritual toward the end of your life, I am, if you like, the soul you have begun to elaborate fire by fire. And yes, I have been to watch over Angelica asleep. As when the flames blew roaring through your woods and my look fell on all you had valued, so tonight I have eyed whom you love. An implacable eyeing – but it is our indifference which binds us each to each, you and I, is it not? A coldness, a slowness to be moved, a tendency to despise whoever lets himself be seen to exult or bewail. Not that you have not committed these follies. But it is from our mistakes that we learn. No, we are not stockbrokers, you and I, those weaklings who in their obsession with coin react with hysterical exaggeration to every hour's small flutters in the world's affairs. I am – put it like this – the slowness to be tempted which you have learned, the indifference you are learning to display and are learning to feel. I am the indifference you love because you have come to admire the Stoical virtues above all others. I am also the indifference you hate because you find it easier day by day, because the subjugation of passions which are

189

dying is no resounding conquest, because to one of your so feebly faltering gusts of sentiment obliteration is very close now. Do not pretend you did not know this. Do not pretend you are not afraid and do not understand why your fear has arisen. Death is very near now. I do not have to raise my voice, my softest whispers reach you. I am beside you. Not touching yet. But here. Now.

So the Angel of Death spoke to Laura as she lay on the chapel bench and fireflies jinked and sparkled and frogs croaked. Her goddaughter might, swimming back-stroke at sunset, have conceived, ethereal, Icarian, that her time partook of eternity now, that as naked she waded ashore eternity partook of her, but Laura knew that the butterfly chapel could be the world's end as well as any more grand and dramatic place, and she knew she was approaching close to the timeless moment she had often dreamed. Slowly time throbbed through her mind. More slowly still. Ah, when it slowed to a standstill . . . !

She would lie here on the bench all night – why not? She would drowse. Already on the dust her dogs were asleep. If the dew wet her she would be honoured. She would wake, perhaps, to the brilliance of dawn which she remembered with her purest love, to the birds chirruping in the thickets, to the radiance in the heavens and the clarity in her head which all the tortuous day she had longed to recover. The tempo in her mind was so slow she believed it had ceased – no! there it echoed, but so softly it must die away soon now. The rhythm of blood and thought was so faint – was she dreaming? was she not even dreaming any more? The refractory elements of her consciousness dissolved, all her cloudy forms dissolved, they dissolved, how much longer could dissolution be stretched out? She was one of the things of time, she would be one of the nothings of eternity soon, soon, soon.

Her Angel had said she was afraid. Was she? She was sad. She was sad to lose, along with the dross of her life, the few ounces of gold. Already her recent years were slipping from her, the events and cares of her old age did not prove interesting enough to remember, she recalled the fire of eleven years before and the fire of today and nothing else, and what were these fires compared with the fire ahead? But long ago . . . Soon after Alexis and she were married they had sailed *Nineveh* home in a rain-storm. They had sailed into the bay with the storm of wind failing but the rain falling torrentially and ever more vertically now, warm summer rain. They had anchored in the bay, they had furled the sails and tidied the cockpit, they had dived into the sea that was still lumpy after the wind though the cloudburst was starting to batter the waves down, it would beat the bay flat, they had swum ashore through the lolloping crests and sidling troughs and through the juddering rain.

She would lie still. She would watch her mind's dissolutions. She would listen to time slowing down, its echoes fading away. She would sleep. Perhaps she would dream.

So still did she sleep that Imogen Scottow, coming around the bell-tower and seeing her lying on the stone in the moonlight, for a moment thought she was dead.

In the hold of the broken-backed tramp steamer on the reef, hardly a sheen of the light of moon and stars penetrated to illumine the water, which lay uneasily calm, imperturbably black. (That wreck had been a local sea-mark for, oh for twenty years he reckoned it must be now, yes, ever since he'd been a lad, Tasso recounted to Dario as, with their nets down sifting the lightless currents of the gulf, waiting to snare octopus by their tentacles, mullet and mackerel and scorpion fish by their gills and their fins, squid by their flanges and fronds, the smack chugged back toward the Rodostamo shore.)

In the *camera obscura* of Laura's stranded mind, dark

waters trembled, shadows fell on shadows and illumined nothing. Was that a footstep on the deck overhead? No. Nothing. Was that murmuring a voice, was it a drowned sailor speaking, telling a story? No. No one. A washing . . . What was it? A splash, it might have been a fish jumping, but in the gloom she couldn't see. (Quietly Imogen sat down by her head. She leaned to look at the lined, grey face. She smiled. "Sleep, my poor old Coz," she breathed. "Sleep, sleep.")

Thus watched over as she lay by the chapel wall and slowly the crescent moon climbed the sky and her spaniels slept with their chins on their paws, Laura, borne helpless on the eddies of her dreams, was a girl in Malta before the war. By serendipity she beheld her father's destroyer flotilla anchored in the sunshiny bay. Wearing a straw hat she watched him play polo, eagerly at the end of the chukker she led away his tired pony and watched him remount. Bathing-dressed, shod with what when at rest were unwieldy planks, bunched up in the water, she called "Ready!" At the helm of the clinker-built speedboat her father accelerated, she rose up from the sparkling ripples, a wild and dripping and childish sea nymph she danced over the blue and white, the mahogany vessel drew her through the splashy rushing air and she sang and her lilting words were lost. Her lilting heart knew there lay no ocean she could not tread, crouching against the pull she swung in fast toward the wake, in the glory of her freedom she jumped into it and scythed across it and leaped clear the far side, following her father she would have trod the seas until they came to the Hesperides had he not steered toward shore and in a curve past the jetty, so reluctantly she had to realise it must be her sister's turn now. She would have followed him to the Blessed Isles, she would, she would! but flung away the rope. The boat's engine faded away, her swishing skis slowed down. In quietness by the jetty's barnacled legs and beneath her mother's approving gaze she wobbled, she sank. Here came the boat with the big inboard engine turning over slowly now, brass cleats all aglitter, her father's voice saying "Well done Laura, soon we'll have to see how you get on with only one ski."

But what are one or two happy dreams? A young man of Venice's Ionian colonies serving with the fleet at Lepanto was early in the day captured by a Turkish crew, and such was their appetite for cruelty that amidst ships cannonading and boarding parties hewing and with the fate of several countries and two religions in the balance they broke off from fighting to torture him to death. Since she had first read of this episode in a history of the campaign, Laura had been horrified by the torturers' impatience. That they had been unable to wait – had not been able to restrain themselves . . . They had tied him down, they had taken out their knives, not distressed by his screams and jerkings and not put off by the bloody mess they had inch by inch peeled off his skin. Had she been awake, Laura would never have compared the mild discomforts of an insensitive organ like the soul to the torments undergone by her husband's fellow islander at Lepanto; but asleep she was fettered, she was skinned. (Hearing her moan, Imogen again bent over her supine form, but the whimpering stopped so she let her sleep on.)

The death of Laura's body might be painful when it came, but it was her brain which was now beginning to be hurt by the preliminary cuts of a slow death. As the mind lives by the play of meanings, so it is tortured by meaninglessnesses, at the end dies of inanity. The sleeper opens the gate of the walled garden of a happy childhood, finds herself on a galley's poop. Laura had infirm enough control over her ideas when awake; now unhindered they had their way with her, with whatever valueless traces of a person may be said to exist when the body has been deprived of feeling and the consciousness of control. From dream to dream her lost soul wandered with no chance of being saved, from vagaries of charm to those of horror, into oblivion and out again, all these passages with just sufficient rhyme and reason to suggest the possibility of meaning but insufficient to substantiate it.

Her sleep had insinuations she could not confound, it convicted her of atrocious crimes of which she was innocent but left her modest ill-doings to flourish uncondemned, grow into healthy vices for angels to cower from and devils to gather round. (Seeing that her godmother lay still and breathed evenly, Imogen stood up, noiselessly she stepped away observed by one of the dogs, a Picardy spaniel much relied upon by Tasso during the winter duck shoots, which raised its head and wagged its tail but did not get up. Imogen walked to and fro in the butterfly glade, thinking.) Her sleep gave Laura everything her heart could desire, it gave her Alexis alive and her hillside never fired, it gave her a true love between Dario and Imogen, it gave her impossibly certain proof of Angelica's parentage; but it gave also the knowledge that dreams are only dreams. Her sleep gave her a labyrinth not of her goddaughter's self-knowledge but of her own, a mazy gaol in which she would twist and turn until death, not because she could not find her way out and forget the self she had alas at last discovered but because she could not want to try. She had become a hankerer after lewd festivals. She suffered a lust to worm deeper into the centre. There was a creature or an object or a practice which she desired with a thudding heart and a dry mouth. There was no cunning she would not develop so she might circle in through the tighter whorls of the vortex, no depravity ahead she would not delight in, no orgy hitherto undreamed of in a moderate and decorous life which now her old flesh shrank from.

The vernal and the macabre sat down together in obscene goodfellowship, the virginal and the syphilitic copulated and Laura knew it was loathsome but she could not prevent herself watching with pleasure. Putrefaction spoke in avuncular tones to little children; with bright eyes they jabbered back, yowling with laughter they leered back. Once she had conceived of death to the music Wagner wrote for Iseult's quietus; but now thoughts of Dionysiac debaucheries kicked her mind along in the dust as boys kick a football; the drugged and incensed revellers began to take their pleasures to murderous lengths, her brain cringed as the victims screamed. Laura's sleep gave her space as coffin-like as that of the man in the iron mask, but space in which nothing could not happen, could not take its ease. Her sleep gave her time of an elasticity incomparably beyond the variations of tempo of her waking mind. No eternity of true love could not in a trice be cast into oblivion, no excruciating foulness not be eternally protracted, and still the firefly flickering past her where she lay would not have reached the cypress. Her sleep gave her fear of death – the Angel had not been wrong – but not the ability to shut out the vision of that suffering and that void, as the Carthaginians before crucifying a man to whom they wished to pay particular attention cut off his eyelids and erected the cross to face the sun. A thousand pains might toy with her and still she lay calm in the moonlight. Knowledge of the joys of the blessed which she would never inherit might visit her and still she breathed regularly.

Laura's sleep gave her herself as she should lie in her grave when water and earth should rot her and maggots should eat her. Her sleep gave her all the world but ceaselessly at the moment of being lost, so that although in life she had had years to mourn Otto less sharply and then further years for her grief for Alexis to take its place among the endurable sorrows, now she hovered before all her inescapable losses at once. And though it appeared that her waking mind might on the threshold of the tomb have been learning to assume a Stoic indifference to the appearances of good and evil as they passed, this could not be said of her mind vulnerably asleep. That Angelica should have no father pierced her with a distress more cutting than ever before, so that stretched on her stone she struggled in the web of her dreams, wildly she flailed for the reason which it seemed she had lost forever. She gasped. Her arms and legs twitched. A dog lifted its head from its crossed paws. The mesh held her yet. And to have lost Imogen!

Laura cried out. Stiff, shaking, she sat up. Her face was rinsed with chill sweat. Her head jerked, she stared at the bell-tower, at the butterfly glade. The moon shed its peace. (Imogen had gone.)

FIVE

"I had a limb corrupted to an ulcer,
But I have cut it off: and now I'll go
Weeping to heaven on crutches."

THE WHITE DEVIL, John Webster

Dario De Corvaro could imagine a ship of death. He could imagine a ship of death and of rebirth which would recede over the night sea, would on the scarcely visible line between glittering dark and glittering dark be extinguished – but would then miraculously come sailing back. Yes, from annihilation the ship of the soul, that noble and inexistent vessel with the Flying Dutchman at her wheel and a crew of the drowned at her winches, would as day broke reappear, would be seen to be making for land. After such lostness, what landfall? What recognition, what homecoming, what joy? Dario could only vaguely conceive. But a course set toward a shore, a return – yes, that he could bring to mind, that he could convince himself with fleetingly, in the nebulous manner of his convictions. With a flush of rose on the tarnished silver of the sea, with her sails fluttering and then filling again, the ship would sail home to her landfall, home to life.

But now at night things were different. Things were not like that. Tasso brought the fishing-smack alongside, Dario jumped from the foredeck to the quay with a warp, made fast to a bollard. He walked back along the stone bulwark, from the stern Tasso flung him another line, he made that fast too. The smack settled against the tyres slung along the quay-side as fenders. The chain on which they were slung was rusty, Dario had noticed in daylight, and the roughly hewn boulders of the breastwork were beribboned with seaweed and studded with limpets, but you could not discern that now.

What about a can of beer, Tasso remarked, would Dario like one too? There was beer in the fridge in the kitchen hut. If he felt like strolling that way, they might sit for a minute under the arbour and drink the cold beer before going to bed. Dario could not think whether or not he would like a glass of beer. He could not think either what he might do if he did not go with Tasso companionably to sit and to drink and to talk – Tasso's English was as serviceable as it was rough and ready – about boats and nets and the ways of fish. He did not think that if he went to bed he would sleep. Perhaps a swim would cheer him up. Possibly an energetic swim would mean he slept for a few hours before they met again at first light and put to sea to raise their nets. Yes, that was an idea. So he told Tasso that he was not thirsty, that he was going for a swim, that certainly he would be back here at the quay at half past five, and he called goodnight as the fisherman and vegetable gardener and carpenter turned away with a cigarette in his hand, he watched him disappear along the winding path into the darkness.

But Dario did not take off his clothes, did not dive into the bay. As if his memory had been jogged by Tasso smoking, he lit a cigarette. He sat on the low wall that ran along the seaward side of Laura Rodostamo's short, stocky, dour grey quay. The sloop *Nineveh* looked pretty, he thought, riding at her anchor; but he did not think much else. After a few minutes he chucked his cigarette into the water, he stood up. Should he go for this swim he had projected? No. Too much effort. And at least, if he could not sleep, if he could not lose what dull profitless consciousness he had, he could lie on his bed in his dim hut, lie on his back, rest. He walked along the quay, came off the stone parapet onto rock and dust, took the path. It would have been more sensible to have acceded to Tasso's suggestion that cold beer would be refreshing. It would have been friendly to sit together and discuss fish. Quietness shared could be friendly too. Oh well. Beneath his shoe a stone slipped, he stumbled.

"Dario!" a voice from behind him faintly called. "Dario!" her voice from the water called.

Ah will you twist your knife in the wound, jerk the blade about in my flesh, pretend to withdraw it, jab it in harder, deeper? The muscles of Dario's heart bunched themselves before he knew it, launched upward a tidal wave of the blood of hatred that hit his mind with such a thump that his vision clouded and his ears rang. Might wretchedness not creep away alone to hide without being shouted at, must he be mocked once more?

When the suffusing wave of evil started to drain down out of his shocked greymatter, when the next heartbeat drove upward its pulse of the malign and he could feel that though malignity was still malignity the first breaking comber of hatred had been unique, Dario saw the black glass of the bay spangled with moonlight and *Nineveh*'s white hull reflected upside-down and Imogen's head which broke the flickering blackness. She kicked her legs, distantly in the silence he heard the splash. She brandished her arm. "Wait!" she called. "I'm coming. Wait, Dario."

To Laura he had promised to remain on her estate that evening, not turn tail till the next day. Grudgingly he had undertaken to stay long enough for her goddaughter to have the opportunity to talk to him if she should wish to. Gruffly, with the merest unadorned essentials of good manners, he had allowed that he would speak if he were spoken to. Speak.

Answer. What his responses to the swimmer's imaginable range of propositions and evasions might be he had not declared, nor could he formulate them now. He listened to his mind arguing stupidly that it must be after midnight. To lay nets he had taken his watch off, left it in his hut, but it must be after midnight by now, he was sure it must. So might he not by dishonest quibbling, by obeying the letter of his agreement with his hostess but abjuring the spirit, now return to his direction? For was it not already tomorrow? And had that voice not had opportunities to address him during the morning, the afternoon, the evening? How the mind scrabbled for any excuse to behave ignominiously! But .night he not get his legs in motion and then somehow keep them swinging forward and back, keep bending his knees and picking his feet up and plodding them down again and stumbling and being ignominious until he reached his hut, until he might open that wood and rush door, go in, shut it behind him, shut out that call from the sea, shut out all the world? (The old lady whose hopes must necessarily founder unless he honoured the spirit of their accord was sitting bolt upright on the bench at the butterfly chapel. So this was the hell reserved for her: consciousness. To dream disgusting things and at last wake herself with her cries and then be afraid to sleep again but even so not to be able even when exhaustedly awake to forget those obscenities. To be herself without intermission, herself out of control when asleep and in futile spasms of partial control when awake. The cold sweat on her face began to dry. She sat, her hands folded in her lap, her back straight, as she had been taught to sit. She looked before her.)

What new unkindness could Imogen have for him? Dribbling down from his poisoned brainpan the blood of hatred left Dario that question, and although successive heartbeats pumped up successive thoughts their oozing away downward did not rinse him of their accumulating bitterness. What further advantage did she with such urgency need to obtain over his inept dithering and his weakness? For such her vindictiveness and his vulnerability impressed him as being, as his body stood stock-still on the path and in his awareness his soul stood with the uprightness and the still poise and the dignity of a blindfolded man tied to a post hearing rifles being loaded. What last humiliation had her spite in its lucid creativity resolved that he should unforgettably suffer before he were permitted, thrashed dog, to drag himself away? Would it be courage to walk down to the beach and cowardice to walk on up the hillside, or the other way around?

The reward of cowardice was a little pain greatly suffered. The reward of courage was pain which, with dangers faced and first wounds endured, increased. Would it be self-betrayal to confront the woman who would wade ashore and freedom to turn his back forever on that barbed wire entanglement her love? Would it be freedom to listen to her voice and meet her eyes? an unoutlivable regret to go his way? His promise to Laura did not matter. That came to him unequivocally now. Laura Rodostamo did not matter. Her feelings had been all very fine in their fashion, but they were past, died away hardly more sonorously than those of her ghastly daughter. And her comprehensions had been so laggardly, her fumblings so interested . . . But why was he worrying about her?

Imogen swam shoreward past the sloop. She must have swum round the bluff and into view of the quay just in time to see him stand up, walk ashore. Could she see him now, halted where the track passed a prickly pear and the moon-shadow of the first olive tree fell? Did she know that although she had not brought him round, had not brought him hurrying down to the shingle, she had stopped him in his tracks? Up out of the tremulous black sheeny mirror again an arm was lifted, waved. Again she called his name. The soul blindfolded and roped to a stake made no answering gesture, gave no cry.

Dario had stood at the cypress helm of the fishing-smack and had jogged the engine into gear and then into neutral and then into gear again so they nudged forward and Tasso could pay out the nets arm's reach by arm's reach, pay them out untangled and so they would not snag on the rudder or foul the propeller, and he had brooded that Imogen had not wished to join them. He had heard his companion say quietly, "Steady," or "All right, ahead now," or "Astern a moment." He had listened to the engine idling, listened to it engage, heard water churn underfoot when the net twisted and he rammed the engine into reverse, then seen the trail of white floats go on slowly lengthening on the calm, seen the effulgence of the lighthouse, and brooded, brooded. "You take a rest tonight!" at dinner she might have cried to Tasso. She was forever blithely crying this to such and such a person and another thing to someone else – why not these words to that man? "You're always out late dropping nets and out early hauling them up. I'll give Dario a hand tonight. I know your father and you believe none of us can catch a tiddler without you, but you're wrong." Something like that.

But she had not said that. Had not said anything. Had not explained that she had been in love with him and he had broken her heart, she had conceived Angelica so as at least to carry away a soul born of that passion, at least bear through the marriageless decades to come a growing, flourishing child, a love child, a great love born of a great love, a standard to bear aloft valiantly, a freedom from lesser attachments, a dedication to a matchless memory. Nor that the conception of her daughter had been an accident and she had not liked to inform him, had seen no reason why he should be burdened with a family when he had shown not the slightest wish ever to have one. Nor that, after leaving the castle for the last time that August of tumid sentiments and over-stretched nerves and the sun itself getting to be just a daily cliché and dust blowing, she had briskly set to work soothing her yanked heartstrings with an amiable past lover or with indecent haste had taken a new one.

Imogen that morning had been irritable, but since then

... What signs had she shown that she was not ready to dilly-dally through summer week after summer week swimming from the same rocks and quay and shingle as he swam from, dining at the same round table under the same tattering arbour, observing him establish the kind of friendship with her daughter that he had with other friends' offspring? She had spoken, it seemed, with her godmother – the recollection of the old lady's keenness at dinner to communicate what she thought she had grasped was depressing – but that was perhaps natural and was certainly beside the point. Doubtless Imogen had wished to kick away the tykes snarling at her ankles and the other tykes that fawned before she raised her weapon, sighted at the condemned prisoner's chest. But of all the – all the what? – all the calculated truths? she might have whispered to him, of all the enticing duplicities or repellent facts, the curt brushings off or the seductive wiles or the dismissive quips or the feigned incomprehensions which reluctantly and with forboding all day and all evening he had waited for – nothing! She might have said that revenge was sweet or that she could not for the life of her think what he might mean by her revenge ... That her child's father's identity was a secret and anyhow was no business of his, truly the arrogant intrusiveness of the male was all it was fabled to be, oh all and more, could not be exaggerated, was of a coarseness ... (Dario could just imagine the cold brazen stare at him with which she would deliver her taut self of this tergiversation.) That a spurned lover surely had a right to privacy in which to lick her wounds ...

Imogen did not wave again, did not again call him by name. She swam strongly. In a minute, two at the most, she would be able to stand.

With forboding he had waited – yes. But with reluctance, honestly? Laura, he remembered, had had slight difficulty only in making him confess that the telephone call from Italy was a put up job, and no more in persuading him to stay till the following day. And ever since just before lunch

203

when he had stood by the fire where on the gridiron the last night's catch was sizzling, had stood in the downpouring sunlight beside the uptowering driftwoodsmoke and had asked Imogen how old her child was . . . At first obscured by the instinct for flight, there had awoken in him a readiness for adventure now becoming ebullient, a sense that it must come even if he were thoroughly vague as to what "it" would be. Ever since she had given him that slow look, answered him with those direct eyes . . . Part of him had ached for her, for an hour with her alone, for her. He had ached for this, precisely this, he now decided, watching the straight furrow she cleft through the water toward him. Swinging between dread and hatred, yes – but he had ached. Determining to defend himself, hoping that if he proudly declined to defend himself she would match him gesture for gesture, disdain for disdain, heart for heart . . . And had her voice when she called to him not been gay? He had been deaf to it and now she swam in silence – but she had called gaily, he was nearly positive she had. Tones of voice were hard enough to be accurate about immediately, one generally heard what one expected to hear or what one longed for, and as for in memory! But surely when she raised her sea-darkened head from the ripples, when she called "Wait, I'm coming!" (had he got even the words right? he *thought* he had) surely her voice had been merry? A happy voice, a voice ringing with gaiety, ringing with love . . .

He had been deaf to it. But should he forever be deaf to the voice that was for him, oblivious of the call when it came? Riding through the snowy woodland his spirit had called to hers. He remembered the white flakes falling softly through the trees and on his horse's head and on his gloveless hands, he remembered the creak of the saddle, the chink of the snaffle, the soft hoof-falls. He had ridden many miles and then in the quietness and stillness and whiteness she had been very near. Almost she had appeared to him – her face, her form, her very life! Snow had brushed his face – a brush of the wing of madness? and was the taloned bird of madness hawking very close to him again now? He had half known Imogen, half loved her. In the snowy wood nearly he had refound her. Her eyes opening, her lips beginning to smile. Then riding in the thaw he had called to her and the voice of the Other had commented that his beloved had answered the call of his heart, but where he was she had found no one. He was absent even from himself. He was an echo-chamber where no echo sounded, he was dead air.

Should he never reverberate again? Already Dario was convincing himself that his long silence was broken, in him a voice was echoing. The man who had imagined his soul blindfolded and lashed to a post for execution now discovered that he could see where he wanted to go and could walk there freely. Come what might, he would go down. He was so near! Twenty strides and he would be on the beach. Twenty strokes and she would be in her depth. Let his mind resound once more – as for what music came pulsing he would take his chance. Never to quiver again to any enchantment, that was death. Let the echo-chamber thrum to airs sweet or airs bitter or airs deceptively sweet, but let it thrum. (That Imogen Scottow was capable of mere discordant unkindness he had forgotten.)

"You are right that her call to you was gay," Dario's dead father's voice said. "But remember, she is an actress. And for heaven's sake remember not to believe every word she says. Still," Eduardo De Corvaro concluded meditatively, dryly, "we may find that her indifference to good and evil marries with yours very well. Has it occurred to you, my dear lad, I wonder, that in your present apparent readiness for any experience whatever so long as it is intense you are skating on dazzling but perhaps treacherous ice?"

Dario's feet crunched on the small stones that sloped down to the lapping sea. He trod on something that did not crunch. Ah, a towel. And beside it, clothes. Another step. Another. He stood still. Imogen was swimming more slowly now. Gingerly in the shallows she found her footing. Slightly unsteadily because her bare feet were on stones she could not see, she stood up. At least, Dario thought, there is no phosphorescence. Moonlight on her wet head and on her wet body is bad enough, phosphorescence streaming off those shoulders and those breasts would have been the limit. Naked, she walked toward him. The water was up to her thighs, then up to her shins. "I don't *think* there are any sea urchins here," she said.

Now here she stood, white, glittering, before him. Her eyes were smiling. Her lips parted. "I thought you might want me," she said. "And I certainly wanted you. So – here I am."

Anna stalked me, she flung her net. Smiling, I stepped toward her, the net fell harmlessly behind me. I was her friend, I smiled. The wretched woman was delighted to consider herself admitted to my confidence. To her commonness, any involvement with the affairs of my heart was welcome. Did she believe my story about Venice I wonder? She thought she was trapping me, forcing me to choose between telling a lie and telling a discreditable truth. If she sensed how I put her aside she was not offended, such is the paucity of her pride. Looking through the auriole of the lantern on the rock, I saw Laura's defeat staining her eyes like blood, like red capillaries snaking all over the whites. I chattered to Anna about the Lido, about which clothes shops and restaurants in Venice we patronised, about the Biennale, about an ivory bracelet. Pleased with chitter which circled around sexual love and childbearing, she gushed, she cooed. "How that brute Dario must have made you suffer, my poor darling!" she cried. And then "Ah, Venice!" and "Ah, but my love, how romantic!" and "Ah, our little angel!" Laura had crept away to deal with her grief alone. I let Anna have her little angel's cot in her hut tonight. I might want to talk to Dario, I said mysteriously. She was willing, she was as conspiratorial as a schoolgirl. Several times she declared that she quite understood.

It was not difficult to guess where Laura would have retreated. You must not perpetually burrow into me as if you were a maggot and I were a dead dog, I should have remonstrated with her – or perhaps I might have found a less lucid way of drawing her attention to her parasitism, indicating that I am not sustenance nor all love consumption. Is it not a higher love to renounce, does not the generous heart give freedom and the noble heart take it? Mercifully, when I came to the butterfly chapel she was asleep. So still she lay on the stone in the moonlight that knowing her weakness, knowing her day's gallantly volunteered-for tribulations and its breathless exaltations, for a moment I thought she might be dead. Mercifully asleep? Well, I did not particularly wish to have to dedicate half an hour to explaining that she ought to know me shrewdly enough by now not to be so appalled that I should, when the object of an unprovoked attack, secure my integrity, my independence. Not the Italian attack on Greece in 1940 that Achilles is forever remembering was a more wanton aggression than Anna's assault on me – nor their invasion of the Horn of Africa either. And if beside the lantern on the rock she had realised that she could not be certain whether what I had told her about Dario being Angelica's father were true . . . should she not have brought that to mind before?

Did I for a moment half hope that she were dead – more than half hope that she had died there by the chapel wall? Only for an instant. I would not have had her go away from me to her burial without telling her not to be such a silly old fool, *of course* she could not dog me through all the twists and turns of this adventure, today's scaling of peaks and plumbing of depths were singularly unsuitable for her comradeship, but *of course* I loved her as excessively as ever, how should I not? Indeed I must not forget to bring her this comfort tomorrow, Lord knows what grotesque emphases she may not have been thudding down here and there.

But then – one mild lit night to die in her butterfly glade . . . Better than being worn down in a hospital, being fiddled with till your heart is no longer in it and gives up. And sometimes when she is trying to focus on the preparations for Anna's wedding, when she is attempting to be systematic, worrying how she can be lavish without being extravagant, she looks so drained that you would be dimwitted not to guess she would uncomplainingly die before the day. What joy will it bring her? A son-in-law who, she suspects, will one day in her olive groves build villas. A joy to hang around for? She sees the way the tide is setting in the Mediterranean, why should she wait to weep over the devastation it wreaks on her little patch of Arcadia? And if Anna presents her with a grandchild I find it hard to believe she will be overjoyed. I too when I am that weary, that sad . . . Give me a chapel on a hillside where only goatherds go. A summer night. A bench of stone.

I strolled in the butterfly glade. The presentness of things which I have felt all day I still feel tonight. The short crooked white-washed belltower, the dappled moonlight in the olive grove, the woman lying by the chapel wall with her dogs asleep, the cypress standing guard – these impressions were incised into my consciousness as the acid sears an etcher's lines into his plate. I walked down to the encampment, took a towel from my hut, came here to this bay. You were out fishing I knew, but I wished to see you when you returned. So much I had resolved – ah not for the first time today! – walking among the moths. For though they come at me with nets, shall I be afraid? Am I not lithe at side-stepping? And when nets have enveloped me, have I not cut myself free? The net which I denominate Wiltshire, or, if you prefer, English society, has never encompassed me; always I have swum to and fro through the mesh. Hooks also I have learned to beware of; even the most succulently baited barbs I avoid, whatever my hunger. Once I saw a moray eel which with a hook bitten deep into its gullet had writhed and fought in the black cold depths in agony alone till by increasing its torture it had driven itself mad with pain, till it had wound the line round and round its throat and in tortured madness had gone on threshing till the knots tightened so that when we heaved it up the fighter had nearly finished cutting off its own head. One learns. As for the net of the past which this morning by the kitchen hut was flung to ensnare me – all day have I not with a sharp blade been hacking at the cords, do I not now stand upright? Time no longer bodes terror for me. All day as well as the presentness of all things to me – as well as, or are they parts of one phenomenon? – my mind has had a supple directness, my blade a cutting edge I have been wielding with verve so that now – no, I do not think there are possibilities I am afraid of. The past I was, the I who confounded me in the morning sun, she who was too innocently duplicitous, she who made the mistake of playing a game she could not play alone, she who left herself vulnerable to ambush, she who could not think of anything more inspired to do with the cornucopia of time than drag it after her like a rickshaw where the ensconced god of exploitation bumpily rides and miscomprehendingly surveys – did I not with Alexis Rodostamo's fascist-slaughtering revolver this afternoon shoot her? And did I not then, cleansing myself in the sea, wash off her grave-clothes, her cerements I had worn too long?

On the shingle I undressed. From the scrub, crickets were churring, then as now. I needed to have no fear of you. Had not this morning the past been thrown to entangle you too? The only difference between us was that I was my own snare, I was hunter and prey. You were not your own snare; I was. And, I reasoned, you were not by nature a spinner of webs, a contriver of man-traps and gins. You would cast nothing at me. You would stand still with your hands at your sides. And see – I was not wrong. It is thus that you stand before me now. You too all day have been angrily hacking at the cords binding you, you have struggled to get your feet under you, your back straight once more and your head up. And you have helped me. You helped me while I swam this afternoon to lift the cornucopia of time to my lips. I wanted to tell you this; I wanted to say thank you.

For the third time today I swam, for the second time I let my mind imagine that you were swimming beside me, that we were swimming stroke for stroke. When before my salt-splashed eyes my hand broke the surface and my Egyptian ring gleamed, I imagined your hand rising from the sea in time with my hand, your father's ring catching pale fire in the same moonlight as Alexis'. It had made you speculate, you once recounted to me, the way before your father set off for the South China Sea that last time he took the family ring off his left hand and gave it to you. And you once remarked to me that my cornelian scarab was beautiful and I replied, "Yes, I'm fond of it, my godmother's husband left it to me." That was how close we came to knowing we had Laura in common. Never would you have come here this summer if you had suspected I might be here, never! No, what happens to us cannot mean much, with chance playing all the crucial moves.

I swam down the shore, happy to be going nowhere. My nakedness in the sea pleased me, I felt smoothed. For the second time I hoped that your spirit and mine might fall into step, might dance in time. At least tonight! I prayed. Give us one night! Let us fall into step with freedom, you and I, and journey a little way. We can always turn off in divergent directions later. What, in a night, do we risk? The high summer nights are so short! I saw the masthead light of the smack approaching. I turned, I started to swim back toward the anchorage. I swam easily. If when I reached land you had gone I should have looked for you, I should have found you beneath the arbour or in your hut. The boat passed fifty or a hundred yards from me, I saw Tasso and you on board, I heard the beat of the engine, felt the wash. You did not notice me.

My hour was just after sunset: ripples that lapped, swifts that skirled, pistol shots, a whingeing dog. But shall not tonight be ours? In myself I have raised a light, I am fit for you now. Our time has come, I called voicelessly as the throb of your diesel died away, and now I stand before you on Laura's beach, I dab myself dry with my towel and I say it aloud, softly but aloud, I try to speak with exactness about these dissolving and reforming feelings.

"Time is freedom to me now," I tell you, "as perhaps in your more harmonious mind it has always been – and this is your gift to me whether you intended such munificence or not, this I owe to your forbearance, to your dignity, to you. All time washes to us here, it laps around us, it laps in and out of our minds. You've forborne with me all day. Minute by minute I waited for you to revile me. I knew how vulnerable I was. I hated that. I saw how you held off. You gave me time, you gave me peace and freedom. It doesn't dismay you, does it, that I've come to you now? At least up there on the path you stopped, you turned back. Oh come on, is it so dreadful to have a naked woman walk out of the sea and stand in front of you? Look, we've got moonlight, we've got starlight, we've got the lighthouse – what more do you want? We've got bats. Sheep-bells too. Listen. Hear them? A long way off."

It is the night of power, I reflect, but not in your reckoning. You stand still. I stand still. We have stood here for – what? five minutes, maybe ten. I have talked. I have given you my reckoning of this, my reckoning of that. You have not touched me. That is not important. When I decide that you shall touch me I think that you will. You listen. When I decide that you shall speak I think that you will. It may even be that I can predict a little what you will say, I may even triflingly ordain what you will say. We shall see. We shall hear. We shall find our ways of being free –

for that, in my reckoning, is the essence of power, is what it means. So you see you do not need to be afraid. I wrap my towel around me, I sit on a rock, I pat the rock beside me. You sit down. You put your hands on your knees; then, settling to our meditations, your elbows.

"I've got no wish to triumph over you," I say. I speak in Italian, as we used to do. All day you have been speaking English. Will Italian be an ease to you, a liberty? "I want to triumph beside you," I say, "and to see you triumph beside me."

At last you speak. "Nothing to do with forbearance or dignity," you mutter. "Just a case of not being able to think of anything to think."

Now, she must convince him. Now. "From the chance of our meeting here this morning can't we evolve destinies as fixed as stars' tracks?" This she suggested; but at once was afraid she had sounded too martial for so diffident a listener. Yet valour was what she longed to instil in him. Yes, but in pacific murmurings only! So gently and with assumed hesitancies she resumed.

"From the day's weaknesses can't we draw strength? Nothing that smacks of self-defence. A greater weakness yet. A vulnerability we each accept for ourselves and leave unwounded in the other. Come, Dario, the daring for an absolute surrender! You don't know whether I'm disposed to overlook your banishment of me two years ago. I don't know whether you're disposed to overlook Angelica. Yes, I think overlook is the right word. Or, perhaps, make light of . . . ?

"I don't know if you've cut yourself free, stood upright, but I imagine you have. Didn't you try to go away, leave me to my course? Haven't you since then in admirably acted indifference come and gone about the estate, been – what are the words? – civil? patient? tolerant? Aren't you even capable of not loving Angelica?" The man who at sea an hour before had wondered the precise opposite straightened his back; he cocked one eyebrow. "Capable, I mean, of not loving her after the standard fashion of father and daughter. There are the conventional loves we all know dispiritingly much about – but aren't there also the far greater number of affections which have escaped labelling? The note we strike has got to be all ours, all new, it's got to be unique, it must be. It's going to have to be . . . I don't know . . . One of the wonders of the invisible world."

Overlook . . . Should she tell Dario what she had already made light of, made nothing of? He would have guessed this, her little surprise would be all spoiled, but never mind. She wanted to tell him; she wanted to confront him with her good faith, so he should trust her. "I would have married you." Ah, not by so much as a flicker in his eyes did he courteously pretend he didn't know! "If you'd asked me . . . Can you imagine how I tried to suppress this longing, to pretend to myself I never had this idea? And at the same time I was summoning the courage to ask you to marry me. I would have asked you, too. The effrontery had been building up in me. When you told me it was all over I'd almost mustered the necessary masochism. For naturally I knew you'd say no. But – is this going to make you smile? – there was something in me that wanted to be refused, wanted to be humiliated, wanted self-pity more profoundly than anything else. Of course I was horrified by these cravings. But then at the same time I didn't find them all that surprising by any means – I found these tastes had a piquancy . . ."

All this she was ready to overlook, she told him. It was simply a question of raising one's gaze, of looking beyond. The sweat on their bodies when on sultry nights they had made love, the things she had done to him to bewitch him, the things she had invited him to do to her. The days he had

213

spent reading or writing, when he answered her remarks in monosyllables or not at all. In early summer, scholarship had not been such a passion; but after the solstice, yes. The days so chokingly sybaritic, the hours so elaborately sexual, that she had felt bound wrist and ankle in the carnal. She had known that for him she was only carnal. She had known that for herself she was only carnal and she had wanted to scream, she had wanted to run away but hadn't had the guts – where the hell had her freedom been then? Well, she had consigned those days to nonexistence.

"One afternoon – you're not to make believe you've forgotten – I drove half the length of Italy to be with you. I wanted to walk by the trout stream with my hand in yours. I wanted the golden freshness of the evening, wanted to watch the midges dance. I thought that maybe by one of the sluice-gates it might be mirrory enough, or by one of the waterfalls it might be splashily musical enough for us to know that . . . Well, I expect you guessed at the time what nonsense I wanted you to know. Because what did you do? Now I can laugh about it, but I didn't then. You decided you had to pass half the evening with your mother, on the subject of your dislike of whom you'd more than once been fulsome, whom for years you'd neglected as stalwartly as I'd neglected mine. If now I bundle that evening off-stage you must allow that I'm of a generosity . . . !

"Overlook . . . Look further . . . What do you see that takes your fancy? What shall we become, who shall we be? This is freedom! I can be anything under the sun, I'm sure I can. Anything! The rigging that's tapping against that mast. I want you to be it with me."

There was no God – apart from maritime pines against a canopy of stars and a white sloop reflected in a black bay, apart from the cry of a gull and a breath of thyme, apart from a flying fish winging away and the gladness in her heart. It wasn't always going to be comfortable or comforting, what they had in common, he and she. Because it was terrible as well as blessed how time had its way with them, called into being in them whatever it pleased, sooner or later satisfied all desires, holy, unholy.

"Can't freedom as absolute as ours disclose itself an absolute innocence? When I lifted my glimmer to gaze into your mind you were dark. But if tonight I do it again will you be light?"

Imogen fell quiet. The lighthouse on the reef opened his mind, it was an incandescence. And here was an owl. How silently he hunted! It was the frog in the swamp he was after, it was that year's hatchling sparrow on the arbutus twig, it was the mouse on the pale dust of the path. She was – she herself would be – what? Oh, let her be the tortoise they could hear pushing his cumbersome progress through the sere khaki stalks of the grass. Dario must be him too, please. She was Stephen in Paris who was dying, she was Angelica whom for the moment they'd agreed to overlook, she was Laura who she hoped died not later in hospital but in her own house soon. There another flying fish took wing – wasn't their flight vibrant, their evanescence silverly lit? The moon was past its zenith. This was the hour when they had been released by one day, not yet embroiled by the next. Dew glistened on rocks, on decks. It was their night, they had shed everything. His self-knowledge and his self-hatred and her self-love – where were they now? The warp between the bollard and the gunwale hung slack. Ripples lapped. Who should they be?

Dario was bitter, he'd take a lot of moving – had she been passionate enough? On the other hand, he had come to distrust her, too much eloquence would leave him colder than before. She let a few seconds tick away. He didn't say anything. He appeared to be looking out to sea. If only he'd meet her eyes! She took a slow breath. Another. A third. She'd try once more, a last time.

"Can I tell you a story?" she asked. "Then I'll have done. But right now with my towel around my waist I'm going to sit cross-legged like Scheherazade and tell you a story.

"There's a pilgrim, a walker of the seas, from whom

215

I've learned. As there isn't a holy land so there isn't a holy sea, all the oceans of the planet are his to journey over. From Archangel to Rio he walks, from Port Moresby to Valparaiso. All gulfs are his and all straits, all channels and bays, all isthmuses and sounds. Just like at sunrise and sunset the Beduin unrolls his prayer-mat on the desert sand – well anyhow, that's what happened in the books I read as a girl – so my pilgrim spreads his mat on the sea, he kneels down. When I was at prep school I thought prayer meant words you addressed to God. Then at public school – you know the funny schools we have in England – I became sophisticated, I worked out that prayer was attention, it was waiting in silence for an unspoken Word. Then for a few years I thought the whole notion was too inane to bother about. But now . . . It seems to me that prayer is power.

"You must wait with me till daybreak, you must imagine with me please. You'll see. The pilgrim will unsling the bundled mat from his shoulder. He'll lay out his colours on the sea. Just a childish myth of mine for heaven's sake, you're not going to be superior about it are you? He'll kneel down. Yes, the moral is all about power. How he prays the sun up from below the horizon, how he wheels it across the sky all day, how he prays it down onto his head at dusk. Of course, the power, the energy, aren't his. But by honouring them he partakes of them. The swinging of solar systems is nothing to a man of his intellect. The daily and nightly creation of an old world renewed are nothing to a man of his soul. Here's the sweetness of the love between man and the world, between mind and sun. You must watch with me. I asked, who shall we be? Well . . . Wanderers of the sea? Will you pray with me?"

Come again, early summer, give me May again, thought

Dario with the winning illogicality of the blessed, of those so newly and overcomingly blessed that they have not yet taken their bearings in the aureate rain from heaven, have not yet in the dazzle begun to calculate moralities or to pontificate, are still innocent. Give me the hillside broom putting forth its yellow flower, give me poppies in the hay field, May birdsong all day, he thought. The air after rain – verdant, aromatic, rinsed. Sunshine after rain, a cuckoo calling. In the grass, lady's smock, orchids, vetch. Cuckoo spit clinging in whitish gobs to a grass stalk, cuckoo spit on my shoes. Acacia groves in filmy white flower where again we will ride our horses. At the ford, the brook swirling round fetlocks. Lean from your saddle again, I will kiss you. At night, frogs, nightingales, bats.

Imogen, it appeared, was content to let him take his time. To tell her story she had indeed sat cross-legged like Scheherazade. Now she raised her knees, folded her arms across them, laid her chin on her arms. Dario walked along the sea's edge, came to the boulders at the end of the beach, walked back. Imogen sat motionless, her head lowered. From the shadows beneath her eyebrows was she observing him? Sometimes, perhaps, and sometimes not. A generous patience seemed incarnate in her slight bowed frame. Sometimes, no doubt, her mind dwelt on him, and sometimes not. When he had finished thinking about May she would be there. He turned – the beach was not long – and trod back along the margin of the sea. After his work with the nets, the water had dried on his hands; he could feel the lingering brineyness. The sea air against his face was briney too; and soft; and warm. Moonlight marbled Imogen's slender white shoulders, ran in rivulets down her sleeked hair.

Dario had, as it chanced, been born in May. In May two years ago he had fallen in love with Imogen, in May with its thrushes nesting in the ivy tumps and its puffs of wind scurrying across the fields of thistled and poppied hay. So now, incapable of thinking of anything but happiness, it was

May the world presented to him on a ruby-encrusted gold salver, it was May he would present to Imogen. They would eat strawberries!

So with bright splashes of sunny colours he began to fathom his transfiguration, amid candled chestnut trees and festoons of wistaria flower he began to see summer after summer. His brain infused with scents of elder-flower and acacia so that rationality was hardly to be looked for, he began to take the measure of – of what? Well, to start with, of Imogen's generosity. At sea an hour before had it not seemed to him that he had never lived? And had she not just now offered him the same vertiginous sensation but as liberation not as dread? To his despondency it had been plain that even those few moments of his experience so intense that surely at least then he had been alive were whipped from him into a limbo where not only he suffered their irremediable loss but with it the ever strengthening doubt that they had ever been his, that he had ever been. The future was one haze of the unknowable and the past was another, but compared to the silent emptiness of the present they were of a solidity and a certainty . . . ! Compared to the split second when nerve quivered to mind they were an assured glory, an inalienable right. All of which Imogen Scottow was mistress of, all of which she turned to good account. Yes, of time she was mistress. This, the good, she delighted in; that, the bad, she ordained should do no more harm. So inexistence was the richest blessing in her gift. The bad days were not, she declared – and she was right, they ceased to be, he would be haunted by them no more. To be charmed by the charming, to shrug off the unpleasant – how obvious! what admirable common sense! Next May too in the hills of Umbria poppies would speckle the hay with their brave red, clouds' shadows would blow across the woodland, the stubs of the pruned vines would sprout green. White fluff would blow off the poplars. On the walls of his stable the roses would bloom. In the orchard the bees would drink deep. Dog-roses would fence the lanes.

Blackbird and thrush and finch would nest, would sing all day. Crossing the brook, Imogen and he would rein in their horses, she would lean from her saddle, he would draw her head toward his. Arrived back at the castle, he would pour two glasses of wine. Trout they would eat, and strawberries. It was as simple as that.

Had Imogen not whispered to him that a freedom as absolute as theirs might disclose itself an absolute innocence? thought Dario, walking in a daze with quick steps and then with hesitations and halts and then again with brisk lighthearted strides along the shingle shore in his salt-stained tennis shoes and his salt-spattered shorts and shirt. At the rocks he turned. Back he paced. His father had died and he had known himself haunted. He had lost Imogen and been haunted. But to look back with gratitude for the good and with forgiveness of the bad, to be shadowed no more . . . ! To look forward without instant instinctive dejection . . . ! Forgiveness? It seemed that, after scorning this generally popular notion for years, Imogen and he were coming to understand it the very same night. They would free themselves from the miscomprehensions and unkindnesses of the past. They would wake up to a new innocence, or to an innocence which had always been there, was as old as the human capacity not to give up, old as the readiness to try again, but to them tonight was new. Was not this what Laura so doggedly dreamed, so fervently desired? Dario's mind was of a sudden suffused with love for the lady who, though he did not know this, had beside his father at an Avignon café table sipped her Pernod and smoked an oval Turkish cigarette in an amber holder. (At the butterfly chapel, she sat with her back straight, her eyes open. Phantasm-stricken, image-ridden, she gazed before her. Imogen will leave, she was thinking. Winter will come. Rain. Short days. Long solitude.)

All afternoon and all evening Laura Rodostamo had striven in the cause of forgiveness – how had he allowed himself to treat with such cool scepticism, with nothing more gallant than courtesy, so indefatigable a battler, such generosity? For yes, she had even possibly a more magnificent flair for giving than her goddaughter, set a standard even more to be honoured and lived up to because wholly unselfish. What had Laura stood to gain by her fatigues? For Angelica alone she had worn herself out – for the child whom Dario now found it as blissfully straightforward to overlook as her mother, inviting him to dedicate his scannings to farther horizons, could have wished for. How had he let such compassion be displayed before his eyes and remained – not exactly unmoved, but – but been, in his responses, perhaps niggardly? Of practically everything under the sun he had spoken to his hostess during their afternoon colloquy, he reflected, except what she must most keenly have longed to have illuminated: his feelings about Angelica; his progress in self-knowledge since at the corner of the kitchen hut he had come face to face with his daemon. Possibly there had for some hours not been any very remarkable progress to report – certainly his hateful inveighings were unworthy of rehearsal – but now!

Tomorrow morning the situation could be, must be, put right. He would make haste to pay tribute to the old lady's great heart. And after that there would be time – with that overdue acknowledgement of how mean of spirit he had been decently performed – there would be time for him to tell her how much he had, at last, learned from her, give her some idea, he hoped, of the depth of his thankfulness. There would be time . . . The luxury of it! Days . . . Nights . . . It was not an achievement to be cursorily said thank you for, the turning of a man toward happiness. No small gift, a self one might with a free heart be, be in peace. And that small grey woman had in a day performed all this! Had got hold of him just in time, had with intelligence and love set about turning him around, had prepared him for this hour. And it seemed that for her goddaughter she had wrought a similar miracle. The Imogen of tonight was of a magnanimity and a clairvoyance which the seductress and would-be captor of two years before had showed scant evidence of even having erected among her ambitions. Well, there would be time to acknowledge and time to thank, that was the great thing. Time . . . For he would not, now, depart in the morning as he had intended to.

Back in the spring, Laura Rodostamo's letter inviting Dario De Corvaro to her Ionian estate had mentioned "three weeks, four – the longer you can stay, the better pleased we shall be." And she had added that if he felt that a month was too indulgent an absence from his desk he was to bring with him a second suitcase full of books and papers. Her library, should he wish to work, would be his for as long as his visit could be protracted. Then after lunch when over the curled and now quiescent black scorpion of the telephone they had confronted each other, when it had been elicited that his mother was no iller than usual and his summons home was a fake – these were still the day's only indubitable revealed facts – Laura had entreated him not to flee so precipitously and he had granted her a day, that meagre reprieve, that stay of sentence so she might labour to foster appeals and engender clemencies. But now, with Imogen bowed on the shingle in patience, now that it awaited him to pick her plenitude up, awaited him too to equal it – should not the summer be resumed as it had innocently, casually, affectionately been planned? (That Laura's intention that Imogen's visit and his should coincide had not been totally innocent Dario had not suspected.) Naturally it should. Imogen and he would have their homage to pay to Laura. The university would not require his presence till late September; his hostess would he was sure be delighted if he remained all summer. It would be the most richly harvested season of his life. No, wrong, too definite. But it might be . . .

If he were to harvest, he too must be harvested, and in equal measure. He must grow, he must crop abundantly. What had he ever grown? What ever given? Laura was right – the imagination in that whitened head, the wisdom in that scored countenance! – he had lain always in a darkened room. A pagan spirit in a mausoleum, he had in the blackness grappled other spirits to him and had had his way with them and when wearied by them had pushed them aside; he had cast off, among others, one spirit of rare temper. He had been a darkened room. Well, that was at an end now. Lights! Might not Eros learn to behave more magnanimously? Psyche had lit her candle, had raised it to look at him. The wax, happily, had dripped. His eyes were open. They saw. And what they saw delighted them. How should that graceful shedder of brilliance not be irresistible? Her wish to behold her love was complimentary enough. And why should the undressy charm of the visionary not be gloried in, her poised sensuality not be enjoyed, the fetching not fetch? Let the candle be held aloft. Let other candles be lit, candelabra be set ablaze. Chandeliers he wanted, Bohemian chandeliers, Venetian chandeliers, let the chambers of the castle be bright. From now on he would do his loving in the light.

What had he ever given? Fortunately self-hatred had at long last served him well, there was no longer any call to imitate the penitent who strips off his shirt, kneels, takes up a knotted scourge, flogs himself before that looking-glass the Church. Instead, the question was: What should he give now? What plenitude might he cast before his daemon that should balance hers, marry with hers? (At that moment, Laura Rodostamo turned her stiff neck, stared toward the east. Dying will hurt, she had been thinking. And to go through that squalor and pain and tedium in order to be extinguished utterly . . . The futility of it was awe-inspiring. After all the thinking and the feeling – nothing, eternally. She was not Darwin, not Einstein. Very soon it would be as if she had never lived. And now, straining her eyes into the starry vacancies, she thought: The light! How long still, two hours, three? And again, between a prayer and a moan, desperately she wondered: And the light?)

Never another winter with the silence of death in his skull

222

would he night after night tramp the stony hill town where he had been born. When they were in Italy, Imogen and he might after a fall of snow stroll forth to see how the willows held their newly bridal arms to the night frost, how blackly the stream tumbled between its snowy banks – but here there should be nothing of isolation and no brushing wing of madness, the echo-chamber would hum with lively airs. Yes, little things like the willows under snow he would give her. And his life would be a steady training in how to grow through giving little things to giving great. A few miles upstream there was a waterfall where, he now recalled, he had never taken her. When the warm weather came next May that could be rectified. Sweet to leave the car and walk arm in arm to where the path came through a stand of beech and hazel and then slanted down to where poplar and willow grew and you heard the water fall. Sweet on the rocks by the roofless mill to undress, to be splashed by the chill cascade as you scrambled to the place – he had done it since he was a boy – where it was safe to dive. Together they would swim into the overgrown mill-race which no longer raced but eddied indolently, was patchworked with sunlight and shade, was the domain of dragonflies and daddy-long-legs and water-boatmen. Then more boisterously they would swim the narrow colonnade made where the crashing water fell from an overhang and left a cool vault lit greenly and splattered coldly; you swam between the rock-face and the débâcle and you emerged to the pool suddenly quietened and to flowings almost still, to light golden and willows shimmering and maybe a newt on a lily leaf. But, now – the greater things that he would give? The great thing?

I have just decided something, Dario addressed his father. I banished her. I shall ask forgiveness. Are you surprised? You cannot, having listened to her, be completely astonished, I think. Or is it perhaps that I am so transformed which seems scarcely credible to you? I assure you the alteration is genuine.

So much have I tried not to want, so much have I tried to believe I did not regret. But, Father . . . All I have denied has not ceased to be, all I have turned my back on has still called to me, tonight calls piercingly, I cannot not harken. In my melancholy for years I considered that certain joys were for others. But now . . .

Hearing, shall I not answer call for call, receiving not give? or at last try to give, at least offer myself, be vulnerable? I know your marriage so bored you that you, who detested the clergy, would urge priests, friars, monks and more than once bishops to visit the castle so that my mother should be occupied, for an hour leave you alone. But perhaps I may be more fortunate. I do not desire to desire these things, believe me, Father. But see, she has stood up. With her towel kilted about her waist, with her head slightly bowed, she is gently stirring the ripples with one foot. Has she not declared that our hearts are beating in time with one another, our thoughts dancing in step? As for her invitation to overlook Angelica, now I see its force. I have looked up, looked over, looked beyond. On my horizon now it is the child whom I make out, I cannot perceive blurredly, cannot mistake what I am before. Why all day was I so tormented? With generosity in my heart, with the same freedom to be what we choose to be pulsing an invincible music in Imogen's head and in mine, the case is all simplicity. Her past actions and her present feelings about them are her concern alone. I have never been invasive, never made demands; I never shall. If she offers me Angelica's fatherhood, I shall accept. If she prefers not to, I shall love the child as a friend – as an uncle, say, or a godfather, or a stepfather.

Look, Father, the white sloop hangs over her white image in the black bay. In the shallows, Imogen wades. The crescent moon begins to descend toward the west. I do not desire to desire these things, but I desire them. Now I shall give. Well, try to. Give not less than everything. From the shadowy shore a grey gull flies. At the end of

the beach for the last time I turn, I walk toward Imogen.
I have a sense of recognition. It is as if the ship of death
had indeed from obliteration sailed back, a ship of rebirth.
This shall be my return to myself, here she waits for me. A
fish jumps. A bat whirls.

Dario approached Imogen along the shore, he stood
before her. She raised her eyes to his. He asked, "Imogen
. . . Will you marry me?"

Scarcely she hesitated. "No . . . Ah, I'm sorry, Dario, but
– no." And then, wryly, "What I'd like to do is make love
with you."

It was only after several minutes that Dario De Corvaro
realised that his ghostly father, when invoked, had not
replied. And if the Other was solely a concoction of
his hankering wits, of an intellect without the fortitude
to stand alone which therefore came up with an alter
ego, he, of enfeebled mental productiveness, downright
brain-sick he shouldn't be surprised, had been unable to
echo back a single word, had not even listened. Yes, that
was it. He who fancied himself a listener to occult musics
had disrupted the world's attentiveness with his blathering,
but had not listened at all.

As for unhappiness, its immediate presence to him was
as gratification. Loss took the form of possession. There
was, it was true, briefly the preliminary conviction that
he did not wish to make love, a conviction doubly backed
up by the certainties that he would never wish to make
love again as long as he lived and that at that moment,
if he were by sophistry to make himself believe he wished
to, he would be unable to. But then, with unappealing
inevitability, there arrived the realisation that he could
make love, was degradingly capable, he wanted to, with

equally unappealing masterfulness he wanted her, was degradingly passionate.

Imogen feline, Imogen provocative. Imogen who did not appear to find anything unappealing about him. Imogen whose attentions and desires were flattering, Imogen silky, Imogen a succubus who would have her way with him, who set about taking her pleasure with frankness and whose generosity toward him now assumed the guise of care that he should take his. A slope of small stones which were hard but not unattractively so. Shallows that were warm, that lapped. Imogen who in the ripples was smooth and slithery, whose face on the stones in the moonlight was a bacchante's mask of mindless abandonment to lust and its satisfaction. Imogen whose delight in the flesh was ravishing and of a good humour which even at the time struck him as, given the circumstances of her having a few minutes before refused to marry him, a flagrant contempt which consorted somehow not ungracefully with a proud assumption that for people of their spirit such trifles could only be made nothing of. Shingle that slipped, the moon-shadow of a gull crossing. Water. Skin. Stone. The sea washing, the sea all about them. Gulls' cries. Cries.

Dario pulled on his clothes. He sat on the shore with his forearms slacked over his knees. Of course loss had first been possession only in order that it should be made not merely sad but loathsome as well. Whether his stupidity or Imogen's cruelty were most to blame he neither knew nor cared. Ah why when from the sea she had called to him had he not turned his back on her forever, pursued a solitary way which now impressed him not as pusillanimous but as resolute. The act of love had been made horrible to him, delight would only ever be satiety. Naturally he would feel sexual cravings in the future and naturally – who was more weak-minded? – he would indulge them; but not without remembering tonight, not without self-revulsion. He had known her ruthlessness, why had he allowed himself to forget it? Recriminations jabbered in his head. Useless to utter them. He must make an end. This was the end. How often had he thought that?

Never would he forget that mask of lust lying on the beach in the silver light. But had he not also thought that there were generosity and frankness and good humour in her love-making? No, no, there couldn't have been, he must have been wrong. Wishful thinking yet again. As for all that bullshit of hers about a pilgrim who walked the seas, about prayer as power, he understood it now. The love of power – that was characteristic of Imogen all right. No wonder there was a religious streak in her, she had the vice of worshipping power rooted deep in her soul's manure, and the old religious trick of adoring power dressed up as weakness too, of inventing an omnipotent humility to prostrate yourself before, these hypocrisies were comfortably within the range of her admirable intelligence. Well, he had understood. An education, this love affair, as well as a travesty. He must stand up. He must walk away.

As for all that twaddle about forgiveness which he had elaborated, it made him ashamed. And to make believe that the trick was to be charmed by the charming and to shrug off the unpleasant, to dream that time could be controlled like that, controlled at all – had he been drunk? Time ran – that was all one knew, all one needed to know, all it was possible to know. And as for dreaming that he might be transformed, that one could leave the past behind . . . ! The past appeared in the morning sun at the corner of a hut; it stood in the dust and smiled; it was death herself; it was that principle, that ineluctable decay in that prison, that smile. So much for wanting to hasten to Laura so he could thank her for leading him to his hour of transfiguration. He would go back to Umbria alone. He would try to stop the bad habit of summoning up his father's image and telling it lies. Or perhaps he would find he was unable to summon it, no beloved voice echoed.

Dario stood up. Imogen was on her feet, had been standing quiet and still, apparently contemplating the fishing-smack. He met her eyes. The day she had left the castle for the last time, he had seen those eyes in tears, their blues glistening. For two years he had longed to find those eyes again, dwell on them, never lose them again. Well, here they were, he was gazing into them. They were not wet, but steady, serene, alight with love. No, they couldn't be, he must be mad.

"I'm at an end," he said. "Goodbye."

Well, Imogen thought, that cleared the air a bit. Passionate love tastes of liberation, the ghost of matrimony has been laid for good – this is progress. Onward! Nor was I in error when I suspected that I could make Dario say what I wanted him to say.

I spoke to him of the unclassified affections, I declared to him that the note struck should be unique, and he proposed to me the commonplace of marriage. To fall for such a cliché – an odd mistake for a man of his brilliance. He had, clearly, listened to elements of what I had said, misinterpreted or neglected the rest. And, of course, in justice, I had wished to decoy him into that trap. I pin that medal for stealth onto my ballerina's girlish bosom. So now we are quits, he and I, and the ghost is laid. There has been a levelling, on this even ground we stand as equals, and this seems to me good. He dresses. I half dress.

When I was a child I had a clarity I have tried to keep limpid, I was clear as air, all the lights and hues and hazes in the sky fell in my mind and played there. Tonight I think that I am still a child. Ruthless, often they have said, and unfeeling . . . But tonight I have come to where I want to be. Laura's love has been a staff on which I have leaned, her interferences have been ruts I have stepped over lightly, without irritation. Dario's forbearance and his quietness and his love have been a revelation which my interested vigil scarcely deserved. Nearly, nearly I have emerged into the freedom I want. Another move or two if I have imagined amply, no, if I have calculated shrewdly, and I shall be there.

That Angelica is Dario's daughter has I judge now been endowed with sufficient credibility, the realness of the fact has been allowed to accrue and has reached the degree which will serve us best. Also that she might not be has been brought to the point at which it will not hinder and may help. More fixity, any fixities, I have not thought I wished for. The question remains – as every day – who am I, who shall we be, who will she be? and I think I can answer, or perhaps I mean that I shall be able to suggest the succeeding questions.

Still he sits on the stones. I stand still a few paces away, I wait. Angelica is still a child; I shall defend her from nets, that later she shall defend herself. Dario is not a net. His offer of marriage was not a net, it was an aberration into which I beguiled him because I am ambitious for this love of ours – also conceivably because my instinct for autarchy is a quivering one, it does no harm to my fighting spirit to be permitted a foray to vanquish in now and then, no harm at all, it is good for my nerves. At any rate, Dario's proposal is another of the things which without difficulty I overlook. Should a woman plod her life staring at the mud before her shoes? And should he, the player who loses a set, not be stimulated to forget it, encouraged to play on to the end of the match? I look over, look far away. For those who wallow in possession, there is the discipline of renunciation. For those who are hounded, there is the cunning to take an unexpected turn, lie low, double back. Yes, I am tired. It has been a day! And Dario sits sunken in weariness. Bowed like Ribera's *Poet* he sits. But I have not been so reduced that I could not renounce – see, I have done it, he will never ask me again, it is done, honour secured. And there are muscles in my legs that can canter a bit further.

On his feet at last, "I'm at an end," he says. "Goodbye," he says.

"No . . . At a beginning, surely?"

"You seem to have forgotten . . ." Dario's voice had been gentle, sad, dignified; but it was hard now, exasperated. "You appear to be pretending to have forgotten what you recently said to me." He shrugged his bitterness, his contempt for himself, for his standing there, his answering her, his not walking away. "Pretending to have forgotten," he added with a laugh of disgust, "everything."

"I won't keep you long. This time," she spelt it out, "I will not keep you long." She smiled. "I know you'll have promised Tasso to lift his nets with him at sunrise. I'll even let you snatch an hour's sleep before then if you like." To be true to an idea of her childhood, to keep faith with that clarity, was not going to be an easy task, with this embodiment of self-hatred, this incarnate temptation to hatred of her, as her interlocutor, as the soul whose assent to hers and whose companionship she needed above all lesser benedictions. She kept her eyes steadily, softly on his. "And I assure you I've forgotten nothing. I remember everything."

"You said we should be vulnerable." He would never raise his voice – was incapable of doing so, had no trace of the bully in his fibre – but still the accusation he could not help making grated. A second time he shrugged. 'Vulnerable! for pity's sake, Imogen. I ought to have guessed. I ought to have remembered. Come, you said, the daring for a night's absolute surrender. You say you remember, probably it's true, probably you like to bring these things to mind, they give you pleasure, but . . ."

"But – I've deepened your vulnerability, haven't I?"

"Mine! But yours?"

Her Italian had always been better than his English. Listening to her now he involuntarily recalled how he had loved her slight accent, her occasional hesitations over the word she wanted – the language was in itself a consonance of theirs. It was as if she had got up from her chair beneath the vine in his Umbrian stable-yard, had stepped inside for a minute, had returned – but somehow in the lapse he had been unstrung, given over to discordancy. "And as for what we've just done . . . !"

"You liked it as gloriously as I did."

"Not gloriously. Bitterly. Intensely, if you insist, I agree. But – I don't know – if something can be vile and irresistible at the same time . . ."

"Of course it can," she responded gaily. She smiled. "Only not all that vile."

"You said our days at the castle were – what were your words? – elaborately sexual?"

"I may have pretended to you, to myself, that I didn't enjoy them as much as in fact I did. I may have had my reasons for doing that."

"To me you were only carnal, you said."

"I was only carnal to myself – I believe I said that too. And anyway I suggested we overlook that. Probably it was my fault, my obtuseness, my not seeing. Psyche's mistake – put it like this – was not first to light up her own mind. Straight away the silly girl had to start inspecting her lover, prying into him, gawping like a tourist. Let's say Eros was sensible not to stand for such a trite form of femininity, well within his rights to decide he was getting fed up, chuck her out. The world is full of nymphs. Why should he let his life become a bore by doting on one of the more vapid ones? Now – do you see how much I'm prepared to discount, overlook? I am, as you're probably about to say with a sarcasm I shan't deserve, rather adept at overlooking things. But I still claim it as one of my few virtues."

"You talked a lot about forgiveness, too. I don't believe in it."

Dario's wretchedness was that again skating alone he had fallen through the ice. In all his years of solitude and uncertainty, never had the black water gripped him with such coldness. Never during his winter nights sitting before a sinking fire or patrolling a darkened town had the splintering rafts of ice cut his hands and arms and chest so sharply. Never had the miry bank with its leafless oaks looked so far off. Never had he fought with more horror of drowning and less wish to battle his way to shore. Never had he hauled his shoulders up onto the ice more exhaustedly, known it give beneath his weight with a more bitter recognition of the way of the world. So he regarded Imogen and could only think: If what she has just said about Psyche is right, she was as coarse then as I suspected. Does that mean it is so excellent a line of action now to let myself fall under her sway again, consciously to neglect to learn from experience? Must I surrender my havering self to her enchantment once more now that her sport is to make speeches of a mystical tenor, to reject my love and then insist on talking to me about herself? Still, she was right about one thing – that the world is aswarm with beautiful young women. This worldly wisdom, which I had learned before, this time I shall be careful not to forget.

"If you don't like the word forgiveness," she was easy, she was all cheerful accommodation, "we needn't use it."

"Does it matter what you say? I can't believe it matters to me. Shuffle your words around as you please. Stupidly, I asked you to marry me. Probably fortunately, you said you would not. Where can we be but at the end? What can we have to say to one another except goodbye? Let's say it now, if you don't mind. I'd be grateful if you'd let me go. Let's say it briefly, just the word itself, say it pleasantly."

"It's you who have been saying unpleasant things tonight. I've said one unpleasant word only; I said No." Imogen laughed. "Aren't women meant to be allowed to say No,

232

even encouraged to make use of this right? I say Yes so much. It seems to me that every morning I say Yes to the world." She had not mislaid her knack of attributing to herself superiorities, Dario noticed. "I open my embrace wide, don't I? get a generous armful of life in my hug? It so chanced that you asked me the one question to which my answer is No."

"It didn't *so chance*."

"All right." She rose to this new openness with barely a hesitation, with gaiety. "It didn't so chance – perhaps I was less innocent than you. But perhaps I had been ill-used in the past – even if I deserved my punishment, the pain was real enough, you'll allow me that. And perhaps you should learn to be on occasion less innocent. And perhaps . . ." Among possibilities she swam with confidence, always had. "Isn't it a clearer air we now breathe? Wait, please, a second. Let me explain. It'd be too easy to say that in your nose it stank. But think – think how many things are *not* in our air, might have been but now mercifully aren't. If we overlook the stupidities of the past and resurrect the blessed moments . . . Do you remember the thunder storm which at seven in the evening conveniently turned into a hail storm so we could dash into the yard and grab up handfuls of hailstones to put in our whisky? If we forgive each other and even ourselves – yes, I'll stick by my words if I may, they're the right words for me tonight – aren't we freed? The past frees us, lets us go. The future, thanks to your question and my answer, is open not shut. Breathe deep, Dario. Taste our air a minute. Dwell on the taste. Is it all that foul? One day you'll thank me for not marrying you."

Dario stiffened. "My rejection is not something I wish to discuss."

At which audaciously she permitted herself her most tinkling laughter. "Oh how stiff and grand you can sound when you decide to! I had no idea you were so conventional." Had she gone too far? He might, so mocked by her merriment, turn, go. He stood with the rigidity of

233

masonry. Certainly he was not savouring the air. "Oh come on, there's nothing which it's unseemly for us to talk about." She must maintain this airiness in her voice, it was her only hope. "There's nothing you and I can't say. How should there be? We've emerged. This is what I meant by vulnerability – our emergence alone side by side. You could hurt me, you know."

"I can't imagine why I should want to bother. To hurt you yet again before we part – that doesn't sound like my behaviour."

"You mean, of course, it sounds like mine? There are, don't forget, pains which are salutary." Lightly she must catechise him; only lightly; with a featheriness . . . ! "There exist depths, don't there, which only cruelty sounds? and perhaps transcendences only reached through suffering? You may, if you wish to," she rephrased it, "hurt me."

"I could hurt you, could I, by simply leaving now, parting with you definitively?"

"That'd be a mere brutality. I wouldn't learn anything very interesting from that. Won't you toy with me more lingeringly, amuse yourself by playing with my nerves more imaginatively?"

The sexuality of mysticism – that was how this tract of her destiny had always presented itself to be crossed – was a resource Imogen had all day been aware of keeping in reserve; but now she could wait no longer, would hazard her all tonight, go openly her most intricate ways since her companion was the right one for this enquiry. His simpler tastes were commendably carnal, were to be exploited, but she hoped she could also fire in him a dedication to the pursuit of a plenitude more abstract than that in any cornucopia grasped so far. Well, the next half hour would show what her luck was to be, show the fall of her fate either way.

Not that they would arrive anywhere tonight. Her ambition was to discover if they were to set forth. For all evening the conviction had been stealing upon her that when she had given birth to Angelica she had not been as culpably innocent as later she had come to fear. It was not naïve to embark on a venture you could not achieve alone. It might be necessary to do just that, human nature being incomplete, as full of lacunae as Gruyère. How she had berated herself earlier in the day! Why, she had stormed at herself, had she not had the nous to conceive a child by a banker in Birmingham, a man it was honestly impossible she should meet again (one simply would have to avoid Birmingham, which would be one of the advantages thrown in gratis) so nobody would ever have had cause to pester her with suspicions or embarrass her with facts? Thus in her alarm she had wailed. Anyhow, here tonight the tract lay before her: a waste of distances and exaltations and deprivations and unspeakable dreams where the traveller went dry-mouthed.

She was, she fancied, at a caravanserai. And here was a possible fellow-traveller for the desert that stretched away – a mystic's arid desert but not without oases of sensuality nor without pleasure to be taken in pain, not without mirages to delude the navigator and to torture the austere with desire. Would he travel beside her? For a marriage of this abstraction she was ready enough. Yes, her nature *was* incomplete. But by tonight refusing to marry Dario had she not prepared herself – it was not an operation others could have helped in – as a bride is prepared, had she not put aside all things but one only hazily visible and nearly silent immanence, renounced all fates but one fate? It seemed to her an act of dedication of which at least to herself she might boast – keep her courage up like that. Her own words of earlier in the night re-echoed in her: the note they sounded together, she had suggested to him, should be one of the wonders of the invisible world. And now, yes, I am in a caravanserai, she thought, seeing it plainly. In the dusty courtyard our jeeps are parked. I did not expect to meet another wanderer here, few come this way. It is late. By a lamp we sit under the crumbling arcade, we talk of sand storms outlived, of wells lost and found, of the forest of Askalon of which the Bible tells but which is desert now. My conversationalist has not suggested that tomorrow we journey together. Soon we will wrap up in our rugs and sleep. If I want to convince him that we should share our travails and our rewards I must do it now.

"I begin to understand the pain," Dario was saying. "And I guess we hardly aspire to happiness. But the pleasure?"

"Oh – you get me. Shadowily, all the time. The real thing on occasion, if you so desire. Sexually, intellectually, any way you fancy, all the ways we come to think of. And I'll get you, I hope, please. As for happiness, I'm not sure . . . No, probably you're right, it's too close to contentment. But – will you . . . ?" She laughed. "Would you settle for ecstasy? I know it's rare. It has to be. And sometimes it appears to be a mirage. But it isn't always not there. It's . . ." She reflected. She smiled. "It's a little less rare than the phoenix."

"I am meant, under these circumstances, to set off in pursuit of . . ." For the first time – Imogen caught the flutter in his voice with triumph – he sounded amused. "In pursuit of a – a feeling? – that isn't *always* a mirage?"

"I'll search for it for you. I'll bring you to it more often than anybody else could. You'll find it for me." She knew where she was going. "I'll be it for you. You'll be it for me. You can't resist. How could you? If for no better reason, play this game with me for Laura's sake."

"Game . . . ?"

"Oh we'll play it with deadly passion, don't you worry about that. And for stakes . . . !" Wickedly she was smiling into his eyes. "Not for the squeamish."

So it was that Laura's prophecy to her daughter that Imogen and Dario were unlikely to become engaged to be married but might conceivably forge an accord so tenuous as to be invisible to Jim and Margaret Scottow began to be fulfilled. So it was that Dario imagined a miracle of

236

one thought, one feeling that might for two thirsts be one brimming glass of the wine of consciousness, and it began to shimmer before the eyes of that seduced pilgrim as an absolute good not only to be desired but to be at least falteringly believed in. That a refusal of an offer of marriage might be a declaration of love – this idea, at first an insult, a carnivalesque reversal of all sane order, started to take the first steps of sense. Angelica herself did not progress more wobblingly, need more guidance and protection – but make headway, however awkwardly, the notion did. Imogen's refusal was a counter-offer – listening to her describing a caravanserai he began to work it out. This counter-offer of what would to all intents and purposes be an invisible marriage had in it the wildest disproportions between presence and absence, warmth and cold, possessing and isolating – this, attending to her proposal of a journey across a desert, he foggily focused on. Had she ever more sublimely played the concubine and story-teller? It was as shameless as it was intoxicating the manner in which, half naked in the warm starlight, pausing only to brush away a mosquito or shake out her damp hair, when she talked about the torments of the desert and the delights of an oasis and applied to both the word exquisite she left it unmistakable that sensual love and its transcendence were inseparable. He who at any stage in his adulthood until a few minutes before would have been appalled that a man should go on conversing with a woman who had just rejected him, might do anything except bid her goodbye and at once depart, now speculated upon what, given that domesticity and security and contentment were not to her taste and were beneath her outrageous dignity, she might, with all her splendid seductiveness, be reckoning to get out of all this.

Imogen would be at her most sublime for a reason. In his experience she soared on her most eagle-like ascents in order the more extensively to map the terrain below, the more minutely to calculate her safest course – for the core of her bravado was caution; she never risked unless she had

237

computed that, however marginally, the odds were in her favour. No, for Imogen glory was a pleasure, certainly, but a dispensable one. Survival was what she was out for. And the first possibility as to her interest which he stumbled upon was that by celebrating this unholy union with him she was, true to her nature, securing her liberty in a large way – for she was expatiating upon their solitudes, giving only glancing attention to their encounters however briefly intense these might be.

Unfortunately these musings came accompanied by the suspicion that already – had half an hour passed? surely not an hour – he was going to have to convict himself of being relieved she would not marry him. So there was that in him too which was glad of an excuse to dodge domestic felicity, was there? Not to mention a fickleness of heart and mind to justify all scepticisms and despairs. So he was not altogether heart-broken to be forced to consummate, if any union at all, one as dubious as the adventurous reciprocity now being outlined, one so hazy as to have some of the merits of the inexistent.

But he must not get entangled in still more self-hatred right now. Further ravelling out of uncertainties could perfectly well be postponed a few minutes or even left till tomorrow. What more urgently battened on his mind was the knowledge that Imogen would go free. Of course she would. She was fobbing him off, just as Anna and Laura had variously been fobbed off, just as Imogen Scottow would always – he was as admiring as he was rueful – fob everybody off, go, go her way wrapped in her mantle of self-sufficiency and with her baby in the crook of her arm – the baby who was the tiny adorable flaw which lent her arrogant independence credibility, was the concession to mere mortal frailty which gave the glittering artefact realism and charm, was the deliberate and infinitesimal imperfection in the pattern of the Arab's carpet which saved it from blasphemy. Imogen might, indeed, be lying. She was a fabulist of proven ability. She might have no intention of ever holding any communication with him again, might be overcoming her day's unexpected difficulties like that, amusing herself by enrapturing him one last valedictory time, knowing that tomorrow, no, later today, he would board the evening ferry for Italy. But it was not this challenge he addressed to her, it was a question.

"Why," he wondered in an amused voice, for ironies were flocking mercifully to his rescue, deflections were saviours, "play this game for Laura's sake?"

"Hasn't she helped us quite enormously?" Either Imogen was truly surprised by his perplexity or she had decided it would be politic to understate her own orchestration of events and emotions, off-load as much responsibility as she could onto her godmother. "I think she has."

"Of course I've known she was trying. All afternoon and evening I've watched her stitching away like a weaver-bird. But I didn't think we wanted a nest. And then I thought we did, and I could hardly believe how – how magnanimous she had been, and how wise. But now . . ."

"All the same, if she hasn't brought us to where we are, she's enabled us to find our ways here. Here . . ." Imogen tasted the word; she repeated it like a charm. "Here where we've come together. Here where we start, now. It's as if – isn't it? – she were somehow blessing us."

Imogen could sense her godmother's benediction in the night air that was now so marvellously cleared, in which neither past nor future would stand like the Fisher and cast a net while the circus of respectable citizenry bayed for the fighter's blood, howled for the death of the rebel who had been captured and made a gladiator and must now pay for her rebellion. Had the old lady not always known that air was her goddaughter's proper element? Had she not often declared that she was light as air, that she was a mere breath, an exhaled intangible invisible word, the freest and most abstract and most powerful – what? – ripple, tremor, beat? That immanence which, by refusing Dario, Imogen was now at liberty to dedicate her life to, glowed momently with richer colours, sounded with a more distinguishable music. Abiding in her was a divinity for which she could take no smattering of credit, was nothing to do with her except that she happened to be its church. To this church – her mental air was so translucent she saw all things clearly, did them justice – Dario De Corvaro would come. Dwelling in him was a divinity she likewise would honour. In each his own. To each the other's. What could be more simple? So resuming where she had broken off she held out her hand to him and said, "Here. Now. You and I. Didn't I say that we hadn't come to an end, we were at a beginning? You'll come with me, won't you?" Dario took her hand in his, and to her walker of the seas her soul cried: I am coming. We are coming. Did I not learn from you how to pray, how to fall into harmony with power? To you I give thanks. And to Dario, whose eyes were on hers, she said, "Don't worry, you won't have to see me very often. And don't pretend you're not already recovering from your disappointment. Just remember, once in a while, that when you gave away your freedom I immediately gave it back. How long were you without it?" she speculated gaily. "A second, two seconds maybe?" But then with a return of seriousness she asked again, "You *will* come with me? There isn't anyone else you'd rather – rather cross these deserts and these oceans with? rather pray with? rather – rather shadow, be shadowed by?"

He shook his head. "There isn't anyone else."

"You'll shadow me," in a whisper she solemnly rejoiced, not noticing that he had concurred only negatively, had not said he would come with her. "We'll keep faith, you and I. I know we will. You'll be true!" with her head thrown back she quietly exulted to the sky. "Ah, I knew it!" And then, mercurial as ever, merrily she demanded, "How shall I shadow you? What do you fancy? Let me think. Well, for a start, at night my ghost will come to your bed. Luckily she knows her way to the castle. She'll walk silently into the stable-yard. She'll climb the stairs . . ."

"The terms," Dario demurred, "are yours. All yours."

"Don't you like them? They must be ours. They can be changed." She was as bold as she was prompt. "Suggest others." She was adamant. "Change them."

He wondered. "Angelica?"

"Angelica . . . ?" With the briefest of hesitations to recover her equilibrium, Imogen echoed his question. "Oh, I don't know. What do you think?" The surest defence would be disarming attack. "What answer would you like me to make?" She would firm up her candour. "I can say anything."

"That's just it. You can say anything. Isn't this why it doesn't matter what you say?" It was the second time that night that Dario had suggested that anything she might say would be meaningless; but his voice was not grating now; collaboration had, it seemed, been agreed on. "Isn't this the labyrinth of words which you've built, into which you've led me? It's a labyrinth because any word may be delusory. Let's say I've come willingly. Let's say I stand here at the heart with you. Speak." It was an invitation. "Let's see if it can matter." And once more, with a wry smile, "Speak."

As it had been the convincing innocence of Imogen's rejoicing a few moments before which had softened Dario's questioning, so now any last hardness in him was melted by his recognition of her finest Daedalian touch, by a twist of genius he could only smilingly admire. The final cunning of the maze-builder had been to make a palace of irresistible joys which no one could ever want to try to leave, where beside her now he stood enchanted, far too happy to desire anything but this. Had the designer caused the air to be drugged? The wine? Was he being nourished on nothing but lotuses? Whatever it was, the tone of their exchange had been established: it was exploratory: he would keep it up to the end.

"Speak?" She was amused. "I could, we're right, say anything. You, for what it's worth, have got the same freedom to choose to believe, or to pretend to believe, what you please. I could tell you I had no doubt but that Angelica was your child or that I had no doubt about the opposite. I could tell you this." She was blithe. "I could tell you that. I could tell you that after I left the castle that last time I drove to Rome, in the next few nights I went to the clubs where you and I had danced sometimes, but I went on my own and by the end of the week I'd made love with enough men to have covered my traces. I could say what I said with gravity – with tears if you like. I could say it frivolously. But . . . Before I say anything . . . While I decide whether I intend to say anything . . . While you decide whether you would rather I kept silent, for it occurs to me you may finish by asking me to say nothing . . . Meanwhile . . . Don't you think I ought to be better informed? After all, it's possible that you'll understand what you want, suggest to me that we agree on that, agree to say this, that, something else, whatever it is you decide on, and that I'll fall in with this, say what you ask me to say, do what you require. Shouldn't I know, for instance, whether or not you want Angelica as your daughter?"

He ought, Dario was aware, to be hearing his mind tell him she was diabolical. But what his mind was stating was that when she juggled with possibilities in her airy style he believed her. He believed that it was very probable that if he opted for a certain outcome she would comply with his wishes. Marry him she would not. Why should she? But in regard to his possible daughter she was ready tonight to cede, if he should ask her to, an independence which for two years she had spiritedly defended, accept a duumvirate in a realm where hitherto she had reigned alone. Likewise

242

if he suggested to her that she say nothing he would be given the silence he asked for, its echoes, possibilities. This was the generosity in her of which he began to take the measure.

There would be time to sit in the castle library and hear his mother dilate on how happy her marriage had been – a version of events which with the passage of years and the accumulations of self-love was growing farther and farther from any reality Dario had ever observed. There would be time to walk again and again in through the gateway of his faculty and breathe the atmosphere of political jockeying and intellectual mediocrity. There would be time to decide his life was over as if it had never been; and later to resolve to consider that things were not quite as deadly as that; and later again to change his mind back and forth innumerable times with no possibility of profiting by whatever he thought and a diminishing ability to be convinced by any mental process whatsoever, because the very act of formulating a notion seemed to make it ring false. There would be time to be miserable because Imogen had refused to marry him; time to feel relieved; time to be ashamed to feel relieved; time again to regret his lost happiness with clear simple pain. There would be time for the parking of cars and the buying of things in shops; time for the finding of girls attractive and the finding of himself ridiculous; time for action; time for futility; time for lying awake; time for voices that fell in his mind like waves on the shore; time for voices that never fell. All these things, therefore, could wait. If they waited forever, if the remains of his life never ensued, he would not be sharply distressed. What he wanted time for now was the labyrinth. Nothing would ever be more vital than his standing here beside Imogen at the heart of her perspectives and obliquities and dubiousnesses. (Was it all just one *trompe l'oeil* after another? in him, the depredations of her whimsies merely?) Nothing would ever match this being at the centre of the wealth of promise he seemed now to sense in her readiness to let him hesitate, take all the time he needed, gaze this way and that.

He took his fill of looking. Yes, promise was everywhere, potentiality lay on every hand. And lest he should doubt her defencelessness she was quietly expounding it. "I'll tell you anything you want. If I know it, that is. Ask," she laughed, "and it shall be given you. Any truth that's in my gift is for you." That this was her declaration of love for him he could not doubt while those eyes smiled into his. "Of course, some things aren't definite." She was amused. "There are, mercifully, ambiguities."

In the presence of such vulnerability – now he understood the word! – yes, in the hushed precincts of such a faith, what answer should he make? That Angelica was his daughter he no longer doubted. Imogen would not offer him the father-hood of another man's child, nor of a child of uncertain parentage, not because she was not capable of deceit but because she would never diminish her independence unless she felt she absolutely had to. And now, apparently, that was indeed her sentiment. Here was a surrender he had scarcely dared dream of, here was a giving! That to all the world but him she should consistently hint that she had veiled Angelica's conception in a good thick mist of obscurities, tell in addition enough open lies to immure the truth safely in her head . . . All this Dario discovered he could forgive – this was another word that he was suddenly comprehending, that maybe held some significance after all – without difficulty, even admire. She had loved him; had borne his child. Tonight she had sought him out; she had offered him, in her fashion, her love – in her fashion which he had mistaken but apprehended vividly now and must learn how to respond to with an equal greatness of heart. How easy it would have been for her to give him no choice, tell him one lie only to believe in or not believe in, send him away with that to live with. But now . . . The labyrinth was only made of words, by morning its unrenounceable delights would have dissolved. Now he must plumb its mysteries, now! Angelica *was* his, wasn't she? and being offered to him?

Yes, Imogen mused, the *Poet* is a portrait of his doppel-gänger, I was right about that. The same sadness and the same gentleness in concentration as my brooding, wondering Dario. He is waking to it all, now, is he not? seeing what is before him? Never have I felt so naked. He offered me his freedom, at once I returned it to him. Now I have offered him mine. I wait. Time beats softly, waiting with me. I shiver.

"Of course I know you know I may not be telling you the truth," Imogen was scrupulous to add, to qualify their balanced hesitations with. "But I am. I am."

And now it seemed that Dario had gazed sufficiently, had judged, in a manner he was learning from her, that their love could not, perhaps, be satisfied, or only by the forgoing of all apparent satisfactions; that satisfactions left so much to be desired that to forgo them gave the promise of a greater and abstract plenitude; that promise was what was exciting to live for, live toward, live in. "Ask," he heard her nervously, smilingly remind him. The labyrinth had superb manifold significances and it had charming jingles, but, yes, it was beginning to fade. Soon silence would fall between them, in him. But an answer he now found he had isolated; whether he ever met her again or not he could meet her on this.

"Nothing. For myself, I ask nothing. As" – it amused him – "you predicted. I ask for silence. Or . . . If anything . . ." He too now could be lighthearted. "Kiss me."

So their renunciation was sealed.

"Thank heaven for Laura," Imogen murmured with the miracle of her renewed freedom radiant in her mind.

"Yes. Bless her."

"Thank heaven for meeting you again, for this, for now." She picked up her towel, in a moment she would leave him, she was pushing her feet into her espadrilles, the shingle shelved. "I wonder . . . What will you do now?"

Dario looked at the fishing-smack. "I shall go on board. I shall sit with my back against the mast, I expect, and watch the sea and the stars. In an hour Tasso will come.

The sun will rise." He turned back to her. "This evening I shall be on the ferry."

"Ah . . ." She did not sound surprised. Everything to her came naturally now. "Yes."

"One thing more, and then I'll let you go. One last question, Imogen. When Angelica asks who her father is, what will you tell her?"

Her eyes gave him then their steadiest look, their slowest smile. "The truth. For your sake, for the sake of tonight . . . I promise you. When she's old enough, when the moment is right . . . The truth."

His thought burnished by the daughter who would grow up, who would one day come to find him, all his consciousness agleam with that future meeting, Dario said, "I'll shadow her. She'll shadow me. And then . . ."

"She'll be free to do whatever she wants – love you or leave you. You're – you'll always be – free to do what you want. I can't," she laughed in her victory, "give you much more freedom than this, can I?"

"It's good enough." It filled him. "It's enough. And when you and I meet, if we ever do . . . ? And when she and I meet, which we will . . . ?"

She was on her way, but for a moment she turned back to him, for the last time smiled. "That'll be – won't it? – another story. Ah, my darling," she breathed, "our haunting has hardly begun."

Watercolour Sky
WILLIAM RIVIÈRE

Under the open skies of north Norfolk, the Dobell family seems to lead an idyllic life, the countryside and its sporting pursuits closely interwoven with the very fabric of existence. Yet happiness eludes two generations; only the natural world remains a passion which sustains expectations in this haunting tale of loss and deep but ill-fated emotions.

'A beautifully written, melancholy tale'
John Nicholson in The Times

'Entrancing . . . Rivière's outdoor scenes are superb. Neither Turgenev nor Hemingway could teach him much about evoking field and water'
Michael Barber in The Listener

'Robust yet delicate, like a good wine. I enjoyed it very much'
John Bayley

'A luminous first novel; it's a love story free of any sentimental clutter. And it's the best evocaation of East Anglia since Graham Swift's *Waterland*'
Company

'The author has a sensitive pen and an ability to portray his characters as real. Again and again we are rewarded by small epiphanies: love's first kiss, an old man scything, a moment watching ghostly owls crossing an open starry sky'
John Wyse Jackson in The Sunday Times

SCEPTRE

A Venetian Theory of Heaven

WILLIAM RIVIÈRE

This moving and elegaic novel charts the sentimental education of Francesca Ziani, a young, naïve student who lodges with her cousin Amedea in a crumbling Venetian *palazzo*. Rich, reckless and unashamedly patrician, Amedea feels trapped by the stagnant society in which she moves and, contemptuous of the effects on her English husband and their small son, makes a dramatic attempt to break free.

'A hymn to beauty . . . The real hero is the city itself, with its dark, thick waters and decaying beauties'
Nicci Gerrard in The Observer

'He writes with authority. He writes beautifully too . . . He dares to treat love, and the death of love, as seriously as lovers treat it . . . I look forward with eagerness and impatience to what he does next'
Allan Massie in The Scotsman

'A beautifully written and captivating tragedy'
Laura Connelly in Time Out

'A marvellous book . . . Subtle and gripping . . . Enthralls and disturbs in the deceptively leisurely manner of Henry James's Venetian idyll THE ASPERN PAPERS'
John Bayley in the Evening Standard

'An interesting and intelligent novelist'
John Melmoth in The Sunday Times

SCEPTRE

Borneo Fire
WILLIAM RIVIÈRE

In the interior the fire had started to burn, but outside the forests no one seemed to be aware of it . . .

When the Japanese invaded Borneo in 1941, Philip Blakeney, fighting thousands of miles away from the country of his birth, was powerless to prevent the deaths of his entire family. Over forty years later, forgotten hero and forgotten poet, he lives vicariously through the adventures of his environmentalist son, Hugh. Yet, when faced with the destruction by fire of his paradisal island, Philip ignores his wartime lessons in the vanity of action and encourages Hugh to set off for the burning interior.

This is the heartrending tale of a man tortured by the past and betrayed by knowledge, and of the intense love which flares up between his son and his adopted daughter, offering the promise of redemption. It is the dramatic story of a brave fight to halt the spread of a vast forest fire, and the authorities' failure in not confronting it. And it is a lovingly drawn portrait of an island of enchanting beauty, many times ravaged by invaders and colonisers. Historical, personal and environmental tragedies are intertwined in this profoundly moving, unforgettable novel.

∫

SCEPTRE